Be Our Ghost

THE DUCHESS HOTEL #2

CARLA LUNA

MOON MANOR PRESS

First paperback edition: October 2025

Cover Design: *Bailey McGinn*
Editing: *Free Bird Editing*
Proofreading: *One Love Editing*

ISBN: 979-8-9894130-7-2 (paperback)
ISBN: 979-8-9894130-6-5 (ebook)

Published by Moon Manor Press
www.carlalunabooks.com

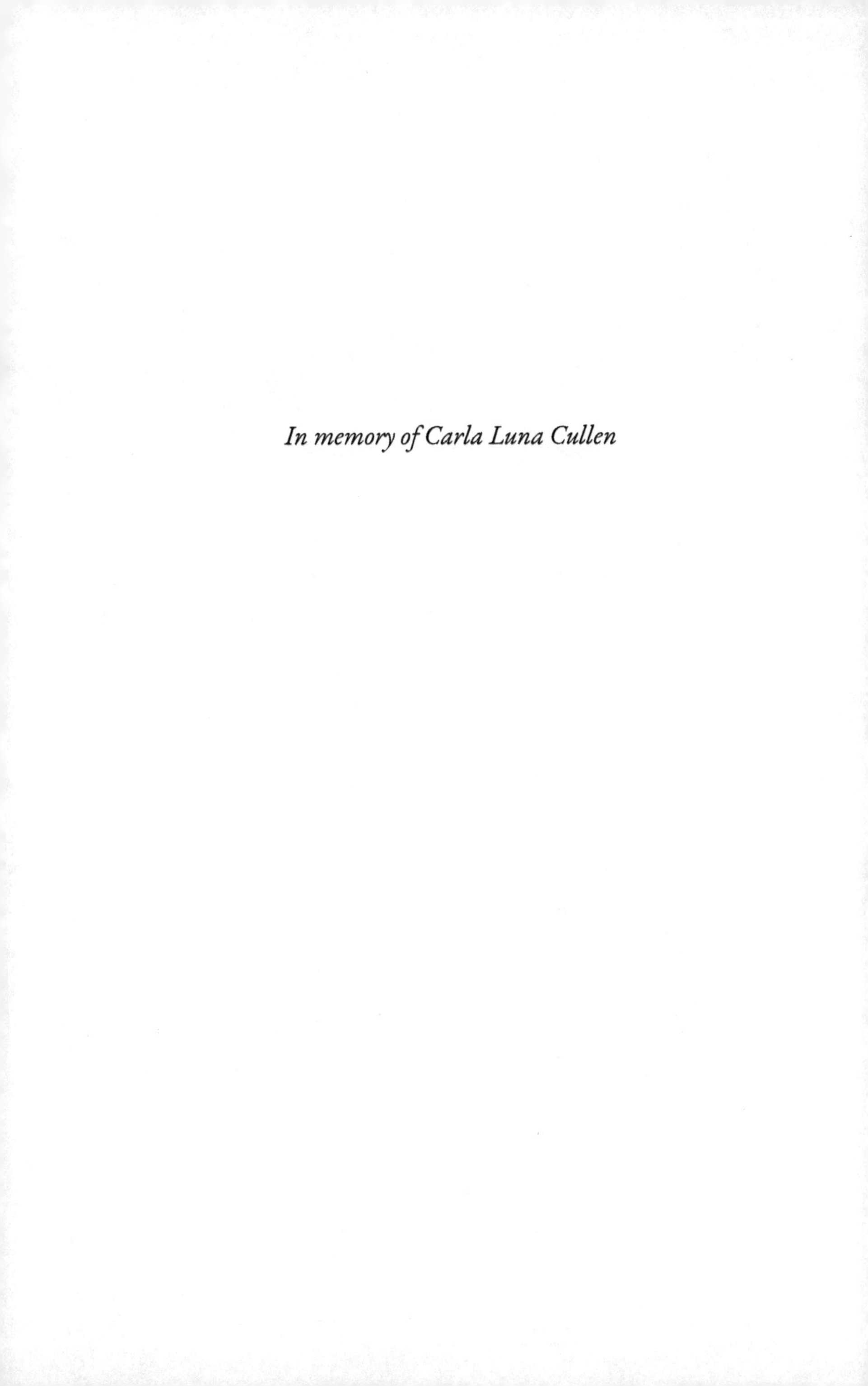

In memory of Carla Luna Cullen

Author's Note

For those of you who might be unfamiliar with Canadian geography, *Be Our Ghost* takes place in the beautiful city of Victoria, which is the provincial capital of British Columbia. It's located on the West Coast of Canada, on the southernmost tip of Vancouver Island (not to be confused with the city of Vancouver, which is on the mainland). I set the Duchess Hotel series in Victoria because I grew up there, and I love going back to visit. In the interest of storytelling, I've taken a few liberties in my depiction of downtown Victoria, including the creation of two fictional hotels: the Duchess and the Grand Duke.

Content warning: While *Be Our Ghost* is meant to provide an enjoyable Halloween romp, the story contains a main character who was cheated on (mentioned in backstory), a main character with a controlling parent (plus an ex who was very controlling), and an incident from the hotel's past involving a tragic murder-suicide that took place in 1924. While this incident is not described in detail, it is mentioned a few times on the page.

One

Thirty minutes until happy hour. The bane of Knox McIntyre's existence.

It wasn't that he disliked his job as head bartender at the Gilded Lily—the swanky cocktail lounge located inside the Duchess Hotel. Unlike the rowdy neighborhood pub where he'd last worked, the Lily had class. But during happy hour, everyone staying at the hotel was entitled to a free glass of wine. Since they weren't paying for it, they rarely felt the need to tip. They also kept him hopping with their demands for the bar's seasonal specials, which were offered at half price.

He frowned as he peered at a note taped to the cash register. It had been left for him by Preston Hargreaves, the Duchess Hotel's general manager, or GM.

Hey, Knox. Just circling back about your request to switch to fall-themed drinks now that September's here. Let's hold off until the weather cools down. Your tropical cocktails have made such a splash we need to keep the momentum going. And keep cranking those Jimmy Buffett tunes! Beach vibes for the win!

Beach vibes, my ass. Knox had spent the past three months mixing up all manner of sweet, fruity drinks. Not ideal, considering the two most popular selections—piña coladas and frozen daiquiris—required the time-consuming use of a blender. And the only blender in the bar was the noisy, janky one his boss was too cheap to replace.

Then there was the matter of Preston's summer playlist. Knox's preferred background music was a low-key mix of vintage jazz and swing. Instead, he'd been forced to endure songs like "Margaritaville" and "Kokomo" on repeat. Both tunes might have been acceptable if he'd been tending bar in Hawaii or Florida. But the Duchess was located in Victoria, B.C. *Canada*. Which was as far from the tropics as you could get.

At least tonight's happy hour would be on the slow side since it was the Tuesday after Labor Day. And if he wasn't elbow-deep in customers, he'd have time to chat with Charlie if she stopped by the bar. The thought of seeing her—even for a few minutes—coaxed a smile out of him. No one else who worked at the Duchess affected him that way. Just Charlie.

His thoughts were interrupted by a voice from the past. "Knox. *Buddy*. How's it hanging?"

He looked up in surprise. How long had it been since he'd seen Logan in person? Three years? Four? His friend looked as slick as ever, designer shades perched atop his wavy blond hair. They'd met while working in Vancouver on *The Hidden Forest*, the award-winning fantasy show where Knox had gotten his big break as a screenwriter, and Logan had learned the ropes as a production assistant. A great gig until Knox's life had gone to shit. After being forced out of the show, he'd moved to Victoria and cut ties with everyone except Logan.

Knox crumpled up Preston's note and shoved it into his pocket. "Good to see you, man. What are you doing in Victoria?"

"I'm here to visit my favorite bartender. Isn't that reason enough?" Logan cast a glance around the cocktail lounge, which was almost empty, except for a couple seated at one of the high-tops. "Classy joint you've got here."

Knox nodded. The Gilded Lily was one of the hotel's best features, designed to resemble a 1920s speakeasy, with a tin-tiled ceiling, green glass pendant lights, and brown leather club chairs. One wall displayed framed newspaper articles and photos from the twenties, along with classic Art Deco posters.

"It's a hell of a lot nicer than the last place I worked," he said. "But I'm not buying your bullshit. You didn't take the ferry all the way from Vancouver just to see my sorry ass."

His friend let out a hearty laugh. "I'm here for work. I've got a new job. Hopefully, it'll last longer than my gig at Sunshine Coast Productions."

Like Knox, Logan had left *The Hidden Forest* a few years ago. But in his case, it had been by choice so he could take on the role of production manager at an up-and-coming studio.

"What happened at Sunshine Coast?" Knox asked.

"You name it. Money problems. Infighting. A CEO who couldn't keep his grabby hands to himself. I'm lucky I got out when I did."

"Glad you landed on your feet." Knox gestured to the wall of bottles behind him. "Want a drink? On the house."

It was the least he could do. More than once, Logan had asked him to come back and visit. Knox always shot him down. Vancouver held too many memories of his old life—the years he'd spent toiling away in a city so tapped into the entertainment industry it was known as "Hollywood North."

Logan settled onto a stool. "I'll have a gin and tonic. Black Fox gin, if you've got it." He took out his phone and set it on the bar top. "Not to be rude, but I'm waiting on a call."

"No problem." For as long as Knox had known him, Logan was *always* waiting on a call. "What's your new job?"

"I'm the field story producer for a ghost-hunting show called *Canada's Most Haunted*. That's why I'm in town. I'm scouting locations for an upcoming episode."

Knox snorted. "Seriously? I didn't think you believed in that stuff." He grabbed the gin and set about mixing Logan's drink.

"I'll believe in anything if there's a paycheck. And there's good money to be made in those paranormal reality shows. Like *Ghost Adventures*. Or *The Dead Files*. Both series have been running forever."

"Never seen either one." Knox garnished the drink with a wedge of lime and passed it to him. "I always assumed they faked their evidence."

Logan took a swig of his drink. "Some of the effects are exaggerated, but a lot of it's real. I've felt cold spots, heard weird noises, and seen stuff I can't explain. We're planning on shooting an episode in Victoria next month."

"You should go on a ghostly walking tour while you're in town. Historic Hauntings does a great job." Despite Knox's skepticism, he'd taken one of their tours and found it entertaining.

"I did that last night. Good stuff. I'd heard of the Grand Duke Hotel before, but I had no idea it was flat-out haunted."

"Yeah, it's part of local lore. Word is, the Duke has three resident ghosts that appear on a regular basis." Yet another thing the ostentatious hotel could brag about. Knox loathed the Grand Duke, as did all his coworkers at the Duchess. Not only was the massive hotel their fiercest rival, but its senior staff were total pricks. "I'm not a fan of the place, but it's worth asking if they'll let you film there."

"I already met with one of their managers. The guy had a stick up his ass." Logan gave a huff of exasperation. "He claimed our show would tarnish their reputation."

"Their loss. But there's gotta be another location that would work. Does the episode have to take place at a hotel?"

"Ideally, yes, since we're focusing on haunted inns and hotels this season. I'm meeting with someone from the Pendray Inn, so that might do the trick, but I'd like more options."

Knox pulled out his phone. "Let me see if there's anywhere

else. After I went on that ghost tour, the guide sent me a link to a few other haunted places in Victoria."

Before he could search for the list, his boss, Preston, entered the Gilded Lily. As usual, he was impeccably dressed in one of his pricey Jack Victor suits. Though he wasn't the worst boss Knox had ever dealt with, he demanded a lot from his staff. Ever since he'd taken the reins of the Duchess a year ago, he'd been on a nonstop mission to boost the struggling boutique hotel's rankings and occupancy rate.

Preston strode up to the bar with a look of grim determination. "*Knox*. Did you get my note? I'd like us to go hard on the beach vibes for at least another week."

Knox resisted the urge to roll his eyes. "Yep. Got it. Once happy hour starts, I'll fire up the blender and switch to your playlist." *But not another minute sooner.*

"Excellent. Just because Labor Day's over doesn't mean we can't enjoy summer for a little while longer. After all, fall doesn't officially start until September twenty-second."

Did that mean another two weeks of frozen daiquiris? *Hell, no.*

Logan tossed back the rest of his drink and set down the glass. "I should head over to the Pendray Inn. Let me know if you think of any other haunted hotels in the area."

"Haunted hotels?" Preston's voice rose in excitement. "Now you've got my interest. I'm Preston Hargreaves, the general manager of the Duchess."

Logan shook his hand. "Logan Cantrell. Knox and I go way back."

Knox spoke up before his friend could reveal too much about their shared past. "We used to work together, but now he's in town scouting locations for *Canada's Most Haunted*."

"I love that show," Preston said. "If you're searching for a place to film an episode, then look no further. Our hotel is second only to the Grand Duke in terms of hauntings."

What the fuck? When Knox had gone on that ghost tour, his guide hadn't mentioned the Duchess.

"I could totally see shooting here," Logan said. "This place has a great old-timey vibe. But we'd need more background material. Usually, when a hotel is haunted, it's because it played host to a tragedy, like a grisly murder or a devastating fire. What've you got?"

Preston's smile faltered. "I...uh...don't have all the details offhand, but I can round up some info. When would the filming take place?"

"In about six or seven weeks, so I'm thinking late October."

Just like that, Preston's smarmy grin was back. "Super. We're planning to 'lean into' Halloween this year. Hosting the show would give us a huge boost."

Logan's phone buzzed. "Shit, I've gotta run." He handed Preston a business card. "Send me all the details. The sooner, the better." He nodded toward Knox. "We need to catch up. You free for coffee tomorrow? Or lunch?"

"Either one's fine. I don't start work until three." Knox could always count on Logan for the juiciest industry gossip.

"Perfecto." Logan shot him a pair of finger guns. "I'll text you."

"Sounds good." Knox took his empty glass and wiped down the bar. He waited until his friend had left before speaking to Preston in a low voice. "The Duchess isn't haunted."

"It could be, right? It's over a hundred years old."

Not everything old is haunted, dipshit. "It's not on the Historic Hauntings tour, and there are no records of any ghostly sightings."

"Maybe we haven't looked hard enough. I'll bet we could find guests who've had some kind of supernatural encounter while staying here. Or we could make something up."

Bad idea. After years of mismanagement, the Duchess was slowly rebuilding its reputation as an iconic boutique hotel. If word got out they were concocting fake ghost stories, they'd be the laughingstock of Victoria's hospitality industry.

Preston rubbed his hands together. "This show could be just what we need to stand out during spooky season. Since you and Logan are old friends, I'd like you to be my point person for this project."

What? This was going from bad to fucking awful. "Me? I've never watched a ghost-hunting show in my life."

"Then you'll have to get up to speed. You'd just need to handle a few things." Preston ticked off the items on his fingers. "Ask the front office staff to comb through past reviews to see if they mention anything out of the ordinary. The spookier, the better. Do some background research into the hotel's history. Then, if we get a green light, coordinate with Logan's team and our facilities staff to set up everything for the filming."

Typical Preston. Every time he came up with one of his "brilliant plans," he delegated it to someone else. But this was a lot on top of Knox's regular responsibilities. "I can't do it. I've got my hands full running the bar."

Preston scowled. "You're not much of a team player, are you?"

Not anymore. Back in Vancouver, as the executive story editor of *The Hidden Forest,* Knox had put in long hours in the writers' room, working with his team to break each episode. They'd bonded over late-night sessions where they'd hammered out story beats, debated character arcs, and brainstormed plot twists. But once he was discredited, he left them all behind. Since then, wherever he'd worked, he kept his coworkers at arm's length. Less to lose that way.

"I do my job," he muttered.

"You'll need to do more than that if you want to keep running the Gilded Lily. If that's not enough incentive, consider this. I know what went down in Vancouver."

The chill icing Knox's spine made him feel like a ghost had passed through him. "I don't know what you're talking about."

"No? When I started working here last year, I did a deep dive into everyone's background. Yours was trickier because you're not online anymore. It took me a while before I discovered your pseudonym. Mac Iverson, one of the creators of *The Hidden Forest*. Formerly engaged to Lila Winstead, who plays Princess Elodie on the show. Impressive stuff."

Fuck. Knox didn't want to remember any aspect of that life. Especially not Lila. "It's no one's business but mine."

"Then I'll keep it to myself. *If* you'll help me with the show. It's not a big ask."

Knox's jaw tightened. It was a *huge* ask.

His anger dissolved when Charlotte Fraser, known to her friends as Charlie, breezed into the bar and headed toward them. Though her brow was creased in dismay, she was so beautiful she took Knox's breath away. Skin like pale cream, a cute dusting of freckles on her upturned nose, jade-green eyes, and short blond hair. Petite and adorable, she was like Tinker Bell, if Tink had been a sweet, sunny hotelier instead of a vengeful fairy with a murderous agenda.

Though he was always glad to see her, he didn't like the thought of anyone making her upset. "Hey, Charlie. Are you okay?"

Preston frowned at her. "Is there a problem at the front desk?"

She blew out a peeved breath. "There's a woman at check-in who insists on talking to the manager. She and her friends booked the Duchess for a girls' getaway through a third-party website. They paid in advance, but now she's insisting we give them a full refund. Apparently, the rooms aren't up to her standards."

Preston regarded her with a condescending smirk. "You're the front office manager. Surely, you can handle it?"

"I can, but the woman said, 'Get your boss out here before I make a scene.' She told me she's a well-known influencer who'd have no qualms about trashing us online." Charlie lowered her voice. "To be honest, if she was *that* famous, she'd be staying at the Grand Duke."

That made Knox laugh. When Charlie favored him with a warm smile, he found it impossible to break away from her gaze. But his blood ran cold when he realized Preston was observing the two of them. Intently.

"I'll head over to the front desk and sort it out," Preston said. "But before I go, I have a quick question. Charlotte, do you believe in ghosts?"

"Ghosts? Gosh, I think so, but I've never seen any."

"I'm asking because a team of paranormal investigators might be coming to the Duchess to shoot an episode." Preston placed his hand on her arm. "Given your background in customer service, you'd be optimally suited to serve as one of the point people for the show."

"Me? I'm a total scaredy-cat. I can't even bring myself to watch horror movies."

Preston raised his eyebrows. "I'm sure it wouldn't be *that* terrifying. Plus, you wouldn't be doing this alone. You'd be working with Knox."

"Oh." Charlie's eyes widened. "Then...I could handle it." She flashed Knox a shy smile. "If it's okay with you?"

Damn it. Somehow, Preston had zeroed in on Knox's two weakest spots—his past and his crush on Charlie—and was using both against him.

Aware she was waiting for a reply, Knox didn't have the heart to turn her down. "Definitely. We'll make a great team."

Two

After Preston left to deal with the demanding guest, Charlie lingered at the bar. Normally, she would have followed right on her boss's heels to see how he handled the situation. But she wasn't going anywhere until she got more information from Knox.

She leaned closer and spoke in a hushed voice. "What's going on? I know Preston wants us to 'lean into' Halloween, but hosting a ghost-hunting show seems pretty extreme."

He chuckled. "You've got that right. He doesn't miss a trick."

That fleeting glimpse of happy Knox—as opposed to regular, grumpy Knox—hit Charlie like a shot of dopamine. It didn't matter that he normally came across as gruff and guarded; she'd harbored a crush on him for well over a year. Unlike the rich, entitled guys she'd dated in the past, he was down-to-earth. Solidly built and bearded, with thick brown hair and warm hazel eyes. The kind of guy who looked like he belonged in a timber camp up north.

Admittedly, she'd had more than a few lumberjack fantasies about him.

But for all the times she'd engaged him in conversation, he'd only divulged a few meager scraps of personal information: he was thirty-three, he'd grown up in a small town in British Columbia's Okanagan Valley, he loved to read, and he had a fondness for vintage cocktail recipes. Anytime she'd probed further, he'd clammed up right away.

More than once, her coworkers had suggested she ask him out, but she hadn't mustered up the courage to take that leap, partly because he didn't seem like he'd be open to it. He'd never mentioned dating anyone. And last February, when Preston had tasked him with creating a few love-themed cocktails for Valentine's Day, Knox had dismissed both the holiday and romance itself as "a total crock."

"The ghost show stuff came about because my friend Logan dropped by," Knox said. "He works for *Canada's Most Haunted.* Ever seen it?"

"No, but if you need me to watch it, I can start binging old episodes. I don't have much going on this weekend." *Or any weekend, really.*

While she was close with a few of her coworkers, her dating life had flatlined three years ago, after she'd broken off her engagement to Randolph. It didn't help that she lived in an apartment above her parents' garage, which meant enduring her mother's intense scrutiny every time she went on a date.

"Watching the show would be a good start," Knox said. "I should do that, too. Gotta admit—as much as I hate the Grand Duke Hotel, they would have been a better choice for an episode. But they turned Logan down."

"I'm not surprised, given what snobs they are." While Charlie rarely disparaged anyone, she thought the Duke's so-called "hospitalitarians" were too high-and-mighty for their own good. "But their hotel is *actually* haunted. Whereas ours is...not. Is it?"

"I don't think so. Not that Preston seemed to care. Once he realized the Duchess could be the location for an episode, he was all for it. He asked me to pitch in because...Logan's an old friend.

But you don't have to help if you're too busy. I don't want to make you uncomfortable, either. Didn't you just tell Preston you don't like watching horror movies?"

Charlie swallowed, unsure of whether Knox was trying to dissuade her. "Yeah, I'm kind of a big chicken. But...um...I'm still willing to help."

Please, say yes.

If she and Knox teamed up to work on this endeavor, they'd get to spend more time together. Maybe then, she'd be able to sense whether he'd be open to dating. And if he was? Then she needed to stop pining for him and *do* something about it—even if it meant stepping out of her comfort zone.

To her relief, he smiled at her, his eyes crinkling at the corners. "Thanks. I could use a partner. If the show decides to film here, it could be good for the hotel."

"Then I'm all for it. I can start watching it on Sunday since I have the day off. For now, I'd better go check on Preston." She peeked at her watch. "Happy hour starts soon, so I'm sure you'll be busy mixing tropical cocktails."

He groaned. "I'm so sick of them. The same goes for those damn Jimmy Buffett songs."

She couldn't resist teasing him. "Even 'Cheeseburger in Paradise'? That one's fun."

"Maybe the first time around, but I've heard it every happy hour." He scowled at her. "Are you admitting you like that song?"

Whenever he addressed her in that extra-growly voice, she broke out in little tingles. Especially when she sensed he wasn't truly angry. "I admit nothing, Mr. McIntyre. Can we talk later about this ghost show?"

"Sure. You know where to find me."

"You got it, partner." She let out an awkward giggle, then gave him a quick wave, trying not to erupt in a squeal of joy as she walked back to the front desk.

What did it matter that she was afraid of ghosts?

She'd be getting to work with Knox on a *very* special project.

ON FRIDAY MORNING, CHARLIE HEADED TOWARD THE Duchess' small conference room, carrying a box of donuts. Once a week, the hotel's four senior managers—the self-proclaimed "Duchess Damsels"—met to discuss upcoming events, specials, sales, and potential crises. Standing at the head of the table was Rosie Gonzalez, the assistant general manager, who was one of Charlie's closest friends. Having just returned to work after a weeklong vacation, Rosie was positively glowing, her light brown skin a shade darker thanks to a newly acquired tan.

After setting the donuts on the table, Charlie gave her friend a quick hug. "Welcome back. How was Banff?"

"It was amazing. I can't remember the last time I got that much sunshine. I could have done with less hiking, but you know Drew. He was totally in his element. We stayed in this adorable cabin just big enough for the two of us." Rosie let out a blissful sigh. "It was hard coming back to work."

"I'm gonna need a full debriefing later." Even if Charlie's dating life was nonexistent, she enjoyed living vicariously through her friend's exploits. Rosie had been dating Drew for almost a year now, and she'd never seemed happier.

"You bet. Thanks for bringing treats. I'm in desperate need of a sugar fix."

"They're nothing fancy. I got pressed for time and stopped at Tim Hortons."

"Who needs fancy? As long as you got me a Boston cream, I'm good."

"Of course." By now, Charlie knew everyone's favorite flavor. For instance, Knox couldn't resist a honey cruller. She'd already set one aside and planned to bring it to him when he showed up for work later.

Selena Reyes walked in, pushing a cart laden with a full coffee service. As the hotel's food and beverage manager, she could be counted on to supply them with decent coffee. "I brewed us the good stuff—French roast from Alma's Beanery." She gave Rosie an appraising stare. "Look at you, with your gorgeous tan. I figured you and Drew would spend your entire vacation in bed."

"I'll have you know we went on five different hikes." Rosie grinned. "Though we did have sex outside once. That's a new one for me."

"You had sex outside?" Laurel Gibson, the hotel's sales and marketing manager, came into the room, carrying a stack of orange folders. "I didn't think you were that bold."

"I'm not a total prude," Rosie said. "Besides, it's not like you've ever had sex outdoors."

"Wanna bet? I grew up on a farm." Laurel gave a toss of her straw-blond hair, then passed out the folders. "There's one for each of you, and it includes a tentative schedule of events for September and October. Fair warning, we've got a lot going on."

Charlie took one and peeked at the schedule. Laurel wasn't kidding. This fall was going to be busier than ever.

"Thanks for getting it all organized," Rosie said. "I'm so glad we're not scrambling to get our events on everyone's radar, like last Christmas. Preston also agreed to increase our advertising budget. As you've probably guessed, he wants us to 'go hard' on Halloween."

"Of course he does," Selena muttered. "He's not the one doing all the work."

"At least he hasn't fired us," Charlie said.

Last November, when Preston had come on board as the hotel's new GM, all four of them had been in danger of losing their jobs. He'd given them a chance to prove their worth when he challenged them to increase the hotel's occupancy rate by making it more holiday-forward. The Damsels' efforts had attracted so many new guests that they'd all been allowed to stay. Ever since then, he'd insisted they "lean into" every holiday.

Laurel pointed to the folders. "Take a minute to look through everything. Now that September's here, we're going to offer fall-themed activities for a few weeks before ramping up to spooky season in October."

Charlie passed the box of donuts around, then grabbed an apple fritter for herself, along with a cup of coffee. As she reviewed Laurel's list of events, she grew excited. Fall was her favorite season in Victoria, and she enjoyed participating in the hotel's holiday activities. Not to mention, she was eager to share her news about *Canada's Most Haunted*.

Laurel called them to attention ten minutes later. "Given that Halloween is one of the biggest holidays of the year, I want to focus on planning for it first. I've probably mentioned it before, but my roommate, Celia, works as a part-time guide for Historic Hauntings, giving ghostly walking tours of Victoria. In exchange for promoting her tours to our guests, she'll offer us a discounted rate. She could even arrange a few private tours, if there's enough interest."

"That's great," Rosie said. "Those tours get super popular around Halloween."

Charlie couldn't wait any longer. She was so antsy she was practically jumping out of her chair. "Speaking of ghosts, I have to tell you about the latest development. I've been sitting on this for three days, and it's killing me. *Canada's Most Haunted* is coming to Victoria."

"Ooh, I love that show," Laurel said. "Where are they filming?"

Charlie felt a touch of pride, knowing she had the inside scoop. "They haven't decided yet, but they're considering shooting an episode at the Duchess."

The silence that followed was...unnerving.

Rosie spoke up first. "You know the Duchess isn't haunted, right?"

"We're not even mentioned on Celia's ghost tour," Laurel added.

Charlie had yet to do any research on the hotel's history, but she'd sought out Knox two days ago to get more information about the show. As she went on to explain the situation to the Damsels, her anxiety kicked in, making her wonder if she'd been too hasty in agreeing to work on this project.

"Are you saying we'd have to pretend our hotel is haunted?" Selena asked. "Are we going to dress up in sheets and frighten people? Or hide out and make scary noises?"

"And why did Preston pick you as the point person?" Laurel said. "Since when are you a fan of spooky reality shows?"

"I'm not, but..." Charlie cringed. "I got roped into it because Preston told me Knox needed my help. So, I..." She trailed off as she caught the others' knowing looks. "What?"

"Oh, hon." Selena sighed. "You don't have to work on this show to get close to Knox. Just lure him into a dark corner and kiss him. Break the spell he's under and turn him from a beast back into a human. Like in *Beauty and the Beast*."

"Are you serious? I can't imagine being that pushy."

"But you wouldn't be helping with this ghost show if he wasn't part of the deal," Selena said. "Right?"

"It's not just that. I'm always up for anything that helps the Duchess stand out. It's an important part of my job." No matter how exhausted or stressed-out she got, Charlie always tried her best to be a goodwill ambassador. To make the hotel an appealing place for everyone who stayed there. From an early age, she'd trained herself to be a people-pleaser, because her mother had only praised her when she presented a positive face to the world.

When no one responded right away, she reached for the lone chocolate glazed donut in the box. Being in the hot seat required a few more carbs. "Anyway, it's too late to back out now. Knox agreed to help Preston, and I agreed to help Knox, and somehow, we have to make this hotel a little more haunted."

"Well..." Laurel stretched out the word. "For all we know, it *is* haunted. I can ask Celia more about it. Even though our hotel isn't on her regular beat, her tour only covers seven spots. Maybe there's a haunting here she's heard of. Since she works at the provincial archives, she might know more about the hotel's history."

"The Duchess has been around for over a hundred years," Selena added. "At some point, it must have played host to a traumatic event or a gruesome murder. Maybe it's been featured on a true crime podcast."

"That would be ideal," Charlie said, then immediately felt guilty. "Sorry, I didn't mean I was hoping someone died gruesomely, but...um..."

"We get it," Laurel said. "Hopefully, you can find something juicy. If it works out, we can include 'as seen on *Canada's Most Haunted*' in our promotional materials. Talk about great publicity."

"Thanks," Charlie said. "I have Sunday off, so I'm going to start watching the show. If any of you want to join me, you're welcome to come over."

Selena gave her a sly smile. "Wouldn't it be more fun if you watched it with Knox? Then you could take notes and discuss strategy. *Together.*"

"I...I don't know. I hadn't thought of it." Could she be so bold as to invite Knox to her place? "What if he turns me down?"

"Then brush it off like it's no big deal," Rosie said. "But you won't know until you ask."

Charlie drew in a shaky breath. "Okay. I'll ask him."

Three

Ten minutes before Knox was due to arrive at her apartment, Charlie dashed into the bathroom and checked her appearance in the mirror again. After trying on multiple outfits, she'd chosen a short-sleeved top with a fun floral print and faded jeans. A little makeup, some hoop earrings, and her favorite beaded bracelets completed the look. A nice change from the blazer-and-skirt combo she usually wore as front office manager of the Duchess.

As she was touching up her mascara, her hands shook so badly she had to set down the tube.

Just breathe.

Why was she so jittery about having Knox over? She'd never had any qualms about popping into the Gilded Lily to chat with him. Or hanging out with him in the staff room on those occasions when their breaks lined up. And last December, she'd persuaded him to work with her on a bunch of the hotel's holiday events. He'd even dropped by her parents' house last year when he helped her haul a fully decorated Christmas tree to the Duchess.

But she'd never been alone with him in her apartment. Just the two of them, without the steady bustle of the hotel to distract them.

A sharp rap on her door made her heart seize up. He was early.

Before she could reach the door, it swung open. Her mother, Irene Fraser, entered the apartment, clad in a pale pink dress and matching kitten heels, a pair of diamond earrings glittering beneath her sleek blond bob.

Charlie walked over to her and caught a whiff of honeysuckle—her mother's signature scent. "Hey, Mom. Shouldn't you be heading to that cocktail thing at the Thomsons'?"

Both her parents had active social lives, filled with golf games, charity fundraisers, dinners, and events at the yacht club, where they were long-standing members.

"Didn't I tell you, sweetie? The renovations on their kitchen still aren't done. It's so hard to find decent help in this city. So, we offered to host the gathering at the last minute. I'd love it if you'd join us." She raked her gaze over Charlie. "You'd just need to change into something...presentable."

Charlie could think of nothing more excruciating than spending the evening with her parents' wealthy acquaintances. "Thanks, but I've already got plans."

"Is one of your friends from the hotel coming over?"

"Yep." She didn't elaborate, hoping her mother would assume she was hanging out with Rosie or Laurel. If she mentioned she was entertaining a male guest, she'd be hit with a barrage of questions.

"Well, if you get done early, you're welcome to stop in," her mom said. "The Bouchards are coming, and they hinted Randolph would be joining them. From what I heard, he's single again. Might be the opportune time to win him back."

Charlie repressed a shudder. "Mom, *I'm* the one who broke things off."

"True, but that was three years ago. After all that time, you haven't found anyone to replace him. Don't you think you might have been a tad hasty?"

Never. If anything, she shouldn't have gone out with him in the first place. From day one, he'd interspersed his compliments with sharp little barbs—about her job, her clothes, and her sweet tooth. Whenever they went out for dinner, he always ordered for her ("the little lady will have the kale salad") and got annoyed if she hinted at wanting dessert. After they'd gotten engaged, he'd pressured her to spend a fortune on designer clothes, salon visits, and expensive gym memberships, just to meet his exacting standards. If she'd married him, he would have stripped her personality down to nothing.

"I'm in no hurry to get married. Not anymore. But thanks for inviting me." *Now, please leave.* She did *not* want her mother still standing here when Knox arrived.

"All right, dear. Have a nice evening." With that, her mother turned to go, closing the door behind her.

Not for the first time, Charlie regretted moving out of the three-bedroom apartment she'd shared with two of her friends. But once Randolph had proposed, he insisted she come live with him. By the time she'd had the courage to end things, her roommates had found a replacement. She'd decided to save money by temporarily moving back home. Though after three years, the arrangement could hardly be called temporary. At least her apartment was in a separate living space, located above her parents' spacious three-car garage. But at age twenty-eight, it was embarrassing to admit she didn't have a place of her own.

Another knock came at the door, and her shoulders tightened. When she opened it, Knox stood there, wearing jeans and a black T-shirt with the *Ghostbusters* logo. In his arms was a paper bag from Fairway Market.

"Come on in," she said. "I love your shirt."

"Thanks. I got it at that vintage place on Johnson Street." He kicked off his sneakers and set the bag next to the coffee table. "I also brought some snacks, though it looks like you've got that covered."

She flushed, fully aware she might have gone overboard. Laid out on the table was a pitcher of ice-cold lemonade, a platter of homemade chocolate chip cookies, and a bowl of freshly popped popcorn, drizzled with butter. "In my opinion, you can never have too many snacks."

"I feel the same way. That popcorn smells incredible." He took out a jumbo pack of Twizzlers, a bag of Sour Patch kids, and another bag of Nestlé miniature chocolate bars.

Had he remembered her sweet tooth? Or did he just love candy as much as she did? "Awesome. Now we'll feel like we're at the movies."

He stuck his hands in his pockets, as if unsure what to say next, and cast his gaze around her apartment. "Cute place."

It was only six hundred square feet, but she'd put every inch of it to good use, filling it full of potted plants, bookshelves, and funky accent pieces, like a fuchsia shag rug, a sunshine-yellow armchair, and a gooseneck lamp with multicolored shades. In one corner was her portable keyboard, which had been gathering dust since Christmas.

"Thanks," she said. "I know it's strange to still be living with my parents, but..."

"No, I get it. Rent in Victoria is ridiculously expensive. It's gotten almost as bad as Vancouver." He walked over to one wall, which held a series of shadow boxes filled with quirky little toys, some dating back to the 1950s. "This is so cool. Where'd you get all these things?"

"Mostly from flea markets or Etsy. My granny started the collection, and when she went into assisted living, she gave it to me. I like adding to it." She loved seeking out new treasures—small china figures, glass animals, tiny dolls, and miniature dollhouse furniture.

"I sometimes hit up flea markets on the weekends," he said.

"Now that I know what you collect, I'll keep an eye out for that stuff."

"Thank you." His comment was so thoughtful it took her aback. Feeling slightly flustered, she gestured to the couch. "Should we get started?"

"Sounds good." He settled himself at one end of it and reached for the pitcher. "Do you want a glass of lemonade?"

"Yes, please. And help yourself to the cookies. I made them this morning."

As she joined him on the couch, she caught the faint hint of cedar and citrus and wondered if he used a special beard grooming oil. Taking a deep, calming breath, she willed herself to relax. But it was hard to play it cool when he was sitting right beside her, his broad frame taking up so much space. He was so close she could easily reach over and touch him.

Not that she would. This was a get-together between two colleagues. If she wanted more from him, she'd have to build up to it. *Slowly.* Which made her feel more like an awkward teenager than a grown woman. But she didn't want to risk anything that would make him retreat into his grumpy shell.

"I did a little research into *Canada's Most Haunted*," she said. "It's been around for five seasons, but I planned to start us off with the first episode of season one."

Knox passed her a glass of lemonade. "That works for me."

She took the glass and handed him a black composition book and a ballpoint pen. "I also got us each a notebook so we could jot stuff down." Even as she said it, she knew she sounded nerdy. Like they were students working on a group project.

He took it from her and set it on his lap. "Let me guess, you were a straight A student?"

"Um...yeah. Kind of."

There was no "kind of" about it. She'd always excelled in school, mostly because her parents had expected nothing less.

"Same here. Except for chem." He offered up a grin. "I hated all those formulas."

Interesting. She filed that tidbit away in the portion of her brain reserved for facts about Knox. He doled them out so sparingly that she treasured them as if they were tiny gems.

Once the show started, she did her best to keep her eyes on the screen. But she couldn't resist sneaking a few glances at him. Though she'd always been aware of his height—he was almost a foot taller than she was—he was usually standing behind the bar, so the difference wasn't as noticeable. Seated on her couch, he looked so solid. Like he could wrap her up in a giant bear hug or pick her up in his arms with little effort.

Focus. If she wanted to know what to expect from the show, she needed to pay attention.

By the end of the first episode, she was able to relax. She even giggled at a few of Knox's snarky comments. Not that she blamed him, since some of the "evidence" the paranormal investigators found looked dubious at best. Like, was that really an otherworldly orb floating by the window, or was it the reflection from a passing car? Was that figure on the road a spectral vision or a random cow?

After three hours, her interest started waning. When Knox suggested breaking for the evening, she turned off the TV. She tried not to ogle him when he stood up, though she couldn't help noticing the way his T-shirt revealed his sturdy biceps and the tattoos on his upper arms. Or the way the dark fabric stretched across his brawny frame.

Down, girl. No staring.

She distracted herself by gathering up the plates and glasses; Knox followed her, bringing the leftover snacks to the kitchen counter. After setting them down, he peered at a shelf where she'd stacked a pile of DVDs. He picked up a thick box set. "You have the first five seasons of *The Hidden Forest.*"

She cringed, hoping he didn't think she was a total geek. "I was a huge fan, back when the show first started. Like, I was flat-out obsessed."

"But not so much anymore?"

"I wanted to stick with it, but the show went downhill in the fourth season. Toward the end of the fifth, I tapped out."

"Yeah, the first few years were the best." He examined the titles more closely. "I'm surprised you have so many DVDs."

"There's something so comforting about owning my favorite movies. This way, I can watch them anytime." Most of her collection consisted of fantasy films and romantic comedies. "But these DVDs aren't my worst addiction."

"No?" He chuckled. "What else are you hiding?"

"You're gonna make fun of me."

When he shook his head, she led him into her bedroom. Other than her queen bed and dresser, most of the room was filled with books. Not just shelves but teetering piles of paperbacks propped up next to her bed. Knox regarded them with such a stunned expression that she almost burst out laughing. Until she realized they were alone. *In her bedroom.*

What the hell were you thinking?

Her bed was *right there*. Worse yet, it was unmade, and her thin cotton nightie was crumpled up beside her pillow, next to a pair of pink panties. She'd tossed them there in her hurry to change this morning. Her face flamed as she ran over to the bed and covered them with her comforter. "Um...so....I love collecting old mass-market paperbacks."

"I can see that." Knox picked one up from the tallest stack. It was an old-school romantic saga from the 1980s with a classic clinch cover, set on a pirate ship. "*Love's Burning Embrace*. Looks spicy."

Now, her cheeks were a fiery inferno. Of course he'd pick that stack instead of the one with her fantasy novels. Though some of those were pretty racy, too. "Historical romance is one of my favorite genres. A lot of these older books are kinda problematic, but I can't help myself. Whenever I see them at library sales and used bookstores, I snap them up and add them to my TBR pile."

"Nothing wrong with that." He set the book back. "I collect paperbacks, too. I own almost everything Stephen King has ever written."

"Whoa. Hasn't he written, like, fifty books?"

"Or thereabouts. I still have two boxes of his paperbacks stashed away in my childhood bedroom. Most of them are from used bookstores. Whenever I buy a secondhand book, I like to imagine all the people who've read it before me."

She allowed herself to relax. Though she'd always known he was a voracious reader—whenever she saw him in the staff room, he was usually caught up in a paperback—she hadn't realized he shared her book-hoarding tendencies. "I've never been gutsy enough to try Stephen King's books. I'm not sure I could handle them."

"You might be surprised. I mean, you just watched three hours of ghost hunting and agreed to help with the show. That counts for something."

Was he teasing her? No, from his sincere expression, she suspected he meant it as a compliment. "Thanks. I'm glad I can help."

Especially since it means spending more time with you

As they stood there, surrounded by all her books, a current passed between them. A tiny spark. She wanted to act on it—to take his hand and pull him closer—but didn't know if he'd welcome her touch.

He rubbed the back of his neck. "I should get going. Thanks for having me over."

"Any time." Though she was tired of watching *Canada's Most Haunted*, she wished he'd stay. She wanted to keep unraveling the mystery that was Knox McIntyre. "Now that we know the basic setup of the show, I guess we should figure out if the Duchess would even qualify for an episode. Laurel said she'd ask her roommate, Celia, if she could look into the hotel's background. She works as a historian for the provincial archives."

He nodded enthusiastically. "Laurel must have already told her what we were up to because Celia got in touch with me yesterday."

"She did? I didn't realize you knew her."

"I met her a couple of years ago when her dad did a signing at Bolen Books. She's also stopped by the Lily a few times after her ghost tours."

Interesting. Knox so rarely spoke about his personal life that Charlie's curiosity was piqued. "You're friends?" Not that it was any of her business.

He shrugged. "I guess you could say that since we share a mutual passion for horror novels. It's always nice to chat with a fellow enthusiast. Anyway, she was excited to help us out, and she'll let me know if she finds anything. Do you want to come if I meet with her?"

Damn right. Even if Celia was probably far gutsier than she was, especially when it came to ghosts, this was Charlie's project. She didn't want anyone to take her place. "I'd like that. I hope she uncovers something spooky. But...um...not *too* spooky. You know what I mean?"

Knox's hearty laugh chased away her momentary bout of jealousy. "I hear you. So, maybe just one or two ghosts? Not a whole fleet of them, like when those ghouls take over New York City in *Ghostbusters*."

"Exactly." She'd never seen him so at ease. Was it because of her? Or because he was off duty? Either way, she wanted more.

She walked him to the door and waited while he put on his sneakers. As he was leaving, she was gripped with the urge to prolong their time together, even for a few more minutes. "I'll walk you out. I could use a little fresh air."

"It's a nice night. Still pretty warm for September."

A surge of self-confidence rushed through her. *I did it. I had*

Knox over, and he wasn't scared off by my shadow boxes, my DVDs, and my raunchy paperbacks.

But when they reached the circular drive in front of her parents' house, where he'd parked his truck, she stopped short. Her parents stood outside their doorway, talking to another couple.

And right beside them...was Randolph.

Four

Knox couldn't remember the last time he'd enjoyed himself so much. While the ghost-hunting show had been cheesy and repetitious, he would have sat through another ten episodes if it meant spending more time with Charlie. He'd thought she was sweet and funny before, but tonight, he'd discovered so many hidden depths about her. Like her obsession with miniature toys. Her collection of old-school romance novels. And her love of *The Hidden Forest*. More specifically, the first three seasons, when he'd worked as the show's head writer.

For a brief moment, he'd been tempted to tell her about his connection to the show. To explain that he'd written some of the episodes she loved. He didn't, of course. After five years of keeping that shit to himself, that was a level of intimacy he wasn't ready for. But after tonight, one thing was certain—he wanted to spend more time with Charlie. Not just at work, either. He liked being able to talk to her without anyone interrupting them.

As they walked along the circular driveway that graced the front of her parents' house, he was struck by the sheer size of the place. Even in the dark, there was no mistaking how massive it was, easily twice as big as the ramshackle home where he'd grown up with five siblings. He was taken aback when Charlie stopped suddenly. The pained expression on her face made it look like she wanted to turn tail and run.

Fifty feet in front of them, a group of people stood next to the front walkway. Before Knox could ask Charlie what was wrong, two well-dressed couples approached them, led by a tall, blond woman in a pink dress. Based on the resemblance, Knox guessed she was Charlie's mother. Trailing behind the couples was a guy his age, dressed in a polo shirt and khakis, all blond and tanned, like he belonged in a Ralph Lauren ad.

Charlie gave them a feeble wave. "Hey, Mom. I wasn't sure if your cocktail night was still going on."

"We're just finishing up. Who's your friend?"

"This is Knox McIntyre. He works with me at the Duchess. Knox, these are my parents and their friends, the Bouchards. And...um...their son, Randolph Bouchard."

Knox had never seen Charlie this ill at ease, not even when dealing with the hotel's most demanding guests. He wasn't sure what was up, but he greeted everyone politely. When he got to Randolph, the guy shook his hand vigorously. The type of handshake meant to indicate *he* was the alpha dog.

"What do you do at the hotel?" Randolph asked. "Are you a front desk clerk, like Charlie?"

Front desk clerk? Charlie was the goddamn front office *manager*, a position she'd worked hard to earn. Even so, Knox didn't correct him. "I'm the head bartender at the Gilded Lily, the hotel's cocktail lounge."

Randolph snickered. "Let me guess—you're not just a bartender. You're also an aspiring actor, waiting on your big break? Or a writer, hoping to sell the great Canadian novel?"

The other adults laughed, as if Randolph's comments were the height of wittiness. Knox had heard it all before. "Nope. I'm just a guy who likes mixing cocktails."

"I guess that's as good a job as any, even if the pay is shit,"

Randolph said. "But you'd never catch *me* serving someone a drink."

"Randolph is in finance," Charlie's mom said. "He and Charlotte were engaged to be married."

Knox reeled inwardly. Not because Charlie had once been engaged, but because she'd contemplated marrying a d-bag like Randolph.

Then again, why was he so surprised? The guy obviously came from money, like Charlie did. Though she never bragged about her family's wealth, the size of her parents' house was a dead giveaway. Located in Uplands—one of the richest neighborhoods in Victoria —it was probably worth a cool three million dollars.

"We're not engaged anymore." Charlie latched onto Knox's arm. "If you'll excuse us, we're heading out."

Knox didn't know what was going on, but he was willing to roll with it. Anything to support Charlie.

"What time will you be home, dear?" her mom asked.

"I'm not sure. See you all later." As Charlie tugged Knox away from the group, she lowered her voice so only he could hear. "Keep walking. *Please.* Once we get to your truck, I need you to drive me around for a bit."

"You got it." He'd drive her anywhere she needed to go. All night, if necessary. When they reached his truck, he opened the passenger door for her and waited until she got inside and put on her seat belt before shutting it. He sensed the group was watching them, but he kept his gaze focused on her as he got in and started the engine. Only after he'd driven a few blocks did he speak up again.

"You okay, Charlie?"

"I...I'm sorry. You must think I'm totally unhinged."

The hitch in her voice was heartbreaking. "You seem pretty hinged to me. I just want to make sure you're all right."

"I am. It's just..." She paused, as if getting a hold of herself. "Randolph and I broke up three years ago. I'm completely over it, but my parents keep hoping we'll get back together. And because they're good friends with *his* parents, I can't avoid him. If we hadn't hightailed it out of there, I would have been forced to make small talk with them, and I just...couldn't." She groaned. "Sorry. That was more information than you needed."

It wasn't too much. Now that he'd gotten a glimpse of the real Charlie—the woman behind the sunny front office manager he'd only known at a surface level—he wanted more. "It's fine. Did you have a destination in mind, or should I drive around?"

"I'm not sure. I don't want to keep you up too late."

"No worries. I have Monday off, so I can sleep in."

"Thanks, Knox."

Her voice still held a slight wobble. Like she was trying to keep everything under control. He wished he could give her a hug, but he wanted to respect her boundaries. "There's a little cove not far from here if you'd like to get some fresh air."

"That sounds great."

They drove in silence until he reached a stretch of road with access to a public beach. One of the things he loved about living on the southern tip of Vancouver Island was the abundance of coves and beaches. Most of them were small and rocky, the water frigid and filled with seaweed, but they were rarely crowded.

After he parked his truck, he went around and opened Charlie's door. "There's a stone stairway going down to the beach just past those bushes."

She eased out of his truck and shut the passenger door behind her, then followed him toward the steps. "I had no idea this place existed."

"It's kind of hidden, but I like coming here." He led her down to the shoreline.

The ground underfoot was made up of small pebbles, with chunks of driftwood scattered around, some pieces the size of tree trunks. It wasn't a beach meant for swimming and sunbathing, but it possessed a quiet beauty, the waves gleaming under the moonlight.

He found his favorite place to sit—a hollow log worn smooth by the wind and water—and gestured for her to join him. She sat beside him, so close their bodies were almost touching. Allowing himself to relax, he inhaled deeply, relishing the briny tang of the ocean.

When she released a drawn-out sigh, he spoke up. "If you want to talk about it, I'll listen."

"Really? You once told me you hated it when people unloaded their sob stories on you."

While she wasn't wrong, he didn't want her to think he was an uncaring jerk. "One of the downsides of being a bartender is that everyone wants to share their woes. Including people you don't give a shit about. So, I make it clear I'm not interested. With you, it's different because...we're friends."

Was it presumptuous to call her a friend? Up until tonight, they'd never hung out after work. But of all the people he knew at the Duchess, she was the one he trusted the most. The one who stopped by the bar to chat with him when she worked the evening shift. Who left him an extra donut every time she brought in a box for one of her meetings. And the only one who'd been able to coerce him into helping with the hotel's seasonal events last Christmas. Just seeing her always brightened his day.

When she didn't respond, he sat quietly, listening to the shush of the waves. As someone with secrets of his own, he would never force her to reveal anything she didn't want to. But the question tumbled out before he could stop it. "Okay, I've got to know. I can understand why you'd date the guy. But to get engaged? He seems like a dick."

Charlie let out a bubbly laugh. "Don't go easy on him or anything."

"I wasn't. I could have called him an asshole, but I toned it down."

Her laughter spilled over, so infectious he couldn't help but smile. "Like I said, I started dating him because our parents spent so much time together. When he asked me out, saying yes seemed like a no-brainer. For once, it was nice to have my parents' approval. They weren't exactly thrilled when I decided to go into hospitality."

"Are you kidding? You're a manager." Fuck these rich jerks who didn't appreciate her.

"Yeah, but I'm in customer service, which they consider demeaning. Dating Randolph was a great way to make them happy. On my twenty-fifth birthday, they threw me a big surprise party, which would have been nice if they'd invited the Damsels, but it was filled with their rich friends. In the middle of it, Randolph got down on one knee and proposed, in full view of everyone. There was no way I could turn him down without humiliating him."

Knox picked up a pebble and smoothed it between his fingers. "So, what happened? Why'd you call it off?"

"As soon as I moved in with him, I realized what a huge mistake I'd made. He'd always been kind of judgmental, but once I was his fiancée, he tried to control every aspect of my life."

Knox's fingers coiled into fists at the thought of anyone mistreating Charlie. He strained to keep his voice even. "He didn't hurt you, did he?"

"Nothing like that. It was more subtle." She looked away, as if too ashamed to face him. "Commenting on what I wore. The kind of food I ate. How often I worked out. Once, when I was sick with the flu, I didn't go to the gym for an entire week. He hounded me about it, telling me I'd get out of shape if I kept skipping my workouts. Or, sometimes, when we were going out for the evening, he'd say, 'Is that what you're wearing?' and I'd get so self-conscious I'd have to change. Then he'd hover over me and insist on choosing my outfit."

"Jesus, Charlie. That's not okay."

She rubbed her hands over her bare arms. "I know that now. But he got into my head, so much that I started feeling physically ill before we went anywhere. And when I told my mom how anxious he made me, she said I was overreacting."

He hated that anyone—especially a parent—had made her question her feelings. "How did it end?"

She gave him a wry smile. "Believe it or not, I broke things off because of the Duchess. He started telling me how happy he'd be once we were married, and I could quit my job. Like my parents, he thought my role at the hotel was beneath me. That's when I told him I couldn't marry someone who didn't support my career."

"You left him?" He could only imagine how hard that would have been—to go against her folks, to leave a secure future, to speak up for herself.

"Bravest thing I ever did." She turned to face him, her eyes damp with tears. "The fallout was rough. My mom nagged me about it for months."

"I'm sorry. For what it's worth, a prick like that doesn't deserve you." He was tempted to tell her about his own broken engagement, but he stopped himself.

It's not about you, dumb-ass. No matter what shit he'd dealt with in his life, he shouldn't be piling it on Charlie. Instead, he needed to support her.

"Thanks. It was hard at first, but I don't regret leaving him." She stood and walked toward the water's edge. Picking up a pebble, she sent it skimming across the ocean. It skipped three times before falling into the water with a splash.

He joined her, tossing his own pebble, then grinning when it skipped four times. "Beat that."

"Getting a little competitive, are we? It's on." She bent down and scooped up a few more stones. "I was just getting warmed up."

Under the faint glow of moonlight, they continued tossing

stones into the water. Charlie's mood turned from sorrowful to exuberant as she went on to beat him nine times out of ten.

Standing beside her, the longing swelled up inside of him, making him *want* something he hadn't dreamed of in years. Ever since he'd left Vancouver, he hadn't pursued a serious relationship with anyone. He'd had a few one-night stands, but he'd never let them develop into anything meaningful. After everything he'd been through with Lila, he hadn't wanted to risk losing his heart again.

But now? Being with Charlie made him wonder if some things were worth the risk.

Five

When Charlie arrived at work on Monday, she was seriously dragging. After Knox had dropped her off at her apartment, she'd had a hard time falling asleep. How could she, when her mind kept replaying their entire evening? Though nothing romantic had happened on the beach, she truly believed they were becoming friends. Not just work buddies, but actual *friends*.

Before heading into the hotel, she dashed over to Alma's Beanery—the coffeehouse closest to the Duchess—and grabbed a mocha for herself and a caramel latte for Rosie. She loved downtown Victoria at this early hour, before the tourists were out in full force. Across from the hotel, the city's popular Inner Harbour—a waterfront area filled with sailboats, small cruise ships, seaplanes, and water taxis—was quiet, no sign of the artists or street musicians who usually lined the causeway. Only the raucous cries of the seagulls overhead broke the stillness.

When she got to Rosie's office, she peeked her head in the doorway. To her surprise, Selena occupied the rolling chair across from Rosie's desk. Usually Selena spent the first few hours of the day in her tiny office near the hotel's kitchen. This way, she could be on hand if any crises occurred while her staff were prepping and serving the Duchess' lavish breakfast buffet. Given that the buffet was one of the hotel's best-reviewed amenities, Selena insisted on maintaining tight quality control.

Upon spotting Charlie, Rosie gestured for her to join them. "Come on in."

"Are you sure? I don't want to interrupt."

"You can stay," Selena said. "This issue actually concerns you, so it's better if I get it off my chest while you're here." She seemed more agitated than usual, a few dark strands of hair falling from her tight bun.

Charlie came in and set Rosie's coffee on her desk. "I got you a caramel latte from Alma's to help you survive Monday. Selena, I'm sorry I didn't get you anything."

"I'm good," Selena said. "I already had three cups of dark roast this morning. Any more caffeine and I'd shoot off into space."

Rosie took a sip of her latte and gave a sigh of satisfaction. "Thanks. This is just what I needed. The first Monday after a vacation is always rough."

Charlie grabbed the extra chair in the corner and pulled it up beside Selena's. "What's going on?"

"I'm so pissed right now." Selena blew out an angry breath. "I fucked up on Saturday."

"You? No way." Charlie had always envied Selena's assertiveness. She'd been at the Duchess for longer than any of them and commanded a fierce loyalty from her staff. But it was more than that. Around the opposite sex, she possessed a confidence Charlie sorely lacked. Selena wasn't the type to spend a year pining for someone. If she wanted a guy, she went for it.

"I blame the tequila." Selena scrubbed her hands over her face. "I was at Pepe's Cantina, waiting on Martin—the guy I've been seeing—but he didn't show. No text, no call, nothing. Two drinks later, I checked his feed, and what did I see but him getting cozy with some 'girl' who looks barely old enough to drink. First of all, if he was going to bail, he should have had the balls to tell me. And second, how dare he trade me in for a younger model?"

"Sorry. That sucks," Rosie said. "How'd you screw up? Did you drunk dial him?"

"I wish. I just ordered a third drink and sat there like a loser. And then—to make my night a complete shit show—guess who walks over to my table?"

"One of your exes?" Charlie asked.

"Nope. Our good buddy, Alejandro Rivera, the assistant manager of the Grand Duke."

"What was he doing there?" Rosie demanded. "Pepe's is *our* hangout."

"Who knows? Out drinking with his minions? Looking for innocent women to lure into his web? But when he saw me, he just *had* to make my night even more unbearable."

Though none of the Damsels liked the stuck-up managers at the Grand Duke, Selena was unrivaled in her hatred of Alejandro. True, he was known for his condescending attitude, but no one had clashed with him the way she had.

"What did he do?" Charlie asked.

"He started bragging about all the prestigious events his hotel was going to be hosting this fall. Like a huge society wedding at the end of September and a fancy Hollywood-type gala in October, for some big-deal fantasy show from Vancouver."

"A fantasy show? Do you mean *The Hidden Forest*?" Even if Charlie hadn't watched it in years, she'd always dreamed of meeting the cast members.

"That's the one. Apparently, they're celebrating their hundredth episode."

"Why are they hosting the event in Victoria?" Charlie asked. "Why not at a hotel in Vancouver?"

"Alejandro said the show's executive producer has ties with the CEO of Royal Host—the company that manages the Duke. Something like that. Anyway..." Selena drew out the word. "I should have stopped after my third drink because I couldn't keep my big mouth shut. Instead, I bragged about us hosting *Canada's Most Haunted*."

No. Charlie's gut knotted into a tight ball. "We're not even sure if they're going to pick us. And we don't have any evidence our hotel is haunted yet."

Selena groaned. "I know, but I had to say something. Which backfired because he laughed at me. He said someone from the show had already met with him, and he'd turned them down."

"I should have told you the Duke was the show's first choice," Charlie said. "That's on me."

"No, this mistake is all my fault." Selena tucked a stray wisp of hair behind her ears. "Now, Alejandro thinks we're even more of a joke. Worse yet, he said he'll be 'watching closely' to see how this plays out."

"You don't think he'll try to discredit us, do you?" Rosie asked.

The concern on her face ramped up Charlie's anxiety. She didn't need their biggest rival spreading rumors that the Duchess was so desperate for attention they'd fake a haunting. "It might be okay. I haven't done any background research yet, so I still might find something. All I did was check out the show with Knox. He came over last night and watched a bunch of episodes with me."

Admitting it filled her with a surge of pride. Like she'd accomplished a huge goal, rather than taking a baby step.

Rosie brightened. "*Yes.* How'd it go?"

Charlie responded with a dreamy smile. "It was so nice. We totally bonded."

"Bonded as in talked, or bonded as in you dragged him into your bedroom and had your way with him?" Selena's grin made it clear she was over her momentary bout of self-loathing.

"Just talked, though he did come into my bedroom. Not to have sex, but...because I wanted to show him all my books. Of course, he noticed the stack with the spicy romances first."

"Girl, your TBR pile is out of control," Selena said. "You're lucky he didn't run screaming from your apartment."

"I know. But he told me he collects paperbacks, too. And then, when we were leaving..." Charlie went on to explain the awkward situation with her parents and Randolph, which had led to her spending an hour with Knox at a nearby cove. "Even if the night didn't end on a romantic note, we definitely connected."

Selena placed her hand over her heart. "I love this for you. But you know this is only the first step, right? You lit the match, and now you've got to fan the flame."

"I agree with Selena," Rosie said. "Stay on him. Since you're working on this show together, you'll have lots of excuses to hang out. The next time you're alone, try dropping a few romantic hints."

Romantic hints? To be honest, dealing with ghosts might be less terrifying.

CHARLIE HAD INTENDED TO HOLE UP IN HER OFFICE AND start researching the hotel's history, but she got stuck dealing with one crisis after another. Like the fallout from a computer glitch that messed up a ton of reservations. And the loss of two newly trained employees, who'd gotten better offers from the Grand Duke. Now, she was filling in at the front desk for a clerk who'd taken off for a few hours to handle an issue with her son's school.

She did her best to greet the guests with her cheerful customer-service smile in place, even though her mind was plagued with worries. Foremost among her concerns was Selena's confrontation with Alejandro. Did they need to do damage control, or was Selena overreacting because she hated him so much?

Charlie's mood worsened when Preston strode over to the front desk with a serious expression on his face. "*Charlotte.* Did you make any progress this weekend?"

No matter how many times she asked him to call her Charlie, he never listened. "Yes. Knox and I watched a bunch of episodes of *Canada's Most Haunted*, and we took notes. We got a good sense of what ghost hunters look for when they visit a haunted location."

Preston waved his hand in dismissal. "That's all very well, but unless we can dredge up some evidence of the supernatural, we'll never land the show. What have you got so far?"

She wiped a thin film of sweat from her brow. "Laurel's roommate, Celia, is checking the provincial archives to find out more about the hotel's history. That should help."

"What about all the reviews the Duchess has gotten? Have any of the hotel's former guests mentioned unexplained phenomena?"

"Not that we've seen. We started combing through our reviews last week, going as far back as the early 2010s, but we haven't had any luck. We still have a long way to go."

There were just *so* many reviews—on TripAdvisor, Google, Yelp, and all the other travel aggregators. Prior to the internet, guests had expressed their feelings via comment cards, which they'd filled out at the end of their stay. At least sixty years' worth of cards were packed into bankers' boxes, located in the hotel's basement storage area. Sorting through all of them would be a Herculean task.

"You need to work faster," he said. "Recruit anyone else from the staff who has time on their hands. It's been almost a week since Logan visited the hotel, and I'm sure he'll make a decision soon. We don't want to miss out."

Charlie sighed. "Are you sure this is a good idea, sir? Since we don't have any proof our hotel is haunted, we don't want to be accused of misrepresenting ourselves. Or have this turn into a big joke." Especially now that the Duke knew about it. Not that she'd share that information with him.

"Nonsense. This could be a huge win for the Duchess. We want this year's spooky season to be the best one ever." He narrowed his eyes at her. "Don't forget your annual review is coming up next month. You wouldn't want to jeopardize it in any way."

Shit. That sounded like a threat. But it wasn't as if she could magically conjure up a ghost or create an eerie legend that didn't exist.

By the time he left, she was more on edge than ever. She was about to take her afternoon break when the desk phone rang. She answered it quickly, hoping it wasn't a guest with a complaint. "The Duchess Hotel, Charlie Fraser speaking. How may I help you?"

The low rumble of Knox's voice put her at ease. "Hey, Charlie. How's it going?"

"I'm doing okay, but I'm bummed I haven't gotten the chance to start in on my research. Right now, I'm stuck filling in at the front desk."

"I assumed as much since you didn't respond to my texts. Do you have a sec, or are you busy with a guest?"

"I'm good. What's up?" The lobby was empty, save for a family of five, who stood near the hotel's entrance, waiting for their airport shuttle.

"I just heard from Celia. She uncovered information about the hotel in the archives."

"She did?" The tension eased from Charlie's shoulders. She'd never expected Celia to come through this quickly. "I can't believe she found something already."

"She said it's good stuff, too. If you can leave work early, she's willing to meet us tonight at five thirty. I asked her if she could push it a little later, but she's giving a ghost tour at seven."

Though Charlie had planned to stay until six, technically, this meeting counted as work. Preston couldn't possibly complain, not when he'd just badgered her about finding more information. "I can make it. But isn't this your day off?"

"It's okay. This ghost stuff is high priority. I'm sure Preston's been riding you about it."

"Has he ever. He stopped by the front desk a few minutes ago." Charlie wrote down the time and place of the meeting. "Thanks for setting this up."

"Glad to do it. I'll see you in a bit."

"See you, Knox."

As she hung up, she could barely contain her exhilaration. Knox had gone out of his way to arrange this meeting—and on his day off, no less. He'd made a point of *calling* her about it. And now, she'd get to spend more time with him.

Of course, there was the remote possibility Celia might have discovered something truly bone-chilling while researching the hotel's history. But right now, Charlie was too excited to worry about that.

Six

At five thirty, Charlie hustled over to the Seagull, a pub located two blocks from the Duchess. It occupied a prime spot on Wharf Street, a bustling road overlooking the Inner Harbour. At this time of day, the area was crammed with tourists, and a few street musicians were out serenading the crowds. Traffic along Wharf Street was backed up due to a line of cars idling behind a horse-and-carriage loaded with people.

The pub's outdoor patio had a lively feel, enhanced by the 1980s pop music playing through the speakers. Knox sat at a wrought-iron table shaded by a big red umbrella. He waved her over. "Hi, Charlie. I'm glad you could escape a little early."

"Me, too. Today's been kind of stressful." She was tempted to tell him about Selena's run-in with Alejandro but decided against it. For now, she wanted to focus on good news, not bad. "I'm eager to hear what Celia found out. I didn't think we'd get any results this quickly."

"Me neither." Knox handed her a menu. "I ordered a beer, but I wasn't sure what you wanted. Happy hour goes until six, and there's a bunch of cocktail specials. But most of them are sickly-sweet frozen drinks."

She grinned at him. "Aren't you glad you're not the one mixing them?"

"Yeah. Why do people drink that crap?" Despite his gruff voice, he had a teasing gleam in his eyes.

"Just for that, I might order a piña colada. Or one of these fruity daiquiris."

"*No*. I know you have more taste than that."

"But if I get one, I can pretend I'm in the tropics."

As she was perusing the menu, a Latina woman with long, dark hair, a multitude of tattoos, and an all-black wardrobe came over to their table. She plopped down in a chair beside them. "Hey, Knox. Good to see you. And you must be Charlie. I'm Celia Ramos."

"Hi, Celia," Charlie said. "Thanks so much for helping us out."

"No problem. Once Laurel filled me in, I couldn't wait to get started. I don't know if Knox told you, but I love ghost stories. Which reminds me..." She reached into her knapsack, pulled out a paperback with a colorfully decorated skull on the cover, and handed it to him. "Last time we talked, I promised you an advanced reader copy of my dad's latest novel. He had a few extras lying around, so I snitched one. You'll have to read it quickly because I need to return it to him next week."

Knox gave her an appreciative smile. "Thanks. I'll have no problem finishing it by then. Knowing me, I'll be up all night reading it."

A surge of jealousy passed through Charlie, so powerful it took her aback. On Sunday night, Knox had made it seem like he and Celia were casual friends. But now, Charlie wasn't so sure. Was he secretly attracted to Celia? Was this the reason he was keen to collaborate with her? If she was into horror novels, she was a better fit to work with him on a ghost-hunting show than Charlie would ever be.

She forced herself to speak up. "Your dad is a writer?"

Celia nodded. "Cristóbal Ramos. Ever heard of him? He's a famous horror author."

"Um...sorry. I mostly read romance and fantasy." Now, Charlie felt even more inadequate.

"Her dad's really talented," Knox said. "But I wouldn't recommend his books unless you're prepared for a few sleepless nights."

"I can testify to that," a male voice said. "I've only read two of them, and the second one gave me nightmares for a week." A lanky guy with messy brown hair and glasses placed his hands on Celia's shoulders and kissed the top of her head. "Sorry I'm late, babe. Work got a little hectic."

She smiled up at him. "It's fine. I just got here. You've met Knox before, and this is Charlie. She works with him at the Duchess. Charlie, this is my boyfriend, Glen."

Boyfriend? Charlie unclenched her hands, suddenly aware she'd been clutching her napkin in a death grip. Maybe it was pathetic, but she was immensely relieved to learn Celia was already involved with someone. "Nice to meet you, Glen. I got roped into this ghost-hunting stuff, even though I'm a wimp when it comes to horror movies."

Glen sat down at their table. "Join the club. I was the world's biggest wuss until I met Celia last year. She's been slowly converting me. When she told me what you and Knox were up to, I had to join in. I've gotten really interested in the supernatural ever since we had a hair-raising encounter at the Grand Duke Hotel last year."

"We were staying there overnight and saw a full-body apparition," Celia said.

Charlie stared at them in awe. "No way. You have proof that ghosts exist?"

"I'm not so sure," Glen said. "As a scientist, I'm more of a skeptic than Celia, but whatever we saw wasn't easily explainable. Since then, I've watched two seasons of *Canada's Most Haunted.*

None of the episodes have shown me anything as impressive as the sight we witnessed that night."

Though Charlie had always been open to the possibility of ghosts, she'd never talked to someone who'd seen one. All of a sudden, her project with Knox was a little more interesting...and a bit scarier.

When their server stopped by, she ordered a frozen mango daiquiri, which made Knox roll his eyes. But it was a playful eye roll—a sign he was getting more comfortable teasing her. She waited until their server had left before turning to Celia. "So... Knox said you already found out something about the Duchess?"

"Yes." Celia smacked her hand on the table. "I thought this might be a wild goose chase, because I've never heard any rumors about your hotel before. I presumed if something *had* happened, the hotel's owners would have played it up. You know, to build up the lore, like the Grand Duke has done. But the gruesome incident I uncovered was deliberately buried. Which isn't surprising, considering how sordid it was." Her eyes sparkled with excitement.

Charlie twisted her cloth napkin between her hands again. She couldn't help feeling guilty that she was pleased at Celia's discovery. "Am I a horrible person if I admit I'm eager to hear the story?"

Knox placed his hand on her arm. "You're not horrible. Preston asked us to dig into the hotel's past. Besides, whatever happened probably took place a long time ago."

"That's right," Celia said. "In fact, I lucked out with my research because I decided to start when the hotel opened in 1922, rather than work backward from the present. In 1924, there was a grisly murder in room 309. The murderess, a wealthy woman named Frances Delacroix, shot two people in cold blood, then turned the gun on herself. Her two victims were her thirty-year-old husband, Howard, and a young front desk clerk named Maeve. My guess is that Frances discovered her husband was cheating on her with Maeve, then tracked him down and killed both of them."

Charlie couldn't believe the Duchess had played host to such a shocking incident. Three lives, all snuffed out in an instant. She pitied the poor room attendant who'd discovered the bodies. That wasn't something you could ever forget.

"That's so tragic," she said. "Why wasn't it a major scandal?"

"Because it didn't make the news," Celia replied. "I only uncovered it after looking through old police records and coroners' reports. I checked the local papers around the date it happened, but nothing was reported. Two weeks after the incident took place, the obituaries for Howard and Frances appeared, but no cause of death was listed. There was no obituary for Maeve, who was a recent immigrant from Ireland."

Charlie was surprised Celia could sound so matter-of-fact about it, but as a historian, she was probably used to reading about people who'd passed on.

Knox scratched his beard, like he was mulling over everything Celia had told them. "I don't understand how a crime of this magnitude didn't make it into the papers."

Celia shrugged. "I can't say for certain, but I'm guessing the hotel's owners paid off Victoria's two local newspapers. They could have offered them a bribe to keep quiet. Don't forget that this was the 1920s. TV and internet coverage didn't exist. If something wasn't in the paper, it wasn't like people could find out about it anywhere else."

"Good point," Knox said. "But those must have been some serious bribes."

"The owners probably thought the expense was worth it. At the time, the Duchess had only been open for two years and was marketing itself as an upscale boutique hotel. If word got out that one of their employees had been caught in a scandalous affair with a wealthy guest, their reputation would have suffered. But the cover-up *isn't* what surprises me the most about all this."

A little furrow crept between Glen's brows, like he was trying to solve a puzzle. "Okay, I'll bite. What do you think is most surprising?"

"That guests staying in room 309 haven't reported any ghostly encounters," Celia said. "At least, none that I've heard of. Usually, I'm the first to learn about this stuff because of my job at Historic Hauntings."

Their server arrived with their drinks, along with a set of plates and a big basket of fries. The fries smelled so good Charlie instantly wished she'd ordered some of her own.

"Help yourself," Knox said. "The fries are for all of us."

"Thanks." Charlie took a handful and set them on her plate, then doused them with malt vinegar. The first bite was crispy and delicious, but so hot it seared her tongue.

She tried to recall what she knew about room 309. In her five years at the Duchess, she'd become very familiar with all the rooms in the hotel. She'd memorized the ones with the best features, like the nicest views and the most square footage. In addition to the regular rooms, each floor of the hotel had four suites. Room 309 was one of those suites, but something about the room number was nagging at her. Until she remembered the layout of the third floor.

"I've got it!" she said. "I know why no one's ever had a ghostly experience in room 309. It's not accessible to our guests because it's part of a storage area."

"For housekeeping?" Knox asked.

"No. We have rooms set aside for that on every floor, next to the elevators, so our attendants can restock their carts. This is different." She wished she had a photo to show them. "It's made up of two adjoining suites, but the wall between them was taken down. It was turned into a big open space that the staff used for storing furniture and random crap."

Knox stared at her in wonder. "Really? I had no idea it even existed."

"That's because we don't use it anymore. It always seemed like an odd place to keep stuff, especially now that we store everything in the hotel's basement.

Celia looked positively giddy. "That explains it. If any ghosts *do* exist, they'd be more likely to appear in that storage room than anywhere else in the hotel. You should ask your housekeeping staff if they've had any sightings."

Sightings? A shiver danced along Charlie's spine. Now that she knew three people had died in that room, there was a good chance it might be haunted. Which was great for the show. But also slightly terrifying.

"Thanks, Celia. Knowing where to narrow my search will make things so much easier." She popped another fry in her mouth. Still too hot. She took a quick sip of her mango daiquiri to cool down, only to be hit with a stunning brain freeze.

"You're welcome," Celia said. "I'll send you an email with all this information so you can forward it to your friend at *Canada's Most Haunted*. I hope he picks your hotel."

"I hope so, too," Knox said. "I can't thank you enough for coming through for us. And on such short notice."

"It was a pleasure. And...just so you know, I have a sixth sense. So, if you want me to check out that storage area, I can do it. Though not tonight because I'm giving a ghost tour."

Charlie nodded eagerly. "That would be great. We don't have a consulting budget or anything, but I could ask our boss if he'd be willing to pay you for your time."

"No need. I love this stuff. Plus, if we do find out the Duchess is haunted, I can add it to my tour. I like injecting my talks with new material." She smiled at Charlie. "You should come on a tour sometime. It's not that frightening, I promise."

Maybe not for someone like Celia or Knox. But Charlie had a very vivid imagination. She caught Knox's eye. "Would you go with me?"

"Absolutely. We can go together as part of our research. Maybe on a Sunday or Monday, when I'm not working at the Gilded Lily."

Yes. Her heart did a giddy skip-jump. Even if it might be mildly frightening, she wasn't passing up another excuse to hang out with him. "I'd like that."

They spent the next half hour chatting, entertaining Celia with tales of the hotel while she regaled them with the full story of her and Glen's experience at the Grand Duke. Throughout their conversation, Charlie couldn't help noticing how comfortable Knox seemed, sharing anecdotes and laughing at everyone's jokes. He'd also acted like this on Sunday, when he'd visited her apartment. Friendly. Compassionate. A good listener.

Yet at the Gilded Lily, he rarely showed this side of himself. Was his mood related to his job? She'd always thought he liked crafting cocktails, but he never seemed truly happy. Though she didn't want to give Randolph any credit, she wondered if he'd been onto something. Did Knox have aspirations he'd never shared with anyone? Given his love of reading, she could easily envision him wanting to pursue a career as a writer.

"Charlie?" Knox's voice startled her out of her reverie. "You okay there?"

She cleared the thoughts from her mind. "I was just daydreaming. Thinking about the possibility of our hotel being haunted."

"Wouldn't that be great if it was?" Celia peeked at her phone. "I've gotta get ready for my tour. Let's grab the bill."

Knox waved her away. "I'll take care of it. In return for all your help."

"Thanks," Celia said. "Let me check my schedule to see when I'm available to visit your storage room. As soon as I'm free, I'll pop over." She and Glen took off, leaving Charlie alone with Knox.

After Knox paid the bill, he turned to Charlie with a devious smile. "Hear me out for a sec. I know you're done with work for the day, but I'm curious about that storage area. Do you want to go over to the hotel and check it out?"

Was he serious? In the three years she'd known him, he'd never suggested anything spontaneous. Nor did he spend time at the hotel after hours. "Shouldn't we wait for Celia? She's the ghost whisperer."

"We can visit it again when she's free. But I'm too intrigued to wait. I've never been in that room before."

What did it matter that this wasn't a romantic proposition? Or that the idea of checking out a room *where people had died* might put them at risk? Charlie wasn't passing up an opportunity to extend their time together.

Her heartbeat quickened. "Okay, but we'll have to go in the back way. I'd rather not have anyone at the front desk see me. Otherwise, I might get stuck there."

"You got it, partner."

Partner. She liked the sound of that.

Seven

After hearing Celia's story, Knox was brimming with curiosity. Usually, he avoided going into the Duchess on his days off. It was yet another way of maintaining the boundaries between his professional and personal life. But tonight? He'd never been so fired up to get back to the hotel.

Since the sun didn't set until eight, it was still light out when he and Charlie walked over to the Duchess. She led him past the loading dock and in through the service entrance. Once they reached her office, she ducked into it and returned with an old brass key, which looked like a relic from the Victorian era. She handed it to him. "Check it out."

He smoothed his hand over the worn metal. "I didn't think you meant an *actual* key."

"I know, right? When the hotel was upgraded in the 1980s, all the rooms switched to key cards except this one. We've only got a few copies."

As they took the elevator to the third floor, Knox felt a surge of adrenaline. Sneaking into the hotel after hours brought back a memory from his teenage years, when he and his older brother had ventured out after curfew and taken their dad's car on a joyride.

They'd covered their tracks so badly their parents had found out and grounded them. But that hadn't diminished the excitement he'd felt at breaking the rules for once.

The storage room was located at the end of the hall, marked by a door that contrasted sharply with those of the guest rooms. Old and weathered, it was a solid slab of wood, outfitted with a brass doorknob decorated in an intricate design. Charlie inserted the key but struggled to turn it. With a grunt, she twisted harder until it produced an audible click. The door swung open to reveal a large, darkened room.

Once they were inside, she flicked on a light switch, then closed the door behind them and pocketed the key. "It might be a bit dusty. It's been ages since anyone came in here."

Knox scanned the room, taking in all the cardboard boxes, old trunks, and ancient furniture. White cloths covered some of the pieces, while others were left to gather dust. Atop a chest of drawers was an old-fashioned phonograph and a stack of vinyl records. "This reminds me of the attic in my grandmother's house. I wonder if any of this stuff is worth something."

"It might be, but I think most of it is junk. From what I heard, this room was used to house things like worn-out linens or furniture that needed mending." Charlie pulled up the shades, allowing the natural light to filter in. Dozens of tiny dust motes danced about in the air.

Knox peeked at a stack of books and brushed off the top one. "*The Savoy Cocktail Book*. This publication is from 1930. I tried to buy a copy on eBay, but I was outbid."

"Take it if you want. Anything here is up for grabs since no one's done a proper inventory in decades." Charlie let out a tiny sneeze, then wiped her nose. "I'm going to see if I can detect any ghostly vibes. Can you let me know if you sense anything unusual?"

Despite all the horror novels he'd read, Knox's worldview skewed toward skepticism. He didn't believe in ghosts, let alone expect to encounter one. For that reason, he wasn't worried, just curious. But Charlie might be more apprehensive. "You're okay with this, right?"

She clasped her hands together. "I wouldn't attempt this on my own, but having you here makes me less nervous."

"Good. I honestly don't think anything bad's going to happen. Let's give it a go."

Closing his eyes, he tried to focus.

What do you feel?

Dust, tickling his nose.

Stifling air, making his forehead bead with sweat.

Otherwise? Not a damn thing.

"I'm not feeling much of anything," he said. "How about you?"

"Not really, but..." She wrapped her arms around herself.

"But what? Did you feel a burst of cold air?" According to the episodes they'd watched, a sudden drop in temperature might indicate a spirit was nearby.

"No, but..." Her forehead pinched in concentration. "I can smell roses. Not the flowers, but a softer scent. Like soap. Can you smell it?"

The only aroma he caught was the musty odor of a room that had been locked up for far too long. "I'm not getting it."

"I'm also feeling..." Her voice trembled. "Kind of awful."

"Physically or emotionally?"

"Emotionally. Like the way I felt after I broke up with Randolph. I knew I'd made the right move, but sometimes I'd lie in bed and wallow in misery and self-doubt. I'd wonder if I could ever trust myself to get involved with anyone again after making such a terrible decision."

Fuck. That sounded miserable. "Charlie, if something—or someone—in this room is messing with your mind, we should leave. It's not worth it."

She shook her head quickly. "It's fine. Really. Maybe I'm feeling this way because we saw Randolph last night."

A plausible explanation, but it didn't satisfy him completely. Wanting to finish up their investigation, he made a wide circuit of the room, peeking under dust cloths and looking behind dressers. Other than a few spiders, he didn't see anything creepy.

He wiped his brow with the back of his hand. "I'm no expert, but I'm not detecting a ghostly presence. I guess we should have waited for Celia."

"It's okay. Coming up here makes me feel brave."

He glanced over at her, relieved her sunny smile had returned. "You *are* brave. Keep telling yourself that."

"Thanks. We should get going, though." She went to open the door, only to tug at the knob in frustration. "Can you help me out? I think it's stuck."

"Sure." He tried turning the knob, but it didn't budge. "It feels more like it's locked, but that doesn't make any sense, unless someone locked us in here from the outside."

"I can't imagine why anyone would do that. Maybe the lock malfunctioned?"

"Do you have your key?" When she handed it to him, he inserted it into the keyhole and attempted to unlock the door. The key wouldn't move. He left it in there, perplexed over what to do next. "Huh. I dunno what's wrong."

Charlie grabbed hold of his arm. "Do you think it's a ghost?"

He was on the verge of teasing her until he realized she was genuinely frightened. "I'm sure this door is just old. Like you said, hardly anyone ever uses this room." He stepped back a few paces, with her still clutching onto his arm. "Let's wait a minute, then we can give it another try. In the meantime, is there anyone you can call? Isn't there an overnight maintenance man?"

Knox couldn't remember the guy's name offhand, but he'd called him last month for assistance when the men's washroom in the bar had backed up.

She perked up. "Good plan. I left my two-way radio in my office, but I can call the front desk and have them send him up here. I'm sure he has a key." When she pulled out her phone, a frown crossed her face. "That's weird. I'm not getting any bars. And the hotel's Wi-Fi isn't showing up either."

He took out his phone but couldn't get a signal. "Same here. This storage area must be a dead zone." As soon as he said it, he regretted his choice of words. "Which...doesn't mean it's haunted. Maybe it's because it was never renovated, like the rest of the hotel."

Her lower lip trembled. "I'm kind of freaked-out. I've always been able to get a signal at the hotel. Even in the basement. And no one knows we're up here. What if we're locked in all night?"

It wouldn't be the worst thing. "I doubt that'll be the case. If it does happen, at least we have each other for company."

Her anxious look filled him with guilt. Even if he didn't mind getting stuck, she wasn't comfortable with it. Coming here after hours had been a big mistake.

"Hang on, okay?" He released her arm and dragged an ancient settee until it was a few feet away from the door. After dusting it off, he motioned for her to sit beside him. "We'll try the key again in a bit. If we can't get it to work, we could look for a way to pry open the door. Does that sound like a good plan?"

"O...okay." Her voice was still wobbly, but she sat beside him.

He took her hand and rubbed his thumb over the soft skin. "Let's talk about something else to take our minds off this room. Last night, you told me you loved the first three seasons of *The Hidden Forest*. Did you have a favorite storyline?"

"Did I ever." A dreamy smile crossed her face. "I was so invested in Princess Elodie and Finn the Woodsman. Even though she was an Elven princess, and he was a mortal, I wanted them to end up together. When they finally confessed their love, it was everything I'd hoped for. I watched that episode so many times." She gave a short laugh. "I'm guessing it was too sappy for you?"

"Nope. I was into it. Like you, I was rooting for them."

During the show's second season, he'd come up with that storyline to reflect his own relationship with Lila, who'd played the princess. He'd fought hard for it, convincing their showrunner the romance would resonate with their viewers. He'd been right. The love story had been a huge fan favorite. Given that his departure from the show had coincided with the start of the fourth season, he wasn't surprised when the romance took a sharp turn. The woodsman had perished, and the princess ended up pursuing a different love interest—a morally gray character who embodied a darker side of the show's fantasy world.

"You shipped Finn and Princess Elodie?" Charlie asked.

"Absolutely. I was all in."

He expected her to be pleased they shared the same opinion. But in the blink of an eye, her expression darkened. He drew away, bewildered by the angry look on her face.

She glared at him. "So, you haven't *always* hated romance?"

"I don't hate it."

"Sure didn't seem like it last Valentine's Day. You called romance a crock."

"No, I didn't." Even as he said it, he remembered complaining about all the shit Preston had asked them to do, just to promote the holiday. He'd insisted they make the hotel the most "romance-forward" destination in Victoria.

"You totally did." Her voice rose in irritation. "You hated mixing all those love-themed drinks, and you said Valentine's was nothing but a Hallmark holiday."

"It *is* a Hallmark holiday."

He was surprised at how agitated she'd gotten. Why did she care if he had a cynical view of romance? Or was this about those spicy books he'd seen in her room? Did she think he was criticizing her choice of reading material?

"Just so we're clear," he said. "I wasn't implying there's

anything wrong with reading romance novels. If they make you happy, then I'm glad you enjoy them."

She glowered at him, her entire body rigid, her hands clenched into tight fists. "I'm not talking about books. I'm talking about real life. About letting yourself be open to romance."

Where was she going with this? "I didn't mean *all* romance is a crock. It's just not for me."

"But..." She wiped her eyes. "Don't you think you're depriving yourself of happiness?"

Fuck, were those tears? "Charlie...are you crying? What's wrong?"

She sniffed. "It's just my allergies. This place is so fucking dusty."

That, more than anything, told him she was truly upset. Charlie hardly ever swore. She'd once admitted she couldn't risk getting into the habit, given her customer-facing role at the hotel.

He wished he could tell her the truth. *Yes, I once believed in love. How else could I have created a storyline that centered around a tumultuous, opposites-attract romance? But when that princess shattered my heart, I never wanted to go through that again.*

After a minute of awkward silence, she spoke up. "Sorry for getting upset. I...just hate that you're denying yourself a chance for a happy ending."

"Even though you haven't gotten yours? No offense, but Randolph didn't sound like a knight in shining armor. More like the evil Fae King that Princess Elodie ended up with."

That made her laugh. "I couldn't stand him. The Fae King, I mean. Though Randolph wasn't much better. But I'm still holding out hope."

He squeezed her hand, wishing he shared her optimism. She was looking at him so intently that he got caught up in her gaze. More than anything, he wanted to kiss her. To tell her he was willing to open his heart to her, just a little, to see where it led.

With his free hand, he drew his thumb across her cheek and wiped away a stray tear. "I'm sorry."

"For what?"

"For bringing you up here without thinking it through. Here you are, worried about ghosts, and I got you locked in a room where we can't even call for help."

She let out a shuddering breath. "I...I don't mind getting locked up with you."

"No?" He leaned toward her and brushed a wisp of hair from her cheek. Cupping her chin, he tilted her head up and drew nearer until their lips were almost touching. Just a whisper away, so close that he could—

A sharp click sent prickles along the back of his neck. The key clattered onto the floor.

He pulled away from her and leapt to his feet. "Did you see that?"

"Y...yes. Can you go check on it?"

When he turned the knob, the door opened easily, ushering in a welcome blast of cool air.

"You did it!" Charlie said.

"I don't think I did anything." After picking up the key, he examined the door more closely. The wood wasn't warped or bent. There was nothing to indicate why it had gotten stuck. "But I'm glad we're not locked in anymore."

"Me, too. I need a dose of Benadryl, stat. The dust is really getting to me."

He looked back at her wistfully. If the door hadn't popped open, he would have kissed her, no doubt about it. But now that they were free, the fleeting spark they'd shared had vanished like a ghost into the night. They left the room together, locking it behind them.

On their way to the elevator, he checked his phone again. Full bars. "My phone's working. I'm going to text Logan and tell him about the storage room."

"Good plan." She let out another sneeze. "I'm heading home. I've been here since eight this morning, and I'm wiped."

Another twinge of guilt tugged at his conscience. If not for him, she wouldn't have been stuck inside a scary, dusty storage area, listening to him grumble about his lack of faith in romance. He wanted to explain why he was such a cynic, but now wasn't the time. Not when she was exhausted and battling allergies. "Okay. I'll be in tomorrow at three. Thanks for coming with me tonight."

"Sure. No problem."

They rode the elevator down to the parking garage in silence. He wanted to say something, to bring back the closeness they'd shared, but he was at a loss. And as she walked to her car, he longed to call her back, to tell her his entire story, to explain why he'd kept his heart locked up tight for so long.

Instead, he just let her walk away.

Eight

ONCE CHARLIE WAS BACK IN HER APARTMENT, SHE MADE a beeline for her bathroom. If she didn't get some allergy meds into her system, she'd be up all night sneezing. After taking a dose of Benadryl, she went into her bedroom to change and stumbled over a stack of books. With a kick, she sent them flying. Stupid romance novels. Why was she still believing that shit?

Maybe Knox was right to call it a crock. After all, it wasn't like she'd found her own happily ever after. The only guy she'd considered marrying had turned out to be a jerk. And the guy she wanted had no interest in her.

And yet...

When Knox had brushed away her tears, he'd regarded her with such tenderness it had taken her breath away. For a brief moment, his lips had been so close she thought he was going to kiss her. Until the key popped out of the lock and shocked them apart.

After that, he'd barely spoken to her. The silence between them had expanded, becoming so agonizing she could hardly wait to leave the hotel.

What did you expect? Out of the blue, you lit into him for not believing in happy endings. He didn't deserve that.

She still didn't understand why the room had affected her emotions so strongly. At first, she'd merely felt uneasy, but her mood had worsened, filling her with a soul-crushing remorse that preyed upon her worst self-doubts. It was as if a little voice had invaded her head, chastising her for all the mistakes she'd made with Randolph. And then her misery had transformed into a sudden, vicious bout of anger. Had she just been tired after a long day of work? Or had her mood swings been caused by a supernatural element? She suspected it might be the latter since it wasn't like her to lose control that way.

When it was time for bed, she didn't reach for one of her romance novels. Nor did she pick a fantasy book, since most of them had a romantic subplot. She pulled out her e-reader, which she kept for backup. Sometimes, she'd download a steamy novella if she needed to satisfy an itch. But tonight, she searched for Stephen King's name and scanned the list of titles. Rather than commit to an entire novel, she purchased an e-book of his short stories.

At this point, she'd prefer nightmares to dreaming about someone who didn't want her.

WHEN CHARLIE WENT INTO WORK ON TUESDAY, SHE'D made a decision. She still wasn't sure why her emotions had gone haywire in the storage room, but she needed to get them under control. Instead of wasting her energy angsting over Knox, she was going to channel all of it into digging deep into the early years of the Duchess. Thankfully, most of the hotel's records, including its employee files, were now kept in the basement storage area rather than in the creepy room on the third floor. After informing her staff she'd be spending most of the day holed up underground, she went to work.

At noon, her phone pinged with a text from Knox:

Logan was excited to hear about the tragedy in room 309. He liked the idea of a haunted storage room.

She replied quickly:

Does that mean we're in?

Knox: Not yet. Logan said they'll know by Friday.

Charlie: Okay, thanks. Keep me posted!

She waited to see if he'd follow up with a personal message. Like a joke about the storage room. Or a vibe check to see how she was doing after their unsettling experience. Text bubbles appeared, then disappeared, filling her with frustration. After ten minutes, she gave up waiting and set her phone face-down on the floor next to a stack of banker's boxes. She kept hoping he'd text her again, but he never did. Though the silence nagged at her, she didn't follow up with another message. Nor did she swing by the Gilded Lily to chat with him before happy hour started. If he wanted to reach her, he knew how to find her.

She didn't talk to him again until Thursday night, when they met up to escort Celia and Glen to the storage room. While the two men had no qualms about joining Celia inside the room while she conducted her observation, Charlie watched from the doorway. This way, she could keep the door propped open and ensure they weren't locked in. She also hoped it would spare her a repeat of the unsettling experience she'd had with Knox three days ago.

Rather than use any ghost-hunting tools, Celia sat on the faded settee and closed her eyes. And just like Charlie, she told them afterward that she'd been assaulted with a powerful barrage of emotions—sorrow, distress, rage. Charlie wasn't sure whether to feel frightened or validated that the room's ghostly presence had affected her and Celia in the same way. Odder still, the men hadn't felt a damn thing. Though the whole scenario was spooky as hell, Charlie couldn't wait to tell the Damsels about it at their Friday morning meeting.

Once Celia and Glen left, she lingered behind, hoping for a chance to chat with Knox, but he had to get back to the Lily since he was on shift until eleven. When he didn't suggest she stop by for a visit, she took that as her cue to head home.

To be fair, both she and Knox had been run ragged this week. The Duchess had been at full occupancy, thanks to Victoria playing host to a huge international wine festival. When not dealing with high-maintenance guests, Charlie had spent every spare minute plugging away at her research. The few times she'd passed the Gilded Lily during happy hour, the lounge had been packed. Normally, she and Knox would have joked about it, but something felt off between them.

Was it because she'd challenged his views on romance? Or because he'd almost kissed her and had immediately regretted it? Either way, she couldn't shake the feeling her baby steps had been erased.

~

By Friday, Charlie had amassed so much information that she'd assembled it on one of the hotel's whiteboards. She'd included staff reports, faded photographs, newspaper clippings, and a photocopy of the third-floor blueprints. The only thing missing was the red string detectives used when they were trying to connect their clues.

When it was time for the Damsels' weekly meeting, she

wheeled the board into the room. The other women stared at her in surprise.

"Charlie, what's with the murder board?" Selena asked. "Are we hunting a serial killer?"

"I'll explain in a minute." Charlie turned to Rosie, who stood at the head of the table. "I know we have a lot of fall events to cover, but is it okay if I go first?"

"By all means." Rosie sat down. "Take it away."

Charlie cleared her throat. "Did you all read the email I sent about the tragic incident Celia discovered?" When they nodded, she continued. "Just to review the facts, the murder-suicide occurred in 1924 and took place in room 309, which was one of the hotel's biggest suites. Shortly after that, it was turned into a storage area, along with the suite next to it. Knox and I went to check it out on Monday night."

"*Yes*," Selena said. "Now we're getting somewhere. Though I remember it being very dusty up there. Not the best place for a steamy hookup."

Charlie frowned. She did *not* want her memory of that almost-kiss messing with her head. "Nothing happened. We were there to see if we could detect a ghostly presence or feel its energy. I definitely felt uneasy. Kind of awful, if I'm being honest. And then, out of the blue, I went off on Knox and yelled at him." Another memory that made her cringe. "But the room didn't affect him at all. When we were ready to leave, the door wouldn't open, and the key got stuck, like it was locked from the other side. We also couldn't get a signal on our phones. Not from the hotel's Wi-Fi or our regular cell service."

She was afraid they might treat her experience like a joke, but no one was laughing.

"That's creepy," Laurel said. "Did you ask Celia to visit the room? She's really attuned to the supernatural."

"I did. She came by last night with her boyfriend, Glen." Charlie shivered at the memory. "She told us she felt an overwhelming sadness. A sense of remorse and misery, followed by a surge of anger. Which were the *exact* same emotions I felt. She also told me she could smell roses. Not the actual flowers, but the soap we once used in the hotel's washrooms. I smelled the same thing when I was trapped in the room."

"*Fuck*," Selena exclaimed. "I would have gotten the hell out of there."

"Believe me, I wanted to. But you know what's even scarier? Before Celia went in to do her observation, Glen asked me *not* to tell her what I'd experienced. He said it would be better if she didn't know what to expect."

Laurel nodded. "That tracks. He's all about the scientific method."

"Right. So after Celia was done, when she told me how she felt, I couldn't believe we'd had the same reactions. There's something haunting that room, I'm sure of it." In all honesty, Charlie had never expected any of this. At worst, she thought they might uncover a ghostly legend. Not go head-to-head with a restless spirit.

"Three people died, right?" Selena said. "Any guess as to which of them is causing this?"

"Celia thought the negative energy might be coming from Maeve," Charlie said. "She's the front desk clerk who was murdered. She was only twenty-one, and she'd been with the hotel since it first opened. You can see her right here." Charlie pointed to a black-and-white picture. "This is a staff photo taken at the Grand Opening in 1922. I'm not sure why she risked her job to sneak off with Howard Delacroix to one of the hotel rooms. Even back then, romantic liaisons between the staff and the guests were strictly forbidden. Did Howard pay her for her services? Offer to make her his mistress? Or was she genuinely in love with him and hoped it would work out? There's no way to know. But she ended up dead because of it." The deeper Charlie probed, the more she sympathized with Maeve's plight.

"That's just heartbreaking," Rosie said. "Did you find out anything else about her?"

"No. Sadly, there wasn't even an obituary. Celia did a thorough search but couldn't locate anyone related to her."

"I wonder if her family was still back in Ireland," Laurel said. "Do you think they ever learned about her death?"

"Imagine having no one to mourn you." Rosie's voice was subdued. "Poor Maeve."

Charlie couldn't help but wonder what had become of Maeve's body. According to Celia, both Howard and Frances had been interred in Ross Bay Cemetery, the oldest burial ground in Victoria. But there was no evidence Maeve had a headstone anywhere.

"So...moving on. I want to talk about the next bit of evidence." Charlie pointed to a series of handwritten pages taped to the board. "I found boxes of old files on the hotel's staff—annual reviews, salary charts, and incidents when they were written up for infractions. A lot of them got in trouble for refusing to go into the storage room. Many claimed they'd been locked in. One woman was fired after she insisted she'd been stuck there for three hours. She was accused of using the room to take a nap, but I have a hunch the door wasn't behaving."

"This is so fascinating," Laurel said. "You're like an investigative reporter."

"Speaking of reporters..." Charlie pointed to a photocopy of a page from one of the hotel's earliest ledgers. "This entry is from 1924, and it's dated around the time of the tragedy. Two lump-sum payments were made to *The Victoria Daily Times* and *The British Colonist*—Victoria's two major newspapers. Neither one ever published anything about the murders."

"Do you think they were paid off?" Selena asked.

"Without a doubt. I scoured the ledgers and didn't see any other instances of a payment like this occurring in 1924 or 1925.

Assuming they were bribes, that could be the reason the papers kept this incident quiet."

"Can we come look at the board?" Laurel asked.

"Sure." Charlie swelled with pride. She'd never tackled a project like this before, and she was pleased at how much she'd discovered in such a short time.

As they crowded around the board, Rosie placed a hand on her shoulder. "I can't believe you pulled this off during a week filled with needy guests. Knox must have been so impressed."

"I guess." Charlie shrugged. "I sent him an email this morning with all my notes. He said he'd forward it to Logan."

Selena pinned Charlie in her gaze. "You didn't show him this fabulous murder board in person?"

Charlie's cheeks tingled with heat. "No. I figured he was too busy. Anyway, I'm done with my presentation. Let's move on to our fall events." She took a seat at the conference table.

Laurel sat back down and passed her a plate of cookies. "Take one. Last night, I needed a sugar fix and made peanut butter chocolate-chunk cookies."

Charlie grabbed one and bit into it, savoring the crumbly texture and the tasty blend of peanut butter and chocolate. "Thanks. Your cookies are the best."

Once Rosie and Selena joined them at the table, Charlie expected them to start reviewing the hotel's upcoming activities. But Selena spoke first. "Charlie, you need to tell us what happened between you and Knox. I thought things were going well."

Charlie flinched, wishing she could fade away like a ghost, rather than endure the Damsels' scrutiny. "They were, but I think it's hopeless. He's not a romantic guy."

"I don't buy it," Selena said. "And I'm not letting you wimp out. Not when you've come this far. You need more courage."

"Courage?" Charlie burst out laughing. "I've gotten out of my comfort zone a lot this month. I invited Knox over to my apartment, I got locked in a haunted storage room, and I'm halfway through a Stephen King book. How's that for courage?"

Selena shook her head. "It's not enough. You need to try harder."

Charlie groaned. Why couldn't Selena understand she'd never have that kind of confidence? "This thing with me and Knox isn't going to happen. Can we please move on?"

"Nope, because we need you to help us out." Laurel passed the plate of cookies to Rosie. "Take another one. Or save one for Drew. I don't need all these cookies tempting me."

"Why do you need my help?" Charlie asked. "Isn't it enough that I spent days researching the hotel's sordid past?"

"We appreciate all the work you did," Rosie said. "But there's one event we want to add to our calendar, and we can't do it unless Knox cooperates. We want to hold a costume contest at the Gilded Lily on Friday, October twenty-third. It would include themed cocktails, fun prizes, and a DJ. The last time I asked him, he said no."

Selena snorted. "He said 'no way in hell,' if I recall correctly. So, we need you to talk him into it. After everything you've done for him, he owes you."

While it was true he owed her, he wouldn't be enthused about holding a costume party at the bar. Even if he liked Halloween, he hated dressing up. "Do I have to?"

"Yes," Rosie said. "We've got plenty of kid-friendly activities planned for October, starting with our first 'Spooky Saturday' on the third. Lots of crafts, cookie decorating, a kiddie costume party, and a magician who dresses in wizard's robes. We've also got two family-friendly ghost tours scheduled with Celia, but we need an adults-only event."

Charlie knew when she was outgunned. If she didn't try to convince Knox, the Damsels would keep hounding her until she conceded.

"Okay, I'll do it. But you're all going to be in my debt."

Nine

WHEN KNOX ARRIVED AT THE GILDED LILY ON FRIDAY, he braced himself for a busy evening. Ever since Wednesday, he'd been slammed, dealing with all the guests who were in town for the international wine festival. Even if a lot of them were self-professed wine snobs, that didn't stop them from turning up at happy hour, intent on pre-gaming with a complimentary glass of the house red. At least he wouldn't be managing the Lily on his own. Miles, who worked as the lounge's other full-time bartender, would be arriving shortly after five.

To add to Knox's stress, Preston had left one of his irksome notes by the cash register.

Hey, Knox. Spending the summer in the tropics has been a blast, but it's time to put away your flip-flops and bring out those fall-themed cocktail specials for happy hour. Pumpkin spice vibes FTW!

The guy was such a try-hard. Not to mention, Knox had already switched up his specials last week. Right now, the most popular drink on the menu was his bourbon-cranberry cocktail, followed by his take on a smoky apple cider margarita.

When his phone buzzed, he grabbed it, hoping Miles wasn't running late. Instead, Logan's name appeared on the caller ID.

"Hey, man, what's up?" Knox said.

"Thanks for sending all that intel on the Duchess. When I talked to a few other locals, no one knew any of that shit about your hotel."

"I'd never heard of it, either. Our local ghost whisperer is the one who uncovered the murders. But the other research? That was all Charlie. She's been incredible." When Knox had gotten her email, with a full report attached, he'd read through it twice, blown away at everything she'd discovered.

"Incredible, eh? Tell me more about this *Charlie*."

"She's just a coworker. That's all."

"Nope. You sounded excited, and that never happens."

Ugh. Knox's voice had given too much away. He infused his reply with an extra level of surliness. "I don't have time for this. Not with happy hour starting soon."

Logan laughed so loudly it made him wince. "Got it. But I'm not letting you off the hook."

"We can talk about Charlie later. Do you have any updates about the show? My boss has been riding my ass."

"Not gonna lie, he seems like an intense dude. But yeah, I called to let you know your hotel is in. We're going with a two-fer —filming at the Pendray Inn *and* the Duchess. Two nights at each place. One for interviews and setup, and the other for overnight observation."

Relief flooded through Knox's veins. Even if he'd initially loathed the idea of being involved with the show, it had brought him closer to Charlie. She'd put in so much work he was glad her efforts would be rewarded. "Do you know the exact dates yet?"

"I'm still firming things up, but I'll send you the filming schedule once I have it. Let Charlie know we'll want to interview her, as well as that friend of yours who works for the archives. The one with the sixth sense. Can you also ask her if she'd be willing to join us during the lockdown?"

"You bet. I'm sure Celia would be into it." For once, Knox

didn't try to hide his enthusiasm. "This is great. I hope you get some decent footage."

By the time he hung up, he could barely keep the grin off his face. Now that he'd done exactly what Preston wanted, his boss might be less inclined to hold Knox's past over his head. And Charlie would be delighted her research had helped seal the deal.

Charlie.

Though he'd barely reached out to her over the past few days, she'd been on his mind constantly. On Thursday night, when they'd taken Celia and Glen up to the storage room, she'd mentioned having a busy week. Even so, she'd seemed more distant than usual. After preparing her meticulous report, she'd emailed it to him, rather than sharing it in person. Which made him suspect he'd done something to upset her.

He tried to pinpoint the moment when things had gone off the rails. It all came back to the storage room. He wished he'd taken the initiative and kissed her. Or explained why he'd built up such an aversion to romance. Even if her outburst had been unexpected, he hadn't handled it well. And after the incident? He'd retreated inside his shell again.

Somehow, he had to make things right. He could start by sending her an update about *Canada's Most Haunted*. While he was at it, he should thank her profusely for all her help. Before he could figure out what to say, a couple came up to the bar and ordered glasses of the Coolshanagh Reserve Chardonnay—a local wine from the Okanagan Valley. They took their drinks over to a corner of the lounge and settled into the leather club chairs.

He brought out his phone again, intent on texting Charlie before happy hour got underway. But he stopped when she marched into the Gilded Lily and approached the bar with a determined scowl. In the three years he'd known her, she'd never greeted him that way.

"Hey, Charlie. You okay?"

"No. I need to talk to you. Not by choice, either. The Damsels made me do it."

Her words dug into him, making him fully aware of how closed off he'd been. "You're always welcome to stop by and chat. You know that, right?"

She plowed on, pointedly ignoring his attempt to bridge the distance between them. "They want you to host a costume contest at the Gilded Lily on October twenty-third. And they need you to be all in."

Though she was trying to come across as assertive, the slight wobble in her voice gave her away. He'd done something to hurt her feelings, and it was time for him to deal with it head-on. "Are you upset with me? I feel like I screwed up, but I'm not sure how to make it better."

"It's not you," she snapped. "I've been working myself to the bone this week. All this research, plus a hotel filled with demanding guests."

"You sure that's all?" It had to be more than that.

"I...I don't know." Her voice broke. "This sounds so stupid, but I haven't stopped by the Lily in three days, and it feels like it didn't matter. You didn't even miss me."

Her honesty shook him to the core. "I did miss you. But..."

"But what?" She put her hands on her hips. "Is this because of the storage room? It wasn't your fault we got locked in."

"I still feel bad about it. I'm the one who put you at risk and..." *I almost kissed you.*

Taking a step toward him, she placed her hands on the bar top until she was only inches away, so close he could make out every tiny freckle sprinkled across her nose. "If it hadn't been for my allergies, I would have been fine staying there. I'm not that much of a wuss. For the past three nights, I've been reading a book of scary stories, and I haven't had a single nightmare."

What? "Scary stories? What are you talking about?"

"They're from a book by Stephen King. *Night Shift.*"

"That's one of my favorites."

Three young women walked into the lounge, but they didn't approach the bar. Instead, they sat down at one of the high-tops, no doubt waiting for happy hour to start.

Charlie nodded, a little less agitated now. "It's been good to try something different. Usually, the books I read end happily. The heroines end up with the heroes. Good conquers evil. But in these stories, I never know if the characters are going to survive. That's a more realistic outlook than always hoping for a happy ending."

No. One of the things he admired about Charlie was her unwavering optimism. "There's nothing wrong with happy endings." He tried to inject some levity into his voice. "Maybe I should try reading one of your romance novels. Just to see what I'm missing."

That eked a smile out of her. "Maybe? But we're getting off topic. Can we please move on from the storage room incident? I don't want it to make things weird."

"Okay." He was so impressed she'd tackled the awkwardness that he wanted to do something in return. "You can let the Damsels know I'm willing to host a costume party at the Gilded Lily. I'll even dress up."

"You will?" All of a sudden, Charlie was back to her sunny self. "What are you going to wear?"

He almost retorted that he had no fucking clue, but a devilish thought took hold. "If you dress as Tinker Bell, I'll go as Captain Hook."

She clapped her hands together. "I love that idea."

"I thought you might. Since you seem to be into pirates." Was he flirting with her? Shit, he *never* flirted.

A burst of laughter tumbled out of her. "You've got that right. I can't wait to tell the Damsels. We're doing happy hour at Pepe's Cantina tonight, and I'm so ready for a margarita. We haven't been in ages."

"You used to go every Friday, didn't you?" he asked. "What happened?"

"Every *other* Friday. We're not total lushes. We tried to keep it going this summer, but we got too busy. I'm so glad we have a reason to celebrate tonight."

Her gleeful expression instantly improved his day. "I can give you one more reason to celebrate. Logan called. His show is going to do a double episode featuring the Duchess and the Pendray Inn."

"Yes!" She pumped her fist. "I'm so excited! We did this, Knox. Can I hug you? I feel like this news requires a hug."

Like he'd say no? He beckoned her over. "Come around the bar. But hurry. Happy hour's starting soon."

She scooted around to his side and flung herself into his arms. And just like that, all his resistance ebbed away. After months of fighting his attraction to her, it was time to act. He held her tightly, utterly bewitched by the feel of her curves and the tantalizing aroma of her lavender-scented shampoo.

"Thanks for all your hard work," he said.

"My pleasure. I can't believe we pulled this off."

When she looked up at him with those big, jade green eyes, he wanted to seize the moment. Kiss her thoroughly and drown himself in the taste of her lips, customers be damned.

The loud chime of the bar's antique grandfather clock struck him like a blow. Five o'clock. Any minute now, the horde would descend. Already, the three women who'd come in earlier were advancing toward him.

"Shit," he muttered. "Happy hour."

"At least you're not stuck making piña coladas anymore." She eased away from him and returned to the other side of the bar.

He didn't want to lose momentum. If he didn't take this chance now, then when would he? "We should celebrate. Do you have Sunday off?"

"Yes, indeed. Want to go out for drinks? We could go back to the Seagull." She flashed him an impish grin. "There are loads of tropical cocktails I haven't tried yet."

"Actually, I'd like to take you out to dinner."

Her lips parted in shock, making him wonder if he'd misjudged her feelings. Then a joyful smile crossed her face, like a ray of pure sunshine. "That sounds wonderful."

"Perfect. It's a date."

A date.

What had he gotten himself into?

Ten

CHARLIE WAS ON A ROLL. SO, NATURALLY, THE UNIVERSE had to take her down a peg.

After a delightful Friday night, celebrating with the Damsels at Pepe's Cantina, she'd woken on Saturday with a splitting headache. At first, she blamed the booze. But by noon, her nose was running, and her throat ached. She dosed with vitamin C, orange juice, and hot tea. It didn't help. On Sunday morning, she felt even worse.

With enormous reluctance, she texted Knox:

I'm so sorry, but I have to cancel. I caught the crud and I'm sick in bed.

Knox: Sorry you're sick. Do you need anything?

Charlie: I'll be okay. I have a can of chicken noodle soup somewhere.

Feeling awash in self-pity, she settled herself on the couch with a couple of blankets, a box of tissues, and a tumbler of ice water. Since she was in a nostalgic mood, she grabbed her box set of *The Hidden Forest* and started watching the third season from the beginning. In her opinion, it was the show's best season, containing her favorite episodes. At some point, she drifted off to sleep, and when she woke at six, she was ravenous with hunger.

This sucks. If she hadn't caught a lousy cold, she would have been dining with Knox at Il Terrazzo—an Italian restaurant ranked as one of Victoria's most romantic dining spots. Instead, she was trying to decide if it was worth the effort to heat up a can of soup. She couldn't even ask her mom for a little TLC because her parents had gone to Vancouver to visit friends.

When a knock came at the door, she grabbed her robe and answered it, unsure of who might be stopping by. Knox stood in her doorway, clad in jeans and a red flannel shirt, carrying a grocery bag. She cringed, wishing she'd taken the time to shower. Truly, he was seeing her at her worst—messy hair, no makeup, wearing her oldest, rattiest pajamas.

"Knox? What are you doing here?"

"I thought you might need sustenance, so I brought you dinner. I can leave the bag on the counter, unless you'd like some company."

The thought perked her up, but she didn't want him to get sick. "Thanks, but I'm probably contagious."

He gave a dismissive wave of his hand. "Don't worry about that. I'm immune to everything."

"Then a visit would be nice."

"Have you eaten tonight?" When she shook her head, he pointed to the couch. "Go lie down. I'll heat up some soup."

His bossy tone was comforting. Like he'd decided to put himself in charge of her care and wouldn't listen to any arguments. She shuffled back to the couch and wrapped herself in a fleece blanket. "I have a can in my pantry."

"Forget the canned stuff. I brought a quart from Chuck's Deli. They make the best chicken noodle soup I've ever had." He walked over to her kitchen counter and set the bag on it. "I also picked up a few essentials from the grocery store."

She watched in wonder as he pulled out a box of saltines, a bottle of ginger ale, a container of instant oatmeal packets, and a four-pack of Jell-O cups. "How did you know what to buy?"

"Everyone likes this stuff when they're sick. I grew up in a house with five siblings, and these were my mom's go-to's whenever any of us got a cold." He rummaged in her cupboards until he found a pan, then set it on the stove top and dumped half the container of soup into it.

"You had five siblings?" She didn't know much about his childhood, except that he'd grown up in Summerland, a small town located in British Columbia's Okanagan Valley.

"Yep. Two matched sets. My mom had the first three kids when she was barely out of university. Then my brother Greg showed up ten years later—an oops baby. So, my folks doubled down. A year after that, they had me, and then my sister followed. They called us the second wave."

A sharp pang of longing gripped her. She'd grown up an only child but had always wanted a sister or a brother. "Were you close to them?"

"The older ones, not so much. Not when I was little. But Greg and I were tight. He was always getting up to shit, and I usually went along with him." He took a couple of bowls out of the cupboard. "Do you want ginger ale, or should I make tea?"

How had Knox morphed into such a nurturing soul? "Um... ginger ale. Please." Now that he was opening up about his past, she wanted him to keep going. "Do any of your siblings live in Victoria?"

"Just Dave. He's the oldest. He came out to UVic for law school and decided to stay. He's got a wife and two kids, though I guess they're not kids anymore. His son, Jordan, is only twelve years younger than me. He's the one who helped us out at the Lily last December, when we were slammed with all those events."

"I remember." At the time, she'd thought it unusual that Knox had a twenty-one-year-old nephew, but she hadn't asked him about it. "Before coming to Victoria, you lived in Vancouver, right? I think you mentioned it once before."

"I went to university at UBC and lived there for six years after that." He ladled the soup into two bowls and brought her one, along with a box of saltines and a glass of ginger ale. "It's not fine Italian cuisine, but it'll do for tonight."

"Thanks, Knox." Though she could barely smell anything, the warm steam from the soup felt heavenly. "You didn't have to do this."

"It's no bother. And I still owe you a real dinner."

She was about to tell him he wasn't under any obligation, that tonight was more than enough, but she stopped herself. If he wanted to have dinner with her, why dissuade him? "Okay. I'll hold you to it." She took a small sip of the soup, which was salty and delicious, filled with big chunks of chicken and thick noodles. "This is so much better than the canned stuff."

He went to fetch his own bowl and plopped down on the armchair next to the couch. "Chuck's is the best. Though I have to admit, we grew up eating the store brand. Or Campbell's, if it was on sale. With so many kids in the house, my parents were always on a tight budget."

She crumbled up a handful of saltines into her soup. Knox's childhood contrasted so sharply with her own. She'd grown up in complete privilege. If she needed anything—new clothes, shoes, money for a school trip—she only had to ask. And yet, Knox had probably been surrounded by more love and warmth than she had.

"Before I forget—this is for you." He reached into the front pocket of his flannel and pulled out a wad of tissue paper, wrapped around something small. Leaning closer to the couch, he passed it over to her.

She tore off the paper to reveal a tiny glass swan, light blue with white wings and an orange beak. "Oh...where did you get this?"

"At a flea market this morning. I was tooling around, looking for used books, and this made me think of you."

Any more kindness from him and she'd burst into tears. "Thank you. It's lovely." She set it on her coffee table, next to the box of tissues.

He glanced at the TV, which still displayed the DVD menu. "What were you watching?"

"Don't judge me, but I was rewatching the third season of *The Hidden Forest*." She ducked her head in embarrassment. "It's kind of childish, but I don't like to watch any further. That way, I can pretend Princess Elodie and Finn live happily ever after."

"I get it. I'm sure a lot of viewers would agree with you."

How did he know this? Had he spent hours perusing the show's Reddit forum, like she had? When he didn't elaborate, she focused on eating her soup, taking careful bites so she wouldn't spill it all over herself. The silence lingered, but it wasn't awkward. More like the kind of quiet comfort shared between two friends who were at ease with each other.

After they were done, he took the bowls to the kitchen and put them in the sink. "Do you want anything else?"

"I'm good for now." Since he hadn't hinted he was in a hurry to leave, she pointed to the shelf containing her DVDs. "If you want to stay for a bit, we could watch a movie. I slept most of the afternoon, so I'm not that tired."

"Sure. Any preference?" He walked over to her collection and perused the titles.

"Whatever you want. Maybe something under two hours?" That way, she'd have less chance of falling asleep.

He took one off the shelf. "See if you can guess: 'Have fun storming the castle.'"

She grinned at him. "*The Princess Bride* is one of my all-time faves." An odd choice for Knox, given that it was centered around an epic love story, but she wasn't about to bring that up.

Once they were seated, with the movie playing, Charlie no

longer cared that she'd gotten sick. She couldn't remember ever enjoying a first date this much.

Knox had seen *The Princess Bride* at least five times. Maybe more. In his family, Friday nights were set aside for movie watching. His mom would make a huge batch of popcorn and—if they were lucky—break out a bag of Kit Kats. They took turns picking the films, and among his sister's favorites was *The Princess Bride*. But if anyone spoke while it was playing, she'd shush them until they stopped. Fortunately, Charlie didn't feel the same way. Like him, she loved talking back to the screen and making snarky comments.

Toward the end of the movie, she grew quiet. He got up to check on her, only to realize she'd fallen asleep. He turned off the TV and covered her with another blanket. She'd probably be more comfortable in bed, but he didn't want to wake her.

Even if the night had ended with her drifting off to sleep, he was glad he'd risked coming over. He could tell she'd enjoyed his visit and had liked hearing about his family. When she'd mentioned *The Hidden Forest*, he'd been tempted to reveal even more about himself. Not just the good parts, but everything that had happened in Vancouver, including his relationship with Lila.

He'd held off because he hadn't felt right unloading all his baggage on Charlie. The full story was a lot for anyone to take in, let alone someone who was battling a nasty cold. But he was so tired of keeping the past locked up where no one could find it. If he wanted a chance with her, he needed to share more of himself.

After waiting another ten minutes, he figured she was out for the night. He could have stayed, but watching her sleep made him feel like the vampire from the *Twilight* movies. He went to the kitchen and found a sheet of note paper in one of the drawers.

After contemplating what to say, he wrote her a letter, folded the paper in thirds, and set it on the coffee table.

The act of writing something—even if it was just a friendly note—felt good. Like using a muscle that had gone dormant.

He cleaned up the kitchen and let himself out. Then he wondered if he'd been too hasty in leaving her that letter. But he kept walking until he reached his truck, parked in front of the Frasers' house.

When he got back to his apartment, he was too fired up to sleep. He opened his laptop and searched through his old files until he found the first draft of a horror screenplay he'd written six years ago. The story held a lot of potential, but he'd never had the time to revise it.

Tonight, there was nothing stopping him.

Eleven

AT SOME POINT DURING THE NIGHT, CHARLIE WOKE IN A state of total disorientation. It took her a moment to realize she was lying on the couch, swaddled in blankets. She stumbled into the bathroom, took a hefty dose of Nyquil, and got comfortable in bed. Before drifting off, she had the foresight to leave a message on Rosie's work voicemail, informing her friend she'd be taking a sick day on Monday. Then she slept like the dead.

When she woke, it was almost noon. A sure sign that skipping work had been the right call. She took a long, hot shower, put on a fresh pair of pajamas, and went into the kitchen. Knox had cleaned up everything and put the groceries away. Yet another considerate gesture she hadn't anticipated. Randolph had never treated her with such tenderness. The one time she'd been too sick to attend a fancy dinner at his boss's house, he'd accused her of being selfish.

After making a cup of tea, she settled onto the couch. Though she felt infinitely better than she had on Sunday, another day of rest was exactly what she needed. The little glass swan from Knox sat beside her box of tissues. She picked it up and ran her fingers along the smooth glass, still awestruck at his thoughtfulness. Next to it was a folded-up piece of paper with her name on it. Had he left it for her?

She opened it and began to read:

Dear Charlie,

Once upon a time...

There was a boy who loved scary stories. He devoured them late at night while under the covers, flashlight in hand. When he got older, he decided to write a few of his own. At first, they were atrocious—excessive adjectives, convoluted plots, an abundance of gore. But he got better. When he was 16, he won first place in a writing contest for a story about a haunted bar, inspired by his uncle's pub.

At age 18, he set out for university to study creative writing. His parents supported his dreams but suggested he have a backup plan. Bartending suited him because people's stories provided great writing fodder. While in university amid the literary types, he met a kindred spirit, Evan Girard, who shared his passion for all things creepy. Upon graduation, they moved into an apartment and embarked upon a lofty goal—writing an unforgettable horror movie that would scare the shit out of everyone. A film that would be regarded with the same reverence as The Shining or Alien.

They wrote four different screenplays. None of them sold. Their fifth one landed them an agent. And it got made. But it was a tiny indie film that barely broke even. It wasn't even worthy of a local film festival.

Out of frustration, they started a new project. Just for fun. But it would change their lives forever.

Intrigued? Google "Mac Iverson." It's the pen name I used, back when I was in Vancouver. Given your superb research skills, I'm sure you'll uncover some of the answers you seek. If you have more questions, you know where to find me.

Your friend in ghost hunting,

Knox.

With shaky hands, she set down the note. Her earlier guess had been correct. Knox *was* a writer. And he'd written under the pen name Mac Iverson. But why did that name sound vaguely familiar?

She entered it into her phone's search engine, waiting anxiously until a quick summary appeared: *Mac Iverson is a Canadian screenwriter from Summerland, B.C., best known as one of the co-creators of the award-winning fantasy television series, The Hidden Forest, where he worked as the head writer for the first three seasons.*

What? Heart pounding, Charlie flung her phone onto the couch as if it were a snake that might bite her.

How was it possible that Knox was responsible for one of her favorite TV shows?

She wanted to spend the next few hours untangling all the threads of this mystery. To read every article that mentioned Mac Iverson.

But...there must have been a reason Knox had hidden this part of his life. How had he gone from being a successful screenwriter to a hotel bartender? Had he done something so heinous he'd been cast out of *The Hidden Forest*? Had he committed a crime?

When her phone rang, she yelped, worried it might be him. Instead, Rosie's name showed up on the screen. "Rosie?" she gasped.

"Are you all right?" Rosie asked. "I didn't wake you, did I?"

"No, I was up. Sorry I couldn't come in today."

"Don't apologize. If you're sick, you need to take time for self-care. I wanted to see how you're feeling."

"Better, thanks. I slept until noon. I'm hoping to be back tomorrow."

"Do you want me to bring you anything?" Rosie said. "I've been craving Thai food, so I was going to pick up an order of green curry. I can drop some off for you. Spicy food is supposed to be good for a cold."

"I'd like that, thanks." If Rosie stopped by, Charlie could ask her to stay while she researched Mac Iverson. Then she wouldn't have to deal with the results alone.

"Great. I'll be there by six thirty. Take it easy."

Now all Charlie had to do was divert her anxiety until Rosie arrived. Since she still had a few episodes to go before she finished the third season of *The Hidden Forest*, she put the DVD back in the player. This time, she paid attention to the credits, where Mac Iverson was listed, along with his writing partner, Evan Girard. Mac had also received the sole story credit for the final episode of the third season—one of the swooniest hours of television Charlie had ever watched. An episode written by the very guy who'd claimed romance was a crock.

Oh, Knox. Who hurt you?

~

BY THE TIME ROSIE SHOWED UP CARRYING A BAG OF Thai food, Charlie was frantic to find out more about Mac Iverson. She didn't want to overwhelm her friend, so she kept things casual at first, asking Rosie how her Monday had gone. She followed up by describing her evening with Knox and emphasized the way he'd taken care of her.

"I can't believe this is the same Knox," Rosie said. They'd finished their curry and were seated on the couch, drinking ginger tea. "Or maybe I can. I've always thought he had a soft side, but he only shows it when you're around."

Charlie took out Knox's letter. "He was so sweet last night. I fell asleep watching the movie, and he cleaned up everything. Then he left me this note. It's kind of personal, but basically, he told me he used to be a writer."

"A writer? Huh. I wouldn't have guessed that, though I've never peeked at his employee file. I wonder if he mentioned it there."

Somehow, Charlie doubted it. "He might not have, since he wrote under a pen name. Have you ever seen *The Hidden Forest*?"

"The fantasy show? I tried watching the first few episodes, but it wasn't for me. You know I prefer car chases and explosions, and it was sadly lacking in both. Why?"

"Brace yourself—it turns out Knox McIntyre is also Mac Iverson, one of the writers who created the show. He's credited with writing a bunch of the episodes, but only for the first three seasons."

Rosie stared at her in disbelief. "Our Knox? Are you sure it's the same guy?"

Charlie was glad she wasn't the only one shocked at his big revelation. "I'm positive. He told me to look up the name online, but I've been scared to do it. There has to be a reason he left the show and ended up at the Gilded Lily."

"Yeah, that's kind of a hard pivot." Rosie set her mug on the coffee table. "If you want to go down the rabbit hole, I'm here for it. I know Knox isn't on social media, but have you looked up Mac Iverson yet?"

"Not yet." Once Charlie followed this path, there would be no going back. But her trepidation was no match for her curiosity. "Let's do it. If he's not online, we can look up his writing partner, Evan Girard."

Heads bent over their phones, they started searching. Rosie held up her screen first. "Did you see these images of Mac? If I hadn't known it was Knox, I might not have recognized him."

"Same here. He looks so much younger without his beard." But when Charlie enlarged one of the pictures, she could see the resemblance in his warm hazel eyes.

Other than a few photos, Mac barely existed online. He wasn't on any platforms, not even LinkedIn. No TikToks, no posts, nothing. His name was only mentioned in reviews of the show's early seasons.

"Whoa," Rosie said. "Mac might be a ghost, but his writing

partner is everywhere. Parties, events, all kinds of shit. And his wife looks like a model. Oh, wait, Evan's married to someone from the show. Lila Winstead."

"She plays Princess Elodie." Charlie pulled up Evan's Instagram feed, but it was too overwhelming. She didn't want to scroll through years of photos just to find one with Knox in it.

Rosie continued her search. "I'm googling Lila now. There are a ton of photos and videos. I also found a link to an interview she did with *Star Style* magazine, just before she got married four years ago." She started reading it, only to let out a yelp. "I'm sending you the link."

Charlie scanned the interview. In it, Lila gushed about her upcoming wedding to Evan, whom she'd met when she was an aspiring actress. They'd grown closer while filming the show and were tying the knot at Hycroft Manor, an Edwardian mansion in Vancouver. When Charlie reached the middle of the interview, a chill passed over her.

Star Style: *I understand you were once engaged to another one of the show's writers. Mac Iverson.*

Lila: *I was, but I broke it off. He turned out to be too controlling, and his temper frightened me.*

Star Style: *He left the show after you broke up, right? After the end of the third season?*

Lila: *Yes, but I'd rather not talk about him. Can we move on?*

"*Fuck*." Charlie spat out the word. "Knox was engaged to Lila Winstead?"

Rosie barely looked up from her phone. "I found another article. A think piece in *Vulture*—'Why Season 4 Muddied the Forest.' It suggests Mac Iverson's departure as the head writer is one of the reasons the scripts went downhill in the fourth season. And why the show's most popular romantic storyline took a dark turn."

Charlie's stomach churned. "In her interview, Lila said Knox's temper frightened her. That's a major red flag."

"It might be, but I've never known Knox to *actually* lose his temper. Sure, he's a grouch, and he has no qualms about confronting aggressive male patrons if they pester our female guests. But the few times things have escalated, he's called for security rather than dealing with it himself."

"That's what I thought. I don't want to discount Lila's experience, but..."

"Maybe Knox has changed since then. Or..." Rosie drew out the word, as if still putting the pieces together. "I usually always take the woman's side in situations like this, but I wonder if Lila said those things so she wouldn't be painted as the villain. From the timeline of this article, it looks like she and Knox were engaged for a year. Once they broke things off, she started dating Evan *immediately*. Right after that, Knox left the show, supposedly to spend time with his family in the Okanagan Valley. Which makes me think he either resigned out of humiliation or was forced out."

This was a lot to take in. Needing a break, Charlie stood and stretched. "Do you want any dessert? Knox brought me some strawberry Jell-O cups."

"No, thanks."

While retrieving her Jell-O, Charlie mulled over everything she'd read. Obviously, she was biased in favor of Knox, but Rosie's take on the interview made sense. It wasn't a good look that Lila had dumped Knox for his writing partner. Especially since Knox's letter made it sound like he and Evan had been more than just co-writers—they'd been close friends. And they'd shared an apartment. Talk about a crushing betrayal.

"I sent you a link to another article," Rosie said. "In it, Evan pretty much accused Knox of being an alcoholic with serious anger issues. He also hinted that the real reason Knox left the show was to go into rehab. I don't buy it. Knox might be a bartender, but I've never seen him get drunk. My take is that Evan made up this shit to cover his ass."

Charlie sighed. "Poor Knox. That really sucks."

"You should talk to him about it. Get the whole story. Clearly, he wants to share this stuff. He's probably tired of keeping it hidden."

"I can't imagine how hard that would be." Charlie sat back down on the couch. "Are you okay if we keep this between us? It's fine if you share it with Drew, but I don't want anyone else to know. Not until Knox is ready."

"I won't breathe a word. And Drew's never seen the show, so I doubt he'd care."

"Thanks. I'm sure Knox is wondering how I'm going to react to all of this. I'm glad he gave me time to process it." If he'd told her outright, she might have been overwhelmed. This way was better.

For today, she'd let it all sink in.

She could call him tomorrow.

Twelve

When Knox woke up on Monday morning, he was still thinking about the note he'd left for Charlie. Had he revealed too much? Too little? Not that it mattered, since the deed was done.

Rather than waste another minute brooding, he drove to Goldstream Park—a wooded area filled with hiking trails—and spent the day taking photos of the striking fall colors. Years ago, he'd bought a Nikon camera and devoted hours to studying photography, just to have another skill set in his arsenal. Though he didn't post his pictures online, he'd framed some of his best ones and given them to family members as gifts.

By the end of the day, he still hadn't heard from Charlie.

Maybe he'd mucked up everything. No doubt she'd found the interview where Lila had accused him of having a frightening temper, or the one where Evan had hinted at Mac's so-called alcohol abuse. But it was better Charlie learn about all of it now, instead of a few months down the road.

On Tuesday morning, he received a text from her. He braced for the worst, but her message revealed very little.

Charlie: Could we meet up before work today? I don't have to go in until 3.

That could mean anything. But whether she intended to deliver good news or bad, he was grateful for a chance to talk to her in person.

Knox: Want to get lunch at Fisherman's Wharf? Barb's Fish & Chips at 1?

Charlie: I love Fisherman's Wharf!! I'll see you there.

Of course she loved Fisherman's Wharf. It was the kind of fun, touristy place that had Charlie written all over it. Located just west of Victoria's Inner Harbour, it was a waterfront area filled with sailboats and fishing vessels, as well as food kiosks and souvenir shops geared toward out-of-town visitors. But the main reason people came to the wharf was to check out the floating homes. Thirty-three tiny houses, decorated in a riot of colors, were moored at various berths in the harbor, easily viewable via a series of wooden boardwalks.

When he arrived, Charlie was already seated at a picnic table by the fish and chips kiosk, wearing sunglasses and a light pink T-shirt with the words "The book was better" written in a stylized cursive. She waved at him. "Hey, Knox. I grabbed a spot for us because it's super busy here. I've been guarding it with my life."

Around them, the other tables were filled with a large collection of elderly folks, all wearing Day-Glo lanyards. Knox assumed they'd come to Fisherman's Wharf as part of a tour. "Thanks. How's your cold?"

"I'm still kind of stuffed up, but I'm much better than I was on Sunday. It feels so good to be outside. Isn't the weather glorious?" She tilted her head toward the sun, as if basking in its warmth. "I love this time of year. Not too hot, but still plenty of sunshine. I stashed my work clothes in my car because I didn't want to wear them until I have to."

"I don't blame you." He couldn't help but notice how her scoop-neck shirt revealed a tantalizing hint of cleavage.

She stood up. "What do you want? It's on me." When he started to protest, she held up her hand. "Nope. You bought all those groceries and took care of me on Sunday. The least I can do is buy you lunch."

"Fair enough. I'll have a large lemonade and the fish and chips basket with cod."

"Nice. That's what I usually get." She inched around the table and headed for the kiosk.

He tried not to stare, but her faded jeans hugged her ass in a way that was far too tempting. She looked so adorable, moving her hands animatedly as she chatted with the man behind the kiosk window.

She returned with a wooden sign and set it atop the table before sitting back down. "Our food will be ready in a few minutes. In the meantime, can we talk about the letter you left me? It was so sweet and thoughtful. Just like the way you treated me when you came over. Sorry I fell asleep before the movie ended."

"I'm sure you needed your rest. I would have stayed, but I felt weird watching you sleep."

"Kinda like Edward Cullen from *Twilight*," she said.

"That's what I was thinking." When she raised her eyebrows, he chuckled. "My younger sister was obsessed with those books. She made me watch all the movies."

Charlie folded her hands and placed them on the table. "Back to your note—I want to thank you for sharing so much with me. I'm sure it wasn't easy. And thanks for giving me a little breathing room so I could take it all in."

Relief washed over him, loosening the knot at the back of his neck. "I wanted to give you a chance to view the story from all the angles."

She nodded. "I appreciate that, but I still have a few questions. Is that okay? If you don't want to answer them, just say 'no comment.' I won't be offended."

"That's fine. Fire away." For the first time in years, he was ready to share this chapter of his life with someone.

A man came over with a tray and set down their baskets of fish and chips, along with their drinks. Knox inhaled the mouthwatering smell of fried cod and wanted to dive in. He resisted the urge, knowing the food would be piping hot.

Charlie thanked their server, then waited until he left to speak up again. "My biggest question is—what happened? Why did Lila agree to marry you and *then* dump you for Evan? Why didn't she go after him from the start?"

Knox took a sip of lemonade, relishing the icy-cold sweetness. "Evan and I met Lila when she was still a struggling actress. We belonged to a motley group of actors and writers that used to get together for coffee every Sunday. We'd exchange tips, share our victories, and commiserate with each other. After Evan and I sold the pilot for *The Hidden Forest* and got the green light for the first season, Lila was cast as Princess Elodie. It was the best kismet, ever. The three of us grew pretty tight."

A seagull swooped down onto their table, but Charlie shooed it away. "Scram! Go bug the tourists. They'll probably feed you."

Sure enough, a group of people at the nearby table were tossing their fries to a squawking gull. Bad move. It only made the pesky birds more aggressive.

Knox continued. "Right from the start, I had a thing for Lila, but I assumed if she was going to pick either of us, she'd go after Evan. He was the fun one, the life of the party, always up for hours of clubbing or a midnight pizza run. Whereas I was an introvert who preferred to hole up in my writing cave. But...Lila was starved for affection. She'd grown up with emotionally abusive parents and needed someone who could cherish and nurture her and offer her the stability she'd never gotten as a child. I fit that role perfectly."

"I can see that. You took really good care of me on Sunday."

I'd do it again in a heartbeat. "I liked looking after you. It made me feel needed."

"I'm pretty sure that soup you brought me had healing powers. I've never recovered from a cold this quickly." She picked up a fry and bit into it, then set it down and took a quick sip of lemonade. "Still too hot. When will I ever learn to be patient? Sorry, keep going."

"Lila and I started dating during the first season of the show. By the second, I was so head over heels that I proposed. Should I have waited? Probably, but I was in too deep to see the red flags." He frowned, remembering how foolish he'd been, thinking he could erase all of Lila's past trauma just by being supportive. "Now I realize I shouldn't have rushed her into such a huge commitment."

"Don't be so hard on yourself. You were in love with her. There was no reason to think it wouldn't work out."

He appreciated that Charlie's voice bore no judgment. Just support and understanding. "By the start of the third season, the show took off. We'd won awards for season two and were getting invited to parties and events. Which I hated."

Her mouth quirked up in a smile. "Imagine that."

"Big social events aren't my style." He broke off a piece of cod, dipped it in tartar sauce, and ate it. The crisp filling melted in his mouth, so delicious he indulged in a few more bites before carrying on with his story. "Evan loved the celebrity scene, so he always offered to escort Lila. I never got jealous because, at the end of the night, I was the one she came home to. She'd fill me in on all the hottest gossip and make jokes about Evan turning into a total player."

He remembered those nights with fondness. She'd join him in bed, giving off the faint aroma of jasmine perfume, and recount the evening in elaborate detail. Together, they'd laugh over Evan's endless quest to find the next A-list hookup.

"A few weeks before the writers' room was scheduled to plot out the fourth season, my grandfather had a heart attack," he said. "I went home to visit him in the hospital, and he passed away three days later. I stayed there for almost two weeks, supporting my mom and helping arrange the funeral. When I got back to Vancouver, I came into the apartment and saw Evan and Lila sitting together on the couch. Like they were waiting for me."

Charlie let out a little cry. "No! That's terrible timing."

"No kidding. Here I was, assuming Evan had invited Lila over to console me, but I'd misjudged everything. She handed me her engagement ring and said that…" He paused, searching for the strength to get the words out. "Even though she cared for me, she didn't feel any passion. Not like she did with Evan, who made her come alive."

"Oh, Knox, I'm so sorry."

His throat clogged with emotion. "What's worse is that they'd been sleeping together for a while. They'd kept it hidden, but now they wanted the world to know." He doused his fries in malt vinegar and ate a few, savoring the salty goodness before getting to the most painful part of the story. "And this is where I screwed up. I should have walked away, but I lost control of my temper and lashed out at them. My behavior was inexcusable."

Charlie flinched. "You didn't hurt them physically, did you?"

The fact that she had to ask struck him like a knife through the heart. "No. I've never hit anyone in my life."

"Then you have nothing to apologize for. Did they expect you to stand there and take it?" Charlie's voice was so loud the people at the next table turned to look at her. "Plus, they hit you with the news right after you buried your grandfather. What kind of selfish assholery is that!"

Her indignation eased a little of his shame, but not much. He still regretted confronting them before he'd had a chance to cool down. "I still shouldn't have done it. Before that, I'd never raised my voice around either of them."

"Well, I want to kick their asses on your behalf. Screw Princess Elodie." Charlie pounded her fist on the table. "I hope a tree falls on her head in the next season."

He gave her a wry smile. "I doubt it, but I appreciate the sentiment. Anyway, after having it out with Lila and Evan, I packed a bag and spent the night at Logan's place. I don't know if I mentioned it earlier, but we originally met when we were both working on *The Hidden Forest*."

Charlie squeezed a wedge of lemon over her cod and took a bite. "I'm glad he had your back."

"Same here. It helped that he wasn't Evan's biggest fan. He'd even tried to warn me against him. I should have listened." Knox waved away another seagull. "The next day, I went back to the apartment to apologize, but Evan shut me down. He insisted I move out immediately and said he'd never work with me again. Then he gave me an ultimatum—if I didn't leave the show, he'd tell everyone I was a raging alcoholic with serious anger issues."

Knox had never imagined his friend would retaliate that way. The threats had hit him with the force of a gut punch.

"But it wasn't true, was it?" Charlie asked. "I know you're a bartender, but you always practice moderation."

He was grateful she knew him well enough to give him the benefit of the doubt. "That's right. Mixing cocktails is something I enjoy. But getting drunk? Losing control of my emotions and my inhibitions? That's not me."

She nodded sagely. "I thought as much. So why would anyone buy into Evan's lies?"

Knox set down his fork, trying to think of how best to explain the situation. "He was so persuasive. The kind of guy who knew how to spin a story to his advantage. When he wielded his charisma, he usually got what he wanted." He barked out a harsh laugh. "Which is why it pissed him off when the producers chose me to be the executive story editor at the start of the second season. He couldn't accept that I'd earned it through hard work and talent. But I didn't realize how much he resented me until he threatened to destroy my reputation."

"That *fucking asshole*." Charlie said it with such force that the group at the next table glared at her. She gave them an apologetic wave and lowered her voice. "I hope you told him to go fuck himself."

The fact that he'd made her swear not once, but twice, brought another smile to his lips. "Sadly, no. I was done fighting. Everyone who worked on *The Hidden Forest* knew Lila and I were engaged, and now they'd see her with Evan. If I'd stayed, the humiliation would have been brutal. And I was heartbroken. Lila had left me for someone I'd trusted like a brother. I had my agent figure out the contract stuff and announced I was leaving the show to be with my family. It was an easy lie to sell, given that I'd just spent the last two weeks helping my parents."

Charlie's eyes misted over. Grabbing a napkin, she dabbed at them. "God, that sucks."

"It gets worse. A month after I left the show, I made the mistake of reading an interview Evan had given. When asked about me, he hinted that the real reason I'd left was to check into rehab. Even though I'd done what he asked, he still discredited me. Part of it was professional jealousy, but I also think he did it so he could justify betraying me."

"I saw that interview. It was awful. But I don't understand why you didn't fight back. Isn't that libel? Or slander? I mean, it was all lies."

"When I first read it, I was furious. I got in touch with my agent and told him I was going to write a rebuttal. But he warned me against it because public opinion wasn't on my side. Then I made the mistake of reading the comments. Some weren't that bad, but others? They just about killed me." Knox could still remember the sickening anguish that had coiled in his stomach. There were some things you could never unsee.

"No!" Charlie let out a wail. "You're not supposed to read the comments."

He scrubbed his hands through his hair. "I know. But I couldn't help myself. That's when I realized my agent was right. He suggested I let things cool off for a while, but I did more than that. I just disappeared."

"I noticed. I couldn't find Mac Iverson online."

"That's because I deleted all my socials, my work profiles, every bit of it." That part hadn't been a hardship since he'd never liked being on social media. "Rather than go back home, where I'd have to deal with a ton of questions, I moved to Victoria and crashed in my brother Dave's basement suite. It was meant to be temporary since I didn't want to put down roots—not until I figured out my next move. In the meantime, I started bartending at a pub in Dave's neighborhood. Once I landed the job at the Duchess, I decided to stick with bartending and got my own place."

Charlie placed her hand over his. "I'm so sorry. You didn't deserve any of this. I just wish you'd gotten the chance to tell your side of the story."

"I should have, but..." He sighed. "The last thing I wanted was more backlash. Instead of getting drawn into an ugly feud, I stayed hidden and tried to rebuild my life."

Did he regret not fighting back? Without a doubt. But he'd been afraid of making things worse.

She nodded. "Can I ask you one last question? Why the pen name?"

"My agent suggested it. Before selling the pilot of *The Hidden Forest*, I'd been using my real name. But since my only writing credit to date was a gory slasher flick, I needed something different. Hence, Mac Iverson was born. That way, I could keep writing horror on the side."

"Do you think you'll ever go back to writing?"

"I might." It was too soon to say for sure. But now that he'd delved into his old screenplay, he wanted to keep going. It was a feeling he hadn't experienced in a very long time.

"I hope you do." She grinned at him. "Though your stuff might be too scary for me."

"Don't be so sure. Now that you've read one Stephen King book, you might get lured into the dark side."

"Since we're on the subject of books, I have something for you." She set a tote bag on the table and pulled out a paperback. The cover displayed a woman in a long, off-the-shoulder gown leaning into a shirtless dude with wavy hair, set against the backdrop of a pirate ship. "This is *Love's Enduring Bounty*. I'm loaning it to you because you offered to read a romance novel."

"So I did." He took it from her, glad she'd remembered his earlier offer. "You think I'll learn anything from it? Any tips?"

Her cheeks reddened, but a smile played at her lips. "You'll have to read it and see, won't you?"

WHEN THEY WERE DONE EATING, CHARLIE WENT TO dispose of their plates and cups in the trash. The minute Knox stood up to join her, another couple swooped over and claimed their table. She was fine relinquishing it since she wanted to stretch her legs before they went to work.

Knox grabbed the steamy paperback and tucked it under his arm. "How about dessert? Want to grab some ice cream?"

"I'd love to, but I already indulged a lot." She had a sudden flash of memory, recalling the way Randolph used to react whenever she asked if they could get dessert. He'd give her a condescending smile and remind her the calories would go straight to her ass. "I shouldn't overdo it."

"You sure about that?" Knox gave her a quick grin. "Because I'm getting a cone, and I don't want you to feel deprived."

She chased Randolph out of her head. Why was she letting him invade her thoughts when Knox was *right here*, treating her with the respect she deserved? "Okay, you convinced me. But I'll hang on to *Love's Enduring Bounty* so you don't get ice cream all over it."

She took back the book and tucked it into her tote bag. They walked over to a kiosk selling ice cream and milkshakes, where he bought them each a cone—sea salt caramel for him and raspberry cheesecake for her. The sweet, creamy treat was the perfect way to top off her meal, even if the warmth of the sun melted it almost as fast as she could eat it. Since they still had a half hour before they needed to leave, they strolled past the floating homes, stopping to look at each one. She paused in front of her favorite, which was painted a vibrant sapphire blue and adorned with hanging baskets filled with colorful flowers.

"I like this one the best," she said. "When I was a teenager, I used to come down here with my friends. We'd each pick a houseboat and envision what it would be like to live there."

"Not me. Too many gawkers. Especially on a nice day like this."

"I don't think I'd be into it now. I like being around people, but this is too much."

As they walked, her mind kept bouncing back to everything Knox had told her. In the past, he'd revealed so little about himself that she'd regarded each tidbit like a tiny gem. But today, he'd opened the whole damn treasure chest.

"Thanks again for sharing all that stuff about *The Hidden Forest*," she said. "It couldn't have been easy for you to relive it."

"The hardest part was deciding whether to tell you about it. Once I left you that letter, I knew there was no going back."

She licked the side of her cone, trying to catch the drips before they fell on her hand. "Who else knows? Besides me and your friend Logan?"

"My family. A few other friends. But that's it." He gave a short laugh. "Oh, and Preston knows, too."

"How'd he know about it? Was it in your employee file?"

"Nope. When I applied to work at the Duchess, my resume only included my bartending experience. But Preston told me he did a deep dive into everyone's past to make sure we weren't hiding any dirty little secrets. He found mine."

Charlie grimaced. Though she didn't have anything to hide, the thought of him scrolling through her social media accounts made her uncomfortable. "I hope he didn't look at all my Instagram posts. Some of my early stuff is pretty cringey."

"I'm not sure how far back he went, but he somehow uncovered my pen name. I was surprised because I thought I'd done a thorough job burying Mac Iverson. Not only that, but I cut almost all my ties to the show. Other than Logan, no one knew how to reach me."

She couldn't imagine isolating herself that way. Even if she someday moved on to another hotel, she wouldn't want to lose contact with the Damsels. "Were you close to your coworkers? Or was it an easy break?"

He stopped beside an aqua houseboat with a red bike parked in front. "It was tough. There were two writers—Zack and Norah —that I really liked. They joined the show right before we started plotting the second season, and we clicked right away. But Evan always disparaged them. I think it annoyed him that the three of us got on so well."

"Would you ever want to get in touch with them?" She didn't want to push Knox too much, but he might benefit from reaching out to a few of his old friends.

"I've thought about it. But I left so suddenly. Then Evan spread all those rumors about me. Maybe the other writers didn't buy into his bullshit, but I didn't stick around long enough to find out what they really thought. Now, it's too late."

"Is it?" She placed her hand on his arm. He'd rolled up his sleeves, and his bare skin was warm from the sun. "It's only been five years. Maybe if you were able to talk to them, you'd feel better. It might give you some closure."

He tilted his head to the side. "You think I need closure?"

His tone wasn't hostile, just curious. Like no one had ever asked him that before.

"Maybe?" She licked her lips, tasting raspberry ice cream on her tongue. "It's not for me to say. If you're fine with your life as is, then I wouldn't worry about it. But it seems like this stuff has been weighing on you for years. Especially since you didn't get to tell everyone the truth."

When he said nothing, she worried she'd gone too far. Here he was, opening up about his past, and now she was encouraging him to make himself more vulnerable.

He nodded slowly. "It would be nice not to have it locked up inside me like an ugly secret. But damn if I know where to start. Besides telling you, I mean."

"You don't have to do anything just yet. Maybe...leave the door open and see what happens." She licked a drop of ice cream from her hand. "I'm such a mess. This is melting all over me."

"You've got a little smear of it on your chin." He reached over and rubbed his thumb against it. "There, that's better."

His gentle touch made her shiver. When he locked eyes with her, she wanted to inch closer and place a soft kiss on his lips. And from the intense way he was staring at her, she was certain he felt the same way. But they were out in public, with people all around them. Not the best place for a first kiss.

What she wouldn't give for a few more hours alone with him. This longing was stronger than the tiny spark they'd shared when he'd come into her bedroom. Or their almost-kiss in the storage room. This time, they both wanted more.

Hopefully, they'd get the chance to act on it soon.

～

FOR THE REST OF THE DAY, CHARLIE COULDN'T GET Knox off her mind. If she'd had any doubts that he liked her, they were gone now. Even though they had yet to go on a real date, he'd let her into his world and shared his secrets. That counted for a lot.

By the time she got home from work and settled into bed, it was half past midnight. One of the downsides of working the late shift was that it messed up her schedule. Not ideal, given that she needed to be at the Duchess at eight tomorrow for an early meeting.

Unfortunately, needing to fall asleep and being able to do it were two different things. After a half hour of tossing and turning, she flicked on her bedside lamp and grabbed *Love's Passionate Conquest*—yet another pirate romance. Since she'd read it before, she knew what to expect and had already memorized the locations of the steamiest chapters. She was halfway through one of them when her phone chimed with a text.

She grabbed it off her nightstand, brightening when Knox's name appeared on the screen.

> Knox: Are you awake? I have a question for you.

Was Knox *sexting* her? Charlie regarded her phone with trepidation, but the urge to text him back was too hard to resist.

> Charlie: I haven't been able to fall asleep so I'm reading for a bit. What's up?

> Knox: How long until I get to the good stuff in this book? And by good stuff, I mean sexy times on a pirate ship.

Oh, God. Knowing that Knox was reading the book she'd loaned him—which was packed full of racy scenes—made Charlie feel both embarrassed *and* aroused.

> Charlie: Patience. The author needs to immerse you in the story first.

> Knox: I'm already immersed, damn it.

> Charlie: Fine. Chapter 8 is where the magic starts. Chapter 14 is smoking hot. By chapter 20 you'll need a fire extinguisher.

> Knox: I'm impressed you immediately knew which chapters.

> Charlie: I might have read that book a few times. Just saying.

> Knox: What are you reading tonight?

> Charlie: Another romance. Same series as yours but set on a different pirate ship. There are a lot of lusty pirate captains out there.

> Knox: Too bad I couldn't work pirates into The Hidden Forest.

> Charlie: I wish! Even without pirates, some of the show was kind of steamy. Like that love scene between Elodie and Finn at the end of season 3.

The number of times she'd watched that scene bordered on humiliating. What she'd loved most about it wasn't that it was explicit, but that it showed so much tenderness between the two characters. Upon first viewing it, she couldn't conceive of *ever* finding a lover who would treat her that way. But now she was wondering if it might be possible. Especially since Knox had been the one responsible for that episode.

> Charlie: You wrote that episode, didn't you?

> Knox: Guilty as charged. Did you like it?

> Charlie: I loved it.

Knox: Glad to hear it. Since you're a romance aficionado, your opinion counts for a lot.

Charlie gulped down a steadying breath. Talking to Knox like this—with a level of intimacy she wasn't used to—had her heart thrumming wildly. In her mind's eye, she could visualize him sitting up in bed and reading *Love's Enduring Bounty*, maybe chuckling over the book's flowery language. What would he think when he got to chapter eight? Or—*Lord, have mercy*—when he reached chapter twenty?

But now she wanted to know what he was wearing. Pajamas? A T-shirt and boxers? Or did he sleep in the buff?

She was tempted to ask him, but that seemed too much like *actual* sexting. Better to douse this fire now than let it get out of control.

Charlie: I'd better get to sleep. I have to go in early tomorrow. Good night.

Knox: Good night. Sweet dreams.

Oh, they'd be sweet all right. Sweet *and* spicy.

Fourteen

Knox didn't mind that it was Friday. Or that happy hour would be mobbed since the hotel was full of insurance agents in town for a convention. He didn't even care that Preston had left another of his try-hard notes:

Hey, Knox. Loving those fall cocktails! Your pumpkin spice white Russian is the bomb! I'm thinking we should start pivoting into spooky season soon. Halloween's only 5 weeks away! Let's make this the most spook-tacular October ever!

For the record, the pumpkin spice drink was disgusting. Knox had only added it to the menu after multiple reminders.

Still, he could get down with creating a few ghost-themed cocktails. Two days ago, Logan had told him *Canada's Most Haunted* would be filming at the Duchess on Halloween night, which was a huge win. Upon hearing the news, Laurel and her marketing team started using it in their publicity. As a result, the hotel was sold out for the entire week of Halloween.

But the show wasn't the only thing causing Knox's uncommonly good mood. Ever since his lunch with Charlie on Tuesday, he couldn't stop thinking about her. Texting her that night had been a risk, but she'd clearly been into it. Then, on

Wednesday and Thursday, she'd stopped by the Lily and flirted with him so brazenly that he knew she wanted more than just friendship. He could hardly wait until their do-over date on Sunday.

"Earth to Knox. Are you listening to me?" Selena stood on the other side of the bar, clipboard in hand. "I need to finish this order. Do you want me to get more of the Whistlestop cider or not? Last week, you told me hardly anyone orders it, and the rep was a pain to work with."

"Whatever you want." He was still trying to decide where to take Charlie for dinner since he hadn't been able to secure another reservation at Il Terrazzo.

Selena smacked her clipboard on the bar top. "What's going on? You're never this agreeable."

He shrugged. "Maybe I've turned over a new leaf."

"Bullshit." She narrowed her eyes at him. "It's Charlie, isn't it? Don't think I didn't notice. When I came into the conference room this morning, she was singing. Like a goddamn Disney princess. You're fucking, aren't you?"

That brought him back down to earth. "Jesus, Selena. There are customers here. Not to mention, Charlie and I haven't even been on a real date yet."

"I just don't want her to get hurt." A glimpse of pain flickered in her eyes. "You know how trusting she is."

"And you're not?"

"Hell, no. I've been screwed over too many times." She fussed with a lock of hair, tucking it back into her bun. "Just...don't be one of those guys."

"I won't. I promise." Even if Selena was butting into his personal life, he appreciated her looking out for Charlie. "I also promise to give you my full attention."

She arched her eyebrows. "Really? You seem pretty far gone."

He was about to deny it, but Charlie chose that moment to sail into the Gilded Lily for her daily visit. The sight of her brought back his sappy grin. "Hey, Charlie."

"Hi, Knox." She set a small Tupperware container on the bar top. "I saved you a treat from our Damsels' meeting. Rosie brought caramel brownies, and they're *so* decadent."

He leaned over and squeezed her hand. "Thanks. I'll have it on my break."

"I had to fight Laurel for the last one, but I told her you needed it because you're going to be slammed tonight." Charlie flashed Selena an apologetic smile. "Sorry to interrupt. If you two are busy, I can come back later."

Selena rolled her eyes. "It's fine. We're not getting much done. Knox seems more...distracted than usual."

"Just leave the inventory sheet for me," he said. "I'll see if there are any suppliers we want to cross off the list, and I'll get back to you."

"Check to see if we need to increase our orders, too." She handed him the clipboard. "Now that we're busy, we can't afford to run short of anything."

"Will do." Normally, he was on top of this shit, and he liked working with Selena, who managed the hotel's beverage inventory. She had a knack for seeking out local breweries, wineries, and cider orchards to ensure the Lily provided visitors with an authentic taste of Vancouver Island.

"All right, I'll let you lovebirds flirt for a few minutes before Knox gets stuck dealing with all those thirsty insurance guys." Selena glanced around the lounge. "Where's Miles? You're going to need backup tonight."

"He'll be here in a bit. He's had some scheduling issues." Over the past few weeks, Knox had tried to rein in his frustration with Miles. While the guy was a decent bartender, he'd recently been struggling to balance his duties at the Lily with a temp job at an office downtown.

"Let me know if that gets to be a problem," Selena said. "You shouldn't be stuck making dozens of pumpkin spice monstrosities on your own."

"You don't like pumpkin spice?" Charlie placed her hand over her heart. "It's the official flavor of fall."

"It's basic as hell." Selena turned to leave but stopped short as Alejandro, the assistant manager of the Grand Duke, walked into the Gilded Lily. "What's that slimeball doing here?"

Alejandro sauntered up to the bar. While the guy was way too smug for his own good, Knox couldn't deny that he was a smooth fucker. Clad in a charcoal gray suit with a silvery blue tie, his dark, wavy hair in a perfect flow, he looked more polished and professional than anyone who worked at the Duchess.

"Good afternoon, ghostbusters," he said. "Who ya gonna call?"

"Jealous, are you?" Selena demanded.

"Of what—your so-called 'haunted' hotel?"

Knox bristled with annoyance. "It *is* haunted. We've got substantial proof."

"Just because a place is old and run-down doesn't mean it's haunted." Alejandro picked up a laminated card from the bar and grimaced. "A pumpkin spice white Russian? How nauseating."

"First of all, don't insult Knox's drinks," Charlie snapped. "Second, I'll have you know our hotel was the site of a tragic incident in 1924. Three people died in room 309, which was later turned into a storage room. A room that shows all the signs of being haunted. Over the years, a lot of our staff have been locked in there, presumably by a vengeful ghost."

Alejandro's smug look vanished. "I don't believe you. If a scandal like that had ever happened, everyone would know about it."

"The hotel covered it up," Charlie said. "It wasn't in the papers, but we found proof in the provincial archives. Plus, I discovered written accounts from staff members who had unsettling experiences in that room."

"But no one's seen a ghost, have they?" he asked. "At the Grand Duke, guests have supposedly witnessed apparitions floating through the hallways."

"And yet you turned down the opportunity to host the show?" Selena crossed her arms. "Bad move on your part. Landing *Canada's Most Haunted* has been great for business."

Upon seeing the sour look that passed over Alejandro's features, Knox swelled with pride. "We've got a full house for the entire week of Halloween."

"Must be a nice change of pace," Alejandro said. "But we've never had a problem attracting guests. And we don't need a fake ghost to do it."

Selena chuffed out a furious breath. "Why are you here? I can't imagine you came for a drink."

Alejandro turned to Knox. "I'm here for you, barkeep. I wanted to offer you a proposition."

If it was a job at the Grand Duke, Knox wasn't interested. No way was he leaving the Duchess, not after he and Charlie were finally connecting. Even so, he was curious. "What is it?"

"We have a huge gala taking place on October twenty-fourth—the Saturday before Halloween." Alejandro gave Selena a condescending smile. "Remember, querida? I told you about it when we ran into each other at Pepe's. Though maybe it slipped your mind, given that you were slightly inebriated?"

"I remember," she grumbled. "You're hosting a party for that fantasy show."

Fantasy show? Knox's shoulders tightened. "Do you mean *The Hidden Forest*?"

Alejandro nodded. "That's the one. The CEO of Royal Host —our management company—is good friends with an exec from the show. They go way back. Because of that, we're hosting a gala celebrating their one hundredth episode. But our event manager dropped the ball. Too many of our regulars already requested off that night because it's so close to Halloween. So, we need an extra bartender with plenty of experience. Despite the fact you work in this dump, I've heard good things about you."

Knox's throat lurched with a hard swallow. If Alejandro had asked him a month ago, his answer would have been "no way in hell." But ever since his conversation with Charlie three days ago, he'd been thinking about everyone on the show that he'd left behind. Remembering the good times as well as the bad. Could he risk attending such a high-profile event? He had no idea what Evan's reaction would be. Would he want to mend fences, or would he have Knox kicked out on sight?

"One more thing," Alejandro added. "Costumes are mandatory for everyone, including the event staff. Something decent, not a cheap number from Party City."

Never in his life had Knox been so grateful for the chance to dress up. With the right disguise, he could observe everyone without attracting attention. If he was lucky, he might get to connect with a few of his former coworkers and tell them he hadn't forgotten them. Maybe then, he could put old ghosts to rest.

"I'll do it," he said. "Just send me the details."

Charlie spoke up quickly. "But you'll probably need help at your station, right?" She turned to Alejandro with her sunniest smile. "Any chance I could assist Knox? I'm a huge fan of the show."

Without asking, Knox knew she was volunteering for his sake. To ensure he made it through the evening without melting down. While it wasn't something he would have asked her to do, he was grateful she'd thought of it.

"We could probably use you, but only if you promise to behave professionally," Alejandro said. "No asking for autographs or selfies. Understand?"

"Of course. I wouldn't dream of doing anything that intrusive." When he didn't respond right away, she clasped her hands together. "*Please*, Alejandro."

He gave a dramatic sigh. "Fine. Decent costumes. Professional behavior. No photographs. Got it?" He turned to Selena. "What about you? Would you like to help? You could dress up as a sexy serving wench. Or a sexy pirate. I'd pay money to see that."

Her dark eyes flashed with anger. "Go to hell. And get out of our bar."

"As always, it's been a pleasure, princesa." He gave a little bow. "Knox, I'll be in touch."

After he left, Selena gritted her teeth. "He's such a prick. I hate those pet names he uses."

"He wasn't that bad," Charlie said. "You have to admit, he's smoking-hot, and that suit looks like a million bucks on him."

"I'll admit he's...attractive. He looks even better without the suit." When the two of them stared at her, a rosy flush crept across her cheeks. "Not that I've seen him naked. He works out at Northlife Fitness, same as me, and we've run into each other a few times."

Charlie grinned. "Uh-huh. Whatever you say."

"I've got to finish up so I can get out of here at a decent hour," Selena said. "Have a good weekend."

"You, too." Once Selena was gone, Charlie leaned across the bar. "Just so you know, I'm not into Alejandro. Not even a little. Sure, he wears a suit incredibly well, and I love his accent, but he's not my type. I like teasing Selena because it gets her so riled up."

Knox loved it when Charlie showed her naughty side. "For someone who looks so innocent, you're actually a wicked little pixie. You'll be perfect as Tinker Bell." He was already imagining how sexy she would look, wearing a short green dress and ankle boots.

Rather than banter with him like she usually did, she reached over and took his hand again, giving it a tight squeeze. "Speaking of costumes, are you sure you want to work at that gala? It could be super stressful."

"Weren't you the one encouraging me to get closure?"

"I was, but this seems kind of risky. I don't want you to get hurt."

"I don't want that, either, but I'm not sure when I'll get a chance like this again. I think if I can find a disguise that covers my face, I'll be safe. If I don't feel comfortable exposing myself, then I'll keep it on all night." With any luck, he'd get the chance to connect with a few of the people he'd cared about, without making himself too vulnerable.

"I can help. Laurel has a friend who works for VOS Musical Theatre, and she's borrowed costumes from them before. I'll have her ask if they have anything we could rent for the gala."

"Sounds good. Are we still on for Sunday? I couldn't get into Il Terrazzo. Anyplace else you'd like to go?"

Her concerned expression vanished. In its place was the sunny smile he knew so well. "How about somewhere in Chinatown? I love Chinese food."

"That works. I'll pick you up at six. All right?"

"You got it, Captain Hook." With a wink, she walked away, giving him an enticing view of her ass.

Sunday couldn't come soon enough.

Fifteen

FOR ONCE, THE STARS HAD ALIGNED IN CHARLIE'S favor. She and Knox had enjoyed a scrumptious meal at the Fan Tan Café, located in the heart of Victoria's Chinatown. After eating dinner, they walked over to the Inner Harbour and talked for another hour. Now that Knox wasn't keeping his past a secret, the conversation between them flowed freely.

During their drive back to her apartment, she wrestled with her next move. She wanted to barrel on full speed ahead and invite him up to her place, but they hadn't even kissed. Shouldn't they ease into things more gradually?

It didn't help that she was woefully out of practice. After Randolph, she'd only been on a handful of dates, and none had progressed beyond a few kisses. She hadn't shared her bed with anyone for three years.

Three years.

It was pathetic.

But sex with Randolph had often been stressful. Especially on those occasions where she felt like she wasn't thin enough to suit him. When he'd make cracks about her stomach being "bloated" after a big dinner or her ass looking too big. Even during the act, she usually pretended to climax so that he'd feel like a masterful lover.

Was it any wonder she'd avoided sex for so long?

With Knox, she sensed things would be different. He'd already proven how compassionate and caring he was. Not that they needed to leap into bed right away, but she wasn't going to let her fears hold her back.

When he parked his truck in the circular driveway, she unbuckled her seat belt, fully intending to lean toward him and initiate a good-night kiss. Before she could take action, he reached into the back seat and pulled out another of those brown paper grocery bags. "If it's okay with you, I thought we could have dessert at your place. I brought supplies."

She was grateful he was in no hurry to end the night. "What did you have in mind?"

"Last time I was here, I noticed you have a fire pit in your backyard. Is it still usable?"

"Sure. We've got chairs and everything."

He handed her the grocery bag. "If you take this, I'll grab the wood out of the back of my truck."

"You chopped wood?" Her secret lumberjack fantasies came racing back. Knox, chopping wood in the forest. Preferably shirtless.

A burst of laughter rumbled from his chest. "No, I bought it at the grocery store. Where would I find a tree to chop down?"

"Oh...right." She eased out of the truck with the paper bag and waited until he'd fetched a large canvas tote containing a bundle of firewood.

They walked toward her parents' spacious backyard. Off the kitchen was a raised wooden deck; the rest of the grounds consisted of a classic English garden filled with flowers and a large stone fountain. At the far end, four Adirondack chairs and two matching side tables were arranged around a steel fire pit. The last time she'd used it had been in July, when she'd invited the Damsels over for a bonfire.

"I thought we could make s'mores," Knox said. "It's not too chilly out, and we've got a full moon. How does that sound?"

"It sounds heavenly." She set the bag on the ground and took out the items, placing them on the side table. He'd thought of everything: marshmallows, graham crackers, four bars of Cadbury's chocolate, two metal toasting sticks, and a bottle of brandy.

Brandy? "Since when do you use brandy to make s'mores?" she asked.

"I don't, but I thought it would complement them nicely. A spiced porter or a stout would make for a better pairing, but I know you're not much of a beer drinker."

"Thanks." Though she normally didn't drink brandy either, the strong liqueur might give her the courage to make the first move. "Want some?"

"You bet. Normally, I'd serve it up in a snifter, but we'll have to settle for plastic cups. I tossed a couple into the grocery bag."

She poured a little brandy into the cups and passed him one. It was so strong it made her eyes water, though it went down easier after a few sips. Rich and velvety, it had a sweetness that wasn't too overpowering. "It's really good."

"It's from Bridgeland Distillery, out of Calgary. I usually prefer bourbon, but this stuff is addictive." After taking a drink, he set the cup on the side table and arranged the firewood, then added kindling and pieces of crumpled-up newspaper.

Charlie watched, mesmerized, as he got the fire started. The crackling flames danced against the night sky, filling the air with woodsmoke. She moved in closer, seeking out the warmth of the fire. Now that the sun had gone down, the air was crisp enough to have a bite. The smoky smell brought back memories of a trip she'd taken while in university, camping with friends at Strathcona

Park. She'd felt so free being out in nature, with nothing but the woods around her.

Knox gestured for her to sit down. "We'll let it burn for a bit, then we can toast the s'mores."

She did as he said but wasn't satisfied. While the chairs were comfortable, they weren't conducive to snuggling. "Knox?"

"What is it?"

"I really want to kiss you. I've been thinking about it all week, and I—"

He stood and reached for her hand, then pulled her up so she was facing him. "You don't have to ask twice."

His hands skimmed her cheeks, just the lightest of touches. Smoothing his palms across her skin, as if mapping her features. Stroking the back of her neck, making little shivers dance along her spine. She whimpered as he drew his thumb across her bottom lip.

"*Please*, Knox."

His first kiss was tender, his lips softly seeking hers. But he was being too gentle. She wasn't some china doll that needed to be handled with care. With a growl, she stepped closer, placed her arms around his neck, and pressed her body against his. She deepened the kiss, eager to convince him how badly she wanted this.

All his hesitancy vanished. He devoured her mouth, kissing her with such ferocity she could barely get in a breath. Each little sensation shot right to her core—the soft scrape of his beard, the taste of brandy on his lips, the heat of his body, warming her all over. His hands tightened around her waist as he kissed her like his life depended on it.

A spark leapt up from the fire and landed on her jeans. With a cry, she pulled away and patted it out. Despite the momentary shock, she was so aroused she wanted to jump his bones right here and now.

Knox raked a hand through his thick brown hair. "You okay? Sorry about that. I didn't mean to get carried away."

"You don't have to apologize. I only stopped because I didn't want to catch on fire." Her heart was pounding fiercely, her pulse racing. When was the last time she'd felt like this with anyone? Hell, had she *ever* felt this way? "Maybe we should let the flames settle so we don't go down in a blaze of glory."

He laughed. "But what a way to go, right?"

Her bashfulness vanished, replaced by the thrill of victory. She'd *finally* gotten Knox to kiss her. Not just any kiss, either, but a five-alarm blaze that had woken every nerve ending in her body. If his kisses were this good, what would he be like in bed?

She topped up her brandy. "Do you want more?"

"Just another splash. Thanks."

By the time she'd polished off her second cup, her limbs were loose and relaxed. She toasted her marshmallow until it was burned to a crisp and sandwiched it between the graham crackers and chocolate. Then she ate every morsel, licking the crumbs and the melted chocolate off her fingers. "Mmm. Nothing beats a s'more."

"We used to do bonfires all the time when I was growing up," he said. "In the summer, we'd have the neighbor kids over and play night games."

"I'm so jealous of your childhood. Do you go back very often?"

Knox broke off a few pieces of chocolate and ate them. "Not as much as I'd like. I was hoping to go home for Thanksgiving on the twelfth, but I can't make it work. The Gilded Lily will be closed, but I'd need more than one day off to trek home and back. And what with Preston leaning into Halloween, October's already hectic enough without asking for PTO."

"It's a bummer Thanksgiving falls right in the middle of spooky season. Americans are lucky. They get to have Thanksgiving in November, when Halloween's over and done with."

Charlie placed another marshmallow on her stick and toasted

it until it burst into flames. She skimmed off the burnt part and popped it into her mouth. "Yum. Just the way I like it."

"You're supposed to toast it gently, not incinerate it."

"Says who? It's way tastier if it's super crispy."

He set down his toasting stick and sat back in his chair. "C'mere."

"Who, me?" She grinned at him. Teasing Knox was becoming her new favorite activity.

"Yes you, sassy pants. Come sit on my lap. There's room for both of us."

She did as he said, squishing in beside him. This time, when she kissed him, he tasted like marshmallows and milk chocolate.

He wove his hands through her hair and placed soft kisses behind her ear. "Sorry in advance if I get marshmallow goo in your hair."

"Like I care about getting sticky? Do you have any idea how long I've wanted you to kiss me? I've had a thing for you since..." As the realization struck her, she put her head in her hands and lowered her voice to an embarrassed whisper. "March of last year."

With a gentle laugh, he tugged on her hands. "Can you speak up? I didn't catch that."

From his teasing tone, she was certain he hadn't missed a word she'd said. "You heard me. I started feeling this way after you saved me from those jerks who were at the hotel for a travel convention. Do you remember? They were part of that rowdy group who decided to throw a Mardi Gras party at the Gilded Lily."

"What I remember most was having to clean up all those beaded necklaces. Those idiots tossed them everywhere. If they wanted Mardi Gras, they should have gone to New Orleans, not Victoria."

"They were so obnoxious. But most of them were harmless, except the two guys who came up to the front desk and started harassing me."

At the time, she'd been in a vulnerable position, covering the overnight shift on her own. She'd initially responded to them with cool politeness, and then with anger, but they wouldn't be deterred. Since they weren't a direct threat to any of the guests, she'd been hesitant to radio one of the hotel's security officers for backup.

Knox had no such qualms. As he passed by the front desk on his way out, he confronted the men and threatened to call security if they didn't back off. Even after he'd gotten rid of them, he kept Charlie company until her shift ended. In typical Knox fashion, he hadn't said much, but his presence had been incredibly comforting.

He placed a gentle kiss on the inside of her palm. "I'm sorry you had to deal with them."

"It's fine, now. But after that night, I couldn't stop thinking about the gallant way you came to my rescue. That's why I started popping by the Lily and bringing you treats. And why I wheedled you into helping me with all the hotel's events last Christmas."

"Well, it worked. When you asked, I couldn't say no. I even wore a red vest with shiny holly berries on it. Just for you. Every time you came in to the Lily to talk to me, it brightened my whole day."

Hearing the words made her heart soar. "But you never said anything. Why didn't you ask me out?"

He cupped her cheek. "I thought about it, but I always figured you were too sunny and upbeat to want a grouch like me. Even when you invited me over to watch *Canada's Most Haunted*, I didn't want to get my hopes up. I'm glad you made the effort."

"It wasn't easy. I was afraid you'd turn me down, but the Damsels talked me into it. And now..."

"Here we are. Right where we're supposed to be." His lips captured hers again, hungry and possessive, like he couldn't get enough.

She didn't care that they were both sticky and that the chair was too snug to accommodate them. Knox's passionate kisses transported her to a place where minor discomforts didn't matter. And when he trailed kisses along the curve of her throat, she groaned and dug her fingers into his hair. She could have gone on like this for hours, until the fire burned down to embers, but she wanted more.

She hit Knox with a come-hither smile. "Do you want to go up to my apartment? This fire is lovely and all, but...we might be more comfortable in my bed."

"You sure? I don't want to rush you."

She loved that he was taking her feelings into consideration. "I'm sure. If you're not ready, we can wait. But I don't feel rushed." She tensed up, hoping he wouldn't turn her down.

"I'm definitely ready. Let's put out this fire and start a new one...in your bedroom." He waggled his eyebrows. "Sorry. That was unbelievably cheesy."

"The worst. Hard to believe you're an award-winning writer." But she didn't care how many cheesy lines he spouted. All that mattered was that he'd said yes.

She went to the shed, where her parents' gardener kept his equipment. After filling up a bucket of water, she brought it over to the fire. Once they were sure it was out, Knox gathered up the s'more supplies and put them back in the grocery bag.

They'd just reached her apartment door when she froze up, her anxiety taking hold again. "I'm not sure what your expectations are, but since you were in the entertainment industry, I don't want you to be disappointed."

He chuckled. "Did you think I was going to sex parties? I was never that adventurous."

A warm flush crept up her cheeks. "The thing is—when it comes to sex, my tastes are kind of...vanilla."

"Don't undersell yourself." He took her hand and gave it a reassuring squeeze. "In my opinion, vanilla is a highly underrated flavor."

Sixteen

At most, Knox had hoped for a good-night kiss from Charlie. Even if he'd spent weeks fantasizing about her, he had no desire to rush her into anything. Hell, he was just grateful she'd agreed to go out with him in the first place.

But if this was what she wanted, then he wasn't about to say no.

Once they got inside her apartment, he set the bag of groceries on the counter, and they took turns washing the sticky marshmallow residue off their hands. Then she led him into her bedroom and turned on the lamp resting atop her nightstand. To his surprise, the teetering stacks of books had vanished.

"What happened to all your spicy novels?" he asked. "You didn't give them away, did you?"

"Nope. I just boxed them up and put them in the garage. It was getting too hard to walk. But I'll never give up on romance. How could I when you're standing here beside me?"

Not two weeks ago, he'd told Charlie that romance wasn't for him. That he was done holding out hope for a happy ending. But her unwavering faith made him think he'd been dead wrong. "You just might make a believer out of me."

"Good, because that's what I was hoping for." With an impish smile, she unbuttoned his flannel shirt, eased it off his shoulders, and let it fall to the floor.

When she ran her hands under his T-shirt, he gave a ragged groan. Her fingers were soft and delicate, tracing patterns across his chest. He pulled his shirt over his head and tossed it aside, exposing the colorful tattoos adorning his shoulders and upper arms. She gazed at them in awe, running gentle fingers over each one before placing a kiss on his right shoulder, embellished with a detailed design of a pine forest set against a mountain range.

"This tattoo is so elaborate," she said. "I feel like I could live in this forest."

He skimmed his fingers through her soft blond hair. "Do you have any?"

"Tattoos? Not a chance. I'm too scared of needles."

"So, if I took off your shirt, I wouldn't see any hidden ink?" He started unbuttoning her blouse. "No tiny tattoo of a butterfly or a heart?"

"Nothing. But feel free to have a look." She slipped the blouse off her shoulders. Underneath it, she wore a lacy pink bra that barely covered her breasts.

He brushed his thumb against one nipple and was gratified when it hardened into a tight little peak. His desire grew as she unzipped her jeans and slid them off her hips, revealing pale pink panties with a row of tiny red hearts around the waistband. The sight of her, stripped down to almost nothing, was so sexy it took his breath away. He wanted to capture this image in his mind, to remember it forever, in case he never got this chance with her again.

The design on her panties made him smile. "These look familiar."

She glared at him in mock indignation. "What are you talking about? When did you ever get a look at my underwear?"

"When you brought me into your bedroom the first time. You had left them on your bed, next to your pillow."

A soft blush stole over her cheeks. "Oh...I was hoping you didn't notice them."

"I noticed them, all right. Very cute and sexy." He took off his jeans and kicked them aside. When she smoothed her fingers over the bulge in his boxers, he sucked in a tight breath. Her touch felt so good it would take all his willpower not to go off like a rocket.

"Before we go any further, I want you to know I have condoms in my nightstand." She gave him a sheepish smile. "I bought a new box yesterday. Just in case."

"A whole box, eh? I'm glad you were thinking ahead." He had a couple in his wallet, but he wasn't sure how old they were.

She threw back the covers and lay down on one side of the bed. When she crooked her finger, beckoning him to follow, he settled in beside her. How many nights had he spent dreaming about her? How many times, after she'd stopped by the bar, had his mind drifted, envisioning what he'd do to her if he ever got the opportunity?

He pulled her closer, savoring the feel of her bare skin against his, and kissed her again. Long, passionate kisses, their bodies pressed together, his hands stroking the soft skin of her back. He could make out the faint scent of the lavender in her shampoo, barely noticeable under the stronger aroma of woodsmoke.

When she let out another of those impatient whimpers, he flipped her onto her back and positioned himself above her. Pushing aside the lacy cups of her bra, he sucked on her nipples. She gave a cry of pleasure and wove her fingers through his hair.

"Take off my bra. *Please*," she begged. "It's just getting in the way."

He unclasped it and flung it as far as he could. "You okay to keep going?"

"Oh my God, yes. Touch me *everywhere*."

That was all the encouragement he needed. He dipped one

hand beneath her minuscule panties and slid a finger inside her, surprised at how drenched she was. She writhed underneath him, letting out little gasps that made him crave her all the more. God, but she was beautiful—her eyes closed, her soft pink lips slightly parted, her entire body responding to his touch.

He kept going, drawing little circles inside her, increasing the pressure as her cries grew louder. She urged him on, bucking her hips and grinding against his touch, until she arched her back and moaned his name. As she relaxed beneath him, coming down from her orgasm, he was tempted to give her another one, but she took hold of his wrist and moved his hand aside.

She locked eyes with him. "Give me a sec to recover. That felt so good I almost forgot to breathe."

Talk about an ego boost. "Take your time."

After a few minutes, she sat up to face him. "I don't want to keep you waiting. If you want to have sex, I'll just grab a condom."

She wasn't getting off that easily. "What I really want to do is spread your legs and taste you until you make more of those delightful little noises. If that's something you'd be into."

"I would, but...are you sure that's what you want?"

What kind of a question was that? Whoever Charlie had been with before must not have given a shit about her pleasure. "Of course. Slide your body over to the edge of the bed."

She scooted down, and he got off the bed and knelt before her. After easing off her panties, he ran his hands along her thighs and parted her legs. "Just a warning—you might get a little beard burn."

"I'm fine with that. But if we're giving out warnings, I can't always climax this way."

"Challenge accepted, sweetheart."

Gripping her ass, he inhaled her sweetness and dove in, licking and tasting, keeping her firmly in his grasp, even as she squirmed underneath him. By now, his dick was aching for release, but he focused entirely on her pleasure, taking pride as she moaned and begged him to keep going. And when she shuddered all over and let out the biggest cry of all, he didn't stop until her cries faded to tiny whimpers of pleasure and she murmured his name like a caress.

No one had ever made Charlie feel this good. Usually, she faked an orgasm so her partner could move on to the main attraction.

With Knox, that wasn't an issue.

After she stopped trembling and caught her breath again, she sat up to face him. And damn if he didn't have the most self-satisfied grin on his face.

With a sly smile, she looked down at his boxers, which did nothing to hide his erection. "Do you want me to return the favor? Because I'd be glad to."

"Another time. Let's put one of those condoms to good use."

"Ooh, yes. Just in the nightstand drawer. Next to..." She stopped cold, remembering what was in there.

He stood and opened the drawer. As he rummaged around in it, his smile widened. No doubt he'd discovered her vibrator. "Very interesting. I'm thinking we should explore that toy later." After bringing out a condom, he took off his boxers.

Whoa. Though Knox was a big guy—over six feet tall, brawny, and sturdily built—she'd never imagined his...equipment...would match his size. She leaned closer and ran her fingers along his rigid length, smoothing them over the tip. She was still tempted to take him into her mouth, even though she had no idea how she'd fit all of him in there.

He pulled away. "Behave, you naughty pixie. I'm never going to last if you do that. Now, stop teasing me and lie down on the bed."

She loved it when he used his bossy voice. "What if I don't behave?"

"Then I might have to put you over my knee and spank your cute little ass. Would you like that?"

Oddly enough, she would. "Um…maybe? Like, if you didn't spank too hard?"

He groaned. "Enough. We'll put it on the to-do list. For now, I want you on your back, legs open, and ready for me. Got it?"

"Absolutely." Bossy Knox was pushing *all* her buttons. She did as he said, resting her head against the pillows, her whole body revved up and ready for more.

"Good girl," he murmured. "I like seeing you that way."

Goose bumps prickled along her arms. *And I like being this way.*

After putting on the condom, he came back into bed. He nudged her legs open a little wider and slid himself inside her. Despite the tight fit, it felt so good.

With a cry of delight, she pulled him closer. "Yes, Knox. *Yes.*"

"Fuck, you feel amazing," he said. "Gotta warn you, this might be kind of quick."

"That's okay." She'd already had two orgasms, which were two more than she usually had with a partner.

She burrowed her face in his shoulder and inhaled the scent of campfire on his skin. This was like her woodsman fantasy come to life, except better because they were in her comfy bed rather than out in the forest, where wild animals could attack them.

Closing her eyes, she let the physical sensations transport her. Nothing mattered right now except this sturdy, wonderful man who cared so deeply about her pleasure. He angled her hips and drove in deeper, and she urged him on, not wanting him to hold back. So, when his movements stilled, she tried not to sound disappointed.

"Everything okay?" she asked.

"I'm getting close. How about you?"

"I'm good."

"Nope." He smoothed his hand against her cheek. "Look at me, Charlie."

She flung open her eyes and met his gaze. "Am I in trouble?"

"Only if you don't tell me what you need. What'll it take to get you there?"

No one had ever asked her that before. The thought of voicing her need intimidated her, but she made herself speak up. "If you suck on my nipples, that really does it for me."

"That's what I like to hear." He teased the taut buds with his tongue and sucked on them hard before picking up the pace.

Awash in pleasure, she tensed up again. She was a live wire, every sense alert as the pressure built up inside her. This time when the orgasm hit, it wasn't just a wave. It was a fucking tsunami. She let it wash over her, coursing through her entire body until she dissolved into a puddle. He thrust into her a few more times before groaning out her name and collapsing on top of her.

"Fuck yes, Charlie."

Fuck yes, indeed.

With exquisite tenderness, he eased off her. "Don't go anywhere. I'll be right back."

He went into the bathroom to dispose of the condom. When he returned, she beckoned him back into bed. He took her in his arms and pulled the comforter over them.

"Is it okay if I stay here tonight?" he asked.

"Please do." She rested her head on his chest, sighing as he stroked her hair.

And as she drifted off, she was immensely pleased she'd had the courage to ask for what she wanted. For once, she hadn't let her fears get the best of her.

In the morning, Charlie recoiled at the sound of her alarm. *Too soon.*

After spending the night in Knox's arms, she had no desire to leave the warmth of his embrace. So, when he suggested they indulge in a morning quickie, she was all for it. And she was gratified to discover that last night's orgasms hadn't been a onetime thing.

By the time she'd shooed him out the door, she was running late, so she took the world's quickest shower. With no time to stop at Alma's for coffee, she brewed a cup and poured it into her tumbler, only to realize she was out of half-and-half.

Battling a sense of trepidation, she left her apartment and let herself into her parents' house via the back door. Though she'd hoped to avoid running into them, they were seated at the breakfast table, drinking coffee.

Her dad looked up from his copy of *The Globe & Mail*. "Good morning, muffin. Coming to join us for breakfast? We've got fresh bagels."

"Morning, Dad. Tempting offer, but I've got to run, or I'll be late for work. I just came to snitch some cream." She took it out of the fridge and added a splash to her tumbler.

"*Charlie.*" Her mother's voice stopped her cold. It was a summons, not a greeting.

"Yes, Mom?"

"Your friend's truck was parked in the drive this morning. I'm assuming he spent the night."

Oh, Lord, here it comes. "Yep."

"I didn't realize you'd been dating him for that long."

The back of Charlie's neck prickled with heat. "Not that long, but we've known each other for a while now. Because of work."

Her mother's steely-eyed gaze bored into her. "And you think leaping into things with him is the right move?"

Just stop. She did *not* want to be having this conversation first thing in the morning. Especially not with her father present.

"Is it serious?" her mother asked.

Was it serious? They'd only spent *one* night together. But it had the potential to turn into something meaningful. "It's still pretty new, but Knox is important to me." She braced herself, waiting for her mother to scold her for making bad choices.

Her father spoke first. "If that's the case, it would be nice to know him better. Why don't you invite him over for dinner next weekend?"

Charlie beamed at him, grateful he'd come to her rescue. "That's a great idea."

To her surprise, her mother graced both of them with the faintest of smiles. "I have an even better suggestion. How about Thanksgiving? Does he have any plans for the holiday?"

Charlie stared at her in shock. Had the world just tilted on its axis? How else to explain her mother suddenly respecting her decision to date a bartender? "He has the day off, but he's not going home for the holidays. Do you want me to ask if he's free?"

"Please do. We'll be going to the yacht club for their Thanksgiving buffet. Our reservation is for October twelfth at six thirty. If Knox is available, why don't you invite him to join us?"

"Um...sure." Charlie couldn't believe her parents were being so welcoming.

Last night, she'd had mind-blowing sex. Knox had slept over. And now, her parents wanted to spend time with him.

Maybe—just maybe—the universe was finally on her side.

Seventeen

CHARLIE SCRAMBLED IN TO WORK A FULL FIFTEEN minutes late, feeling like the frenetic White Rabbit from *Alice in Wonderland*. While trying to open her office door, she dropped her car keys. A stack of file folders followed, sending papers scattering across the floor. She bent down to scoop up everything, only to freeze when an authoritative male voice addressed her.

"Good morning, Charlotte."

Shit. Of all the days for her boss to arrive early. She bundled the wayward files into her arms and straightened up quickly. "Good morning, Mr. Hargreaves. Sorry I'm late. I...ran into some complications."

"Nothing serious, I hope?"

"Nope, it's all good." *I just couldn't bear to get out of bed with Knox.* "Was there something you wanted to talk to me about?"

"Laurel just showed me the fliers she mocked up for the Gilded Lily's costume party. I understand you're responsible for getting that event on the calendar."

"Actually, Knox is the one who agreed to host the party. All I did was give him a nudge."

"Either way, I'm impressed with your efforts. Not only for

getting him on board, but also for helping us secure a spot on *Canada's Most Haunted*. Rosie told me you did most of the research. You've really been going above and beyond."

Her boss's praise caught her so off guard she was momentarily tongue-tied. "Um...thank you, sir. I've enjoyed my deep dive into the hotel's history. Today, I'm interviewing a woman who worked at the Duchess in the late 1950s and had an unpleasant experience in our haunted storage room. We're hoping to use her testimony for the show."

"Excellent. When I spoke with the hotel's owners last Friday, they were delighted we finally have a ghost story worthy of including in the Historic Hauntings tour."

"They didn't mind that it was associated with a huge scandal? Back in the day, the hotel tried to cover it up."

Preston chuckled. "It happened over a hundred years ago. These days, a little notoriety can be highly profitable, if marketed correctly. Anyway, keep up the good work."

She watched him walk away, slightly stunned she'd earned his favor. And on a day when she'd shown up late, no less.

Thanks, universe.

After unlocking her office door, she shrugged off her jacket and set down her coffee. Rather than get started on her lengthy to-do list, she decided to pop in on Laurel. This was the kind of Monday that couldn't be tackled head-on. She needed to ease into it, partly because she was still recovering from her incredible night with Knox. Everything about their date had exceeded her wildest expectations, including the sex.

Especially the sex.

She poked her head into Laurel's office. "Good morning. Do you have a minute?"

"For you—always. Come on in." Laurel motioned her inside.

Charlie plopped down on the chair across from her desk. "Preston mentioned you mocked up the fliers for our costume contest."

"See what you think." Laurel handed her a couple of fliers. "I made two different versions. The first one will be included in the hotel's welcome packets, and the second will be posted at places around town. That way, we can draw in a mix of guests and locals."

As usual, Laurel had done a masterful job. "These look great. We still have to work out the logistics, but I'm thinking we'll give out cash prizes. Selena also said she'd get us a deal on a photo booth, like the one we used for last year's Christmas activities."

"Those are always so popular. Does Knox have any spooky drink ideas?"

Charlie passed the fliers back to her. "Preston's already been on his case about the menu. Knowing Knox, he'll come up with something creative."

Laurel gave her a sly look. "Speaking of Knox..."

"Yes?" Try as she might, Charlie couldn't play it cool. Already, a sappy grin was spreading across her face.

"How was your big date? It was last night, right?"

"It was. And it didn't end until...this morning." Charlie put her face in her hands. "Don't judge me."

"Are you kidding? I love this for you."

"Thanks. I got a disapproving vibe from my mom this morning, so I'm feeling a little sensitive."

"You told your mom about it? Wow, you two must have a very open relationship."

Charlie laughed. "Hardly. She saw Knox's truck parked in the drive and just *had* to comment on it. I should have had him park a block away."

That earned her a snort from Laurel. "Back when I was sixteen, I was dating this guy my parents hated, and we always had to sneak around. I used to wait until after dark and climb out my bedroom window to meet him."

"The thing is—I don't want to hide my relationship with Knox. I'm glad we're together."

"It's about time. We've all been rooting for you." Laurel set down the fliers. "Before I forget, I met with my friend from VOS Musical Theatre on Sunday, and we came up with an idea for your big event at the Grand Duke. We wanted to stick with a couples theme, but it was tricky finding a costume that would hide Knox's face but not impede his vision." She pulled out her phone and passed it to Charlie. "What do you think?"

Charlie let out a squeal. "*Phantom of the Opera*? I love that musical. These costumes look fabulous, especially since the Phantom's ensemble comes with a mask." Even if it didn't cover his face completely, it was a decent disguise. Not to mention, his appearance had changed since his days on *The Hidden Forest*; back then, he'd been clean-shaven.

Laurel beamed. "They're from a production the company did two years ago. There were a few different outfits for the show's heroine, but I thought this dress was the most fun. It's from the masquerade scene, and it comes with a Venetian carnival mask, in case you need a disguise."

"Thanks so much." While Charlie wasn't sure if Knox had ever seen the musical, she could suggest they watch the movie version together. She'd always thought the Phantom was kind of sexy, despite his questionable behavior.

"That's not all. The company did *Peter Pan* last summer, so I arranged for you to borrow Tinker Bell and Captain Hook costumes for our party at the Gilded Lily."

"Awesome! Just let me know how much your friend wants for the rentals. This is way easier than hunting down the costumes on my own."

"No charge. I'm working with the theater to promote their production of *Little Shop of Horrors* by offering discount tickets to the hotel's guests."

"You're crushing it. I'll bet Preston's thrilled."

"Yeah, he was in an unusually good mood, which was a much-needed boost." Laurel's sunny expression clouded over. "I'm not at my best this morning."

"Are you stressed because we're getting so busy? I don't think it's going to ease up between now and New Year's. You remember what last December was like."

Preston had demanded so many activities that the Damsels had pushed themselves to the breaking point. He'd told them it wouldn't be as bad this year, but Charlie had her doubts.

"It's not that." Laurel picked up a pen and twisted it between her fingers. "It's my roommate, Celia. She told me she's moving out at the end of November."

"Sorry. I thought you two were close." Though Charlie had only met Celia twice, she'd liked her a lot.

"No, we're great. Celia's a bit of a slob, but other than that, she's been an ideal roommate." Laurel took a sip from her to-go cup and wrinkled her nose. "Ugh. Too weak. That's what I get for buying the cheap stuff from 7-Eleven. I need a hit from Alma's Beanery."

"Then let's go. I brought coffee from home, but I don't think it's going to cut it. Preston's in such an upbeat mood that he won't care if we slip out for a few minutes."

"Okay, you convinced me." Laurel stood and grabbed her coat from the back of her chair.

Once they got outside, Charlie wished she hadn't left her fleece jacket in her office. Despite the bright sunshine, the brisk wind off the ocean made for a chilly morning. Rubbing her hands along her arms, she hustled to keep up with Laurel as they headed to Alma's.

"What's up with Celia?" she asked. "Why is she abandoning you?"

"You met Glen, right? The guy she's dating?"

"Yeah, he seemed nice." During their meet-up at the Seagull, Charlie had noticed the affectionate way he'd treated Celia, with little touches and shared smiles. At the time, she'd felt a twinge of envy, wishing she and Knox had that kind of relationship.

"Right now, Glen's renting a studio apartment in Vic West, but his lease is up at the end of November. So, he and Celia decided they'd get a one-bedroom place together, starting in December. On the one hand, I'm happy for her, but on the other..."

"You'll have to find a new roommate. That's tough." Charlie shivered as a gust of wind hit her in the face. "Can you afford your own place?"

"Not really. Plus, I like having someone around. It's more fun that way."

As they entered Alma's, Charlie inhaled the delectable smell of French roast mixed with freshly baked cinnamon rolls. "Maybe you can see if anyone from work needs a roommate."

Laurel shrugged. "I guess, but it's not just that. Everyone's pairing up. Celia and Glen are moving in together. Rosie and Drew are madly in love. And now, you and Knox are a couple."

While Charlie loved hearing her name paired alongside his, she was scared of jinxing it. "This thing with me and Knox is brand-new."

"Yeah, but we all know how long you've been into him. And it's obvious he feels the same way." Laurel sighed. "Sorry for the self-pity. I'm not trying to bring you down on a Monday morning."

"I don't mind listening. How about I get the coffee as a thank-you for finding those costumes? And how about one of those fresh cinnamon rolls? Even if it's a temporary fix, carbs and coffee make any Monday infinitely better."

"Thanks. That sounds great."

To Charlie's delight, Monday was buy one, get one free day, and she'd accumulated enough "Beanery Bucks" to get both cinnamon rolls for two dollars. As they walked back, she sipped her pumpkin spice latte contentedly. There was no saying how long this run of luck would last, but she was going to enjoy every minute of it.

CHARLIE STOOD NEAR THE FRONT ENTRANCE OF THE hotel, waiting for Gertrude Fletcher—a former employee of the Duchess who'd worked as a room attendant in the late 1950s. When an elderly woman came inside and began peering around the lobby, Charlie suspected it was her. The woman's maroon sweater, which was decorated with embroidered fall leaves around the neckline, reminded Charlie of something her granny would have worn.

She came forward. "Mrs. Fletcher? Hi, I'm Charlie Fraser, the front office manager of the Duchess. I'm the one who contacted you."

The woman placed her hand over Charlie's and gave it a light squeeze. "Good afternoon, dear. Please, call me Gertrude. It was such a surprise to receive your call. I hadn't thought about the Duchess in years. I'd heard the old girl had gotten a tad run-down, but she's looking spiffy."

"I'm glad you think so. The lobby was just upgraded this past January."

After the hotel's prosperous Christmas season, the owners of the Duchess had finally given the lobby a refresh, replacing the worn gray couches with brand-new ones, adding navy armchairs in a distressed velvet fabric, and bringing in some large, artfully potted plants.

"Would you like to chat in my office? Or would you rather have a drink?" Charlie checked her watch. "Our cocktail lounge opened at four, and it's usually fairly quiet until happy hour gets underway at five."

"Ooh, yes, I'd love a glass of wine. A bit early for tippling, but why not?"

"Why not, indeed." Charlie led her into the Gilded Lily, where Miles was on duty. While his demeanor was friendlier than Knox's, his craft cocktails paled in comparison. After ordering a glass of chardonnay for Gertrude and a Diet Coke for herself, she ushered her guest over to a corner of the lounge, where a couple of leather club chairs faced a tiled fireplace.

"This is lovely," Gertrude said. "Back in my day, the Lily wasn't nearly this classy. The servers wore skimpy outfits, and everyone smoked. But now, it has a touch of elegance. The Art Deco posters are a particularly nice touch."

"I like them, too." Charlie took out her phone, feeling for all the world like a journalist conducting a groundbreaking interview. After reading dozens of staff reports mentioning the storage room, she was eager to hear more about Gertrude's experiences in it. "Is it all right if I record you? This way, I won't forget anything. If the show's producers decide to include your testimony, they might want to talk to you in person, but it's your call. No pressure."

"Record all you want." Gertrude laughed. "My great-grandchildren thought it was marvelous I was being interviewed for a TV show, but I doubt anything I say will be that earth-shattering. In all honesty, I spent years keeping the storage room incident a secret since it cost me my job. But these days, ghost sightings are all the rage."

"It's pretty wild, isn't it? I had no idea how popular ghost-hunting shows were until I started watching *Canada's Most Haunted*."

Gertrude took a sip of her wine. "All right, I suppose I should get started. I worked here in housekeeping for three years. At the time, we used the storage room on the third floor to stash odds and ends, like furniture or draperies in need of mending. Everyone hated that room. We'd all heard odd noises and felt cold drafts of air, even with the door closed. Whenever I went in there, my mood always worsened. Of course, none of us knew the room had been the site of such a shocking tragedy."

"I was stunned when I learned about it, but it seems the hotel covered up the story. That's why it's not part of local lore, like the ghosts at the Grand Duke."

Gertrude nodded. "I've heard the stories about the Duke. I even went on one of those ghost tours. But that tour wasn't as frightening as getting locked in the storage room."

Charlie leaned forward. "So, what happened?"

"Usually, when we needed to go into that room, we went in pairs. One of us would stand guard outside in case the door didn't cooperate. There were so many times when it wouldn't open from the inside, even when we used the key. I was sent to look for something—a lamp, maybe—and couldn't find anyone to go with me. 'Fine,' I thought. 'It'll just be a quick in and out.' But as soon as the door shut behind me, I knew I'd made a mistake. I spent three hours trying to get out of there."

"I'm so sorry." Charlie's experience had been mild by comparison, plus she'd had Knox for company. "I was only locked in there for a short time, but I was plenty scared."

"So you know what it feels like. I pounded on the door and yelled loudly, but no one heard me. While I was trapped in there, my emotions careened about wildly. One moment, I was bereft, and the next, I was livid with rage. Which was quite ridiculous since my darling Rupert had finally proposed, and we were getting married in three months' time."

Charlie recalled her argument with Knox when they'd been locked up together. At the time, she hadn't understood why she'd gotten so upset, but now she suspected the room's ghost had been manipulating her emotions. "I had a similar reaction. This might be an odd question, but can you recall a specific smell when you were inside the room?"

"*Yes*. Roses. Just like the soap we put in all the washrooms. I assumed there were boxes of it somewhere. But it was very potent."

More than ever, Charlie was convinced the scent was associated with Maeve. "I smelled roses, too, as did the other woman who visited the room. Sorry, carry on with your story."

"There's not much more to tell. My supervisor finally figured out where I was and came to fetch me. She fired me on the spot—

accused me of using the room to take a nap, of all things—and refused to believe my explanation."

"That's so unfair," Charlie said. "You shouldn't have been punished for something that wasn't your fault."

"But it happens, doesn't it, dearie?" Gertrude graced her with a benevolent smile. "In any case, it made no matter because I was soon to be married. I went on to have four children, nine grandchildren, and six great-grandchildren."

"That's so inspiring. Did you ever tell any of them about the storage room?"

"I mentioned it once, when my daughters and I were watching a movie about a haunted house, but they thought I was joking. I'd put it out of my mind until you called me." Gertrude held up her wineglass in a salute. "Now that it's in the past, I don't mind discussing it."

"Thanks." Charlie shut off the recorder on her phone. "If you want to share any other stories about the Duchess, I'd be happy to listen. Not for the show—just for me. I've had so much fun learning about the hotel's history. But if you're too busy, I understand."

"Busy? Hardly. Buy me another glass of wine, and I'll spill all the tea you want." She winked. "That's what the kids say, isn't it? Spilling the tea?"

Charlie laughed. "That sounds about right. Let's do it."

With a touch of wariness, Knox regarded the
costume he'd be wearing for the gala at the Grand Duke. While he
couldn't deny that it was professional-grade quality, he doubted it
would fit him. When he and Charlie had watched the 2004 version
of *The Phantom of the Opera* last night, the titular character had a
lean physique that didn't resemble Knox's body type in the
slightest.

Even so, he appreciated the effort Laurel had made in finding
him a stylish costume that fit the Grand Duke's requirements *and*
covered his face. When she'd dropped off the outfits this morning,
she'd asked him and Charlie to try them on as soon as possible.
Though the big event was still two and a half weeks away, Laurel
wanted to allow time for any necessary alterations.

"Here goes nothing," he grumbled.

To his surprise, the costume had been designed for someone
his size. The black tuxedo jacket, starched white shirt, and tailored
black pants fit him to a T. He placed the long black cape across his
shoulders and grinned at his reflection in Charlie's bathroom
mirror.

"Are you ready?" she called out. "I want to see you."

"Hang on." He emerged from her bedroom and gave an elaborate bow.

Charlie squealed. "Oooh! You look so dashing!" She ran up to him and stroked the lapels of his tuxedo jacket. "I love this on you. I wish you didn't have to put on the mask."

He let his gaze roam over her. She'd told him her dress was based on the masquerade scene from the original Broadway show; on her, it was stunning. The dark blue bodice hugged her breasts and enhanced her cleavage, and the low, ruffled sleeves showed off the curve of her bare shoulders. A pink tulle skirt, adorned with silver stars, fell just above her knees, revealing her shapely calves.

He let out a low whistle. "You look like a fairy princess, only much sexier."

"I'm glad you approve. I feel like I should be twirling about onstage." She picked up the sculpted white Phantom mask and handed it to him. "Here. Try it on to make sure it fits."

While it wasn't that comfortable, at least it didn't block his vision. "I don't love how it feels, but that's not important. I need to make sure most of my face is hidden. Can you tell it's me under the mask?"

"Sorta? But if I was a guest at the gala, I'd have no idea, especially since Mac Iverson didn't have a sexy lumberjack beard like you do now. Does any part of the costume need adjusting? Laurel needs to know right away."

He took off the mask and wiped the sweat from his brow. Wearing it for six hours would be a test of his endurance. "Everything fits, but I'm going to change back now. The less time I spend dressed like this, the better."

She leaned toward him and placed a quick kiss on his lips. "I think you make a totally swoon-worthy Phantom. These costumes are gorgeous, but I can't wait until we get the ones from *Peter Pan*. Think how sexy that's going to be." She lowered her voice. "Imagine Tinker Bell, down on her knees, pleasuring Captain Hook."

Jesus. They'd already had sex once this morning, but the thought of her kneeling before him, dressed in a sexy pixie outfit, made his dick spring back to life. "There's probably a porno out there with that exact scene. But if you're offering, I'm gonna hold you to it."

"Please do." She gave him a saucy wink. "Let's go get changed. Remember to hang up your costume after you take it off. I want to keep it as pristine as possible. And don't forget you promised to take me out for bagels this morning."

Taking her hand, he pulled her close until her body was pressed against his and gripped her ass. "You sure that's what you're hungry for?"

With a laugh, she swatted his arm. "Behave. I want to have time to eat breakfast before I go in to work. I'd also prefer not to show up late." She eased out of his grasp. "I wish my schedule wasn't so intense. I guess I should be grateful Preston isn't making either of us work on Thanksgiving. I'm glad we get to spend the holiday together."

He'd been pleasantly surprised when she'd invited him to join her parents at the yacht club, but something about it didn't sit right with him. "Are you positive your folks want me to come for dinner? I got the impression your mom wasn't thrilled at meeting me."

"She was just caught off guard. Plus, she was still hoping I'd get back together with Randolph. By now, she has to realize that ship has sailed. I don't care if I ever see him again."

Same here. "How about you spend the night at my place afterward? You still haven't seen it yet."

"I'd like that. I've been dying to get a peek into your lair."

In the three years he'd lived there, he'd never brought anyone back to spend the night. He'd preferred to keep it private, like so much of his past. But now that he'd slept over at Charlie's place a few times, he wanted to reciprocate. By having her over, he'd be revealing even more of himself, but he was ready to take that step.

~

Knox wished he and Charlie could have spent a leisurely morning together, but after he'd taken her out for bagels, she headed in to work. Since he had the day off, he decided to enjoy the glorious fall weather. He drove to Beacon Hill Park, a huge expanse of green space near downtown Victoria, filled with winding paths, flower gardens, stone bridges, and duck ponds.

Now that October was here, the air was crisp, the ground carpeted with scattered leaves in shades of red and gold. Squirrels darted about, gathering nuts and scrambling up and down the trees. He took his time capturing all of it with his camera—the brilliant foliage, the playful ducks, and the colorful peacocks strolling through the park.

Charlie would have loved it, particularly his visit to the park's petting zoo, where he took photos of the baby goats. More often than not, their schedules conflicted, but they were making it work. And every time they spent the night together, they grew closer. The only thing he regretted was all the months they'd wasted pining for each other, both of them too gun-shy to make the first move.

He was passing by one of the park's playgrounds when his phone rang and Logan's name appeared on the screen. "Hey, man. Got any updates for me?"

"I sure do. I'll send all the details in an email, but I can give you a quick overview. On the first day—Friday, October thirtieth—we'll do a preliminary walk-through of the hotel's storage room, set up our cameras, get baseline readings, and conduct our in-person interviews. The following night, three members of the team will spend four hours holed up in the room, while myself and another member monitor them from one of the third-floor guest rooms. You took care of that?"

"It's all set. I booked your group into three rooms, right down the hall from the haunted storage area. For the interviews, we've got Celia and Charlie, plus an eighty-nine-year-old woman who worked for the hotel in the 1950s."

"Perfecto. Celia sent me a bunch of photos from the archives. I didn't realize until now that she led the ghost tour I took in September. For a Goth chick, she's kind of hot. Do you know if she's single?"

Knox laughed. "She's with someone."

"What about Charlie?"

"Also taken," he snapped. "Don't even think about it."

"Aha! I knew I'd get you to admit it! What's the story there?"

Normally, Knox would have told him to back off. Or blatantly ignored the question. But his relationship with Charlie was going so well he was willing to talk about it. "We're dating. And I'm trying my hardest not to muck it up."

"I don't see how you could, given your charming personality."

"Fuck off," Knox growled. But he didn't mean it. He was starting to feel the way he had back when Lila had first taken an interest in him. All mushy and hopeful.

"I'm glad for you," Logan said. "It's about time you got a break."

"Thanks." Leaving the playground area, Knox crossed a stone bridge, passing a family of four who were tossing bread at the ducks. "Gotta say, it's a nice change being with someone who's not connected to the industry."

"That reminds me. There's another reason I called. It's about *The Hidden Forest*."

His somber tone made Knox uneasy. "What's going on?"

"I hate to be the bearer of bad news, but I just learned the cast and crew are coming to Victoria in a few weeks. They're having a big gala at the Grand Duke Hotel to celebrate the show's hundredth episode. I doubt you'll run into any of them, but I wanted you to be prepared."

Knox parked himself on a wooden bench, uncapped his water

bottle, and took a long drink. "Well, actually...I'm working at the gala. As a bartender."

When Logan didn't respond, Knox checked his phone to make sure he still had a signal. "Did I lose you?"

"Nope. I'm trying to make sure I heard you correctly. Did you say you're voluntarily working at the event?"

"Yep. But since it's a costume ball, I'll be going in disguise."

"Are you out of your fucking mind?" Logan yelled.

Knox winced. Logan wasn't the type to raise his voice. Back when his friend had worked on *The Hidden Forest*, he'd often been the calmest one on the set. "I know it sounds insane, but hear me out. A couple of weeks ago, I told Charlie all about Mac Iverson. I didn't spare any details."

"Damn. You must really like her."

"I do. It helps that she's so compassionate. Once I got it out in the open, I felt like this huge cloud had lifted. It was so freeing not to hide all that shit. Anyway, we got to talking, and I admitted I felt bad about the way I'd left things. Cutting off people. Making it impossible for them to find me." Knox dug his fingers along a groove in the bench. "I know you told me as much, and I should have listened, but..."

"I'm sure Charlie was way more persuasive. And I think she's right. But if you want to connect with some of the writers from the show, I could help you track them down. Going to this gala could put you in Evan's crosshairs, and you don't want that. He *hates* you."

Though Knox had heard as much before, Evan's prolonged animosity seemed unjustified. "I don't understand why he's still pissed off. He got everything he wanted and sent me into exile. I'm hardly a threat to him."

Logan barked out a sharp laugh. "Are you serious? He's never gotten over the fact that you were the one with all the talent."

"Evan had talent. The show's initial premise—that was all him.

No one was better at pitching a story than he was." Knox had always envied Evan's ability to work a room.

"For the first year, maybe. But after that, you were the creative force that shaped the next two seasons. You might have started off as equals, but your writing was ten times better than his would ever be. And he knew it. Everyone did."

Knox sighed. During the first season of *The Hidden Forest*, he and Evan had been a dynamic duo. Just the two of them, with Evan providing the creative spark and Knox writing most of the episodes. Due to the show's unexpected success, the second season had been far more ambitious, making a writers' room a necessity. When the show's producers chose Knox to be the head writer, Evan had flown into a rage. Though Knox had offered to share the title and the responsibilities with him, the damage had already been done. From then on, Evan was convinced that Knox planned to move up the ladder without him.

"I kept telling Evan I had no desire to be a producer. I just wanted to write. But whenever I got called to the set to work with the cast on the episodes I'd written, he accused me of hogging the spotlight." Knox frowned. "Do I look like a spotlight guy to you?"

"Hardly. Besides, you made sure the other writers got that experience, too. Evan had just as many opportunities as you did, but he didn't want to put in the work. And then he had the balls to force you out and spread those shitty rumors about you."

Of all the things Evan had done, that had hurt the most. He'd trashed Knox's reputation, painting him as a total fuckup with a terrible temper and addiction issues.

"The rumors just about killed me," Knox said. "But do you know what hurt even more? After I left, the show did fine without me. My absence barely made a dent." While the fourth season had stumbled badly, with fans protesting the darker storylines, the show had eventually recovered and won more awards.

"Sorry. If it's any consolation, most of the other writers on staff didn't buy Evan's bullshit. That's why he canned a bunch of them after the fourth season ended. So, he's not someone you want to fuck around with. Not if your life's back on track."

Knox stood and resumed walking along the path. "The thing is, there's not much he can do to me. I already lost everything."

"Man, that sucks."

"It's okay. I'm doing better now. Telling Charlie about it really helped. I know working at the gala could be risky, but I'd like to catch a glimpse of the cast and crew again. Maybe connect with a few old friends, if they're still around. It might help me move on for good."

Now that he'd set his course, he wanted to see it through. Though staying hidden had initially served him well, it hadn't allowed him to heal completely. Like Charlie said, he needed closure. And this event just might give it to him.

Nineteen

Charlie peeked at her phone again. If Knox didn't show up soon, they'd be late for dinner. Today of all days, when her parents would be observing him closely—and no doubt judging him—she wanted him to shine.

Two minutes later, his truck pulled into the circular drive. She waited for him to get out, hoping he'd remembered the yacht club's dress requirements. When he emerged from the truck, she stared at him like a lovestruck teen. Dressed in a sport coat and tie, his hair and beard neatly trimmed, he looked hotter than ever. It was as if a big, burly woodsman was playing at being a sexy professor. All he needed was a pair of wire-rimmed glasses to complete the look.

Back when she'd told him the yacht club required male guests to wear a jacket and tie while in the formal dining room, she wasn't sure how he'd react. He'd just given her a slow smile and said, "Don't worry about it. I can handle dressing up, sweetheart."

Sweetheart.

It was one of his pet names for her, along with "pixie," which was a particular favorite when they were in bed together. She'd never been with someone who was so affectionate. It made her realize how much she'd compromised, dating men her mother had foisted upon her, who had treated her like little more than arm candy.

He gave her an appraising look. "Nice dress. That's a great color on you."

"I saw it at the Bay Centre last week and couldn't resist." She twirled for him, letting the full skirt flare out. The crimson fabric resembled the maple leaves scattered around the front yard. A matching set of dark red pumps and a pendant necklace displaying an amber acorn completed the ensemble. "Thanks for picking me up. My parents went on ahead to have drinks with friends, so I thought we'd be better off meeting them there."

"No problem. You still okay sleeping at my place tonight?"

"I've got my bag right here." After enduring one too many comments about Knox's truck, she was grateful for a chance to dodge her mother's scrutiny. She picked up her duffel bag and slung it over her shoulder.

He opened the passenger side door. "Let's head out. I've never been to a fancy Thanksgiving buffet before. I'm not sure what to expect."

"It's your basic mix of turkey and side dishes, but without doing any of the work. I'm guessing your family probably celebrated the holiday at home."

"Oh, yeah. It was a big deal. My folks usually hosted, so we had our family of eight, plus a bunch of aunts, uncles, and cousins. And my grandparents. There was a ton of food, and the kitchen was sheer chaos."

A familiar pang of longing tugged at her heart. Had her parents *ever* hosted a Thanksgiving dinner? The yacht club's extravagant buffet had always been their go-to. Even when Randolph and his parents had joined them, dinner there was a subdued affair.

During the drive, a sudden bout of nerves took hold of her. She didn't know why she was so anxious. It wasn't like she was springing a new boyfriend on her parents without warning them first. And they were the ones who'd extended the invitation. Even so, she'd be glad when dinner was over and she could retreat with Knox back to his apartment.

Once they arrived, he handed his keys to the valet and helped her out. The sight of her parents, waiting outside the entrance, made her wonder if there was an issue. Had their reservation been canceled? Taking Knox's hand, she walked over to join them.

"Hi, guys. You remember Knox McIntyre, right?"

"Of course." Her dad stuck out his hand and gave Knox a firm handshake. "Glad you could join us."

"I appreciate the invitation," Knox said. "All my family's in the Okanagan Valley, and it's a hel—heck—of a drive. I've never been to the yacht club before."

"Are we okay to go inside?" Charlie asked.

"We already have a table," her dad replied. "Your mother thought it might be nice if we greeted you out here. To make Knox feel extra welcome."

"Oh...kay." An odd move, but she wasn't going to question it. Maybe they'd been worried Knox wouldn't be wearing the proper attire. "Can we go in now? I'm ravenous."

Her mother frowned. "Hang on, Charlotte. You've got a smudge under one eye. It might be mascara. Let's head over to the little girls' room and clean it up." She gestured to her husband. "Art, you can take Knox inside and get him settled."

Charlie followed her mother into the ladies' room. Though she'd checked her makeup before leaving, she might have rubbed her eyes during the drive. She peered at her reflection in the mirror but didn't see anything amiss. "Mom? Where's the smudge?"

Her mother grabbed her arm. "There's no smudge. I need to talk to you before we go inside. The Bouchards are here."

Shit. What were the chances?

Actually, the chances were pretty good, considering

Randolph's parents were yacht club regulars. "That's okay. As long as we don't sit too close to them, it shouldn't be that awkward."

"I don't think you understand. I invited them here." At Charlie's stunned expression, a furrow crept up between her mother's brows. "Don't look so surprised. They've joined us for the buffet before."

"But that was when Randolph and I were together." Cold dread ran through Charlie's veins. "Wait. Is he with them?"

"Yes. I made sure of it."

Charlie stared at her in disbelief. "Why did you invite him if you knew Knox was coming?"

Her mother lowered her voice to a furious hiss. "So you could see the difference for yourself. I'm not pleased you're dating a man with no discernible future. How do you expect a bartender to take care of you? If you size him up next to Randolph, you might realize what a huge mistake you're making."

No. Charlie's stomach twisted into a knot. She'd invited Knox, believing her parents *wanted* to meet him. Not so he could be subjected to her mom's warped agenda. "Does Dad know about this?"

"Of course not. He's utterly clueless. But he doesn't understand what's at stake."

"Knox doesn't deserve to be treated this way." Charlie gouged her nails deep into her palms. "We're leaving."

"You most certainly are not. Imagine how embarrassing it will be for everyone if you march into the dining room and drag Knox out of there. Do you really want to subject your 'boyfriend' to that kind of humiliation?"

A sob clogged Charlie's throat. She needed to stand up for herself. To show a little backbone. But from the time she was old enough to join her parents on their grown-up outings, she'd been taught never to make a scene.

"Fine," she said. "But if I keep dating Knox, you can't pull this again. Do you understand?"

Her mother laughed. "Of course, dear."

An agreement that counted for nothing. How could it, when Charlie had no leverage?

It's your own damn fault for still living with your parents.

When she went into the dining room, Knox was seated beside her father. Around the table were Mr. and Mrs. Bouchard and their son, Randolph. He looked as slick as ever, in a dark gray suit that probably cost a small fortune. She sat beside Knox and squeezed his hand in solidarity. To her dismay, he didn't return the gesture—a sure sign he wasn't pleased with the setup.

Randolph fixed his gaze on her. "Hello, Charlie. It's nice to see you again. We were just trying to decide what kind of wine to order with dinner. Perhaps your bartender friend could offer a suggestion."

"His name is Knox," she snapped.

"I'm not a wine connoisseur," Knox said. "But with turkey, I'd suggest a light-bodied red, like a Pinot Noir. If you want a local wine, you could ask if they have something from the Okanagan Valley. The Quails' Gate Pinot is one of my favorites."

"Thank you, Knox," her dad said. "We'll see what they have and order a couple of bottles. Kids, why don't you get started on the buffet?"

Charlie waited until Randolph had gotten up, then followed close behind Knox. She whispered into his ear. "I'm sorry. It was an ambush."

"Right." His voice was gruff. "I'm guessing your mom's going for the whole 'compare and contrast' thing?"

"We can leave if you want." Even as she said it, she hoped he wouldn't force the issue. Her mother would never let her hear the end of it.

"I'm good. Remember, I spent years in the entertainment industry. I've dealt with all kinds of criticism."

But you shouldn't have to deal with it here. "Okay. Thanks." If

Knox felt like he could hold his own, forcing him to leave might undermine his self-confidence.

At least the food looked mouthwatering—a carving station with slices of turkey breast, two kinds of stuffing, cranberry sauce, roasted carrots and Brussels sprouts, mashed potatoes, and a few other side dishes. Plus pumpkin pie, apple pie, and butter tarts for dessert. She'd just have to hope that her parents—and Randolph, in particular—would treat Knox with respect.

At first, everyone focused on the food and the wine—which proved to be an excellent choice. The conversation stayed polite and impersonal as they chatted about the unseasonably warm October weather and discussed a recent scandal involving a prominent member of B.C.'s legislature. No one appeared to be judging Knox or finding him lacking.

Clearly, her mother wasn't satisfied because she turned to Randolph with a simpering smile. "I understand you received a significant promotion at work this month. That's so impressive."

"Thanks," Randolph said. "Considering how many hours of sweat equity I've put in, it was long overdue. I don't want to toot my own horn, but it feels damn good to be making seven figures."

"Seven figures," her mother said. "Quite an accomplishment at your age."

"It's too bad I don't have a partner to enjoy it with." He caught Charlie's eye. "Remember how much you used to love our weekend getaways to Whistler? When's the last time anyone took you skiing?"

Just stop. Charlie was about to change the subject, but her mother was relentless. "A salary like that must come with a lot more responsibility. Why don't you tell us about it?"

No. If there was one thing Randolph loved, it was flaunting his achievements and bragging about his "toys," like his Beneteau sailboat and his fancy BMW. He never knew when to shut up. As he droned on about the intricacies of the financial markets, she poked at her food. Why had her mother thought this tactic would work? If anything, Charlie was more grateful than ever she'd ended things with Randolph.

She'd all but zoned out when he focused on her again. "Being financially stable is so important. That's why I'm surprised you're still hanging on at that dump of a hotel."

She bristled with anger. "I wouldn't call it a dump. It's an iconic boutique hotel with over a hundred years of history."

He snickered. "No one *I* know would ever choose to stay there. Didn't you once tell me it was in danger of closing?"

"That was years ago, back when our GM was borderline incompetent. Our new manager has a much better handle on things. We had a wonderful Christmas season, and our Halloween activities have attracted a lot of new guests." Now that she'd captured the attention of everyone at the table, she decided to go all in. So far, she hadn't told her parents about the ghost-hunting show for fear they'd disapprove. "As a matter of fact, *Canada's Most Haunted* is coming to our hotel to film an episode. They're a show based in Vancouver that conducts paranormal investigations."

A look of horror crossed her mother's face, like she'd spotted a cockroach in her food. "A tawdry reality show? Oh, Charlotte, your hotel is truly scraping the bottom of the barrel."

"Plus, it's no secret those shows are fake," Randolph said.

Like he was a big expert? Charlie reached for the wine bottle and refilled her glass. "Says who? Some of the episodes have produced incontrovertible evidence."

Her mother gave a nervous laugh. "Sweetie, you'll believe anything. I remember when you used to have that imaginary friend. What was her name—Mitzi? You were convinced she was real."

Charlie's face prickled with heat. She'd only created Mitzi so she'd have a companion when she got lonely. Which had happened far too often when she'd been dragged along on her parents' adult-oriented vacations.

"I don't have an issue with the supernatural element," her dad said. "It's the idea of concocting fake ghosts that bothers me. There's nothing in your hotel's history to suggest it's haunted."

Knox cleared his throat. "You might be surprised. Would you like to hear the story?" His tone was measured and even, like he was in complete control of the situation.

"I'd love to hear it," her dad said. "I don't know if Charlie told you, but I'm something of a local history buff."

"Well, then," Knox said. "Let me tell you *exactly* what happened."

Even though Charlie knew the story better than anyone else at the table, she listened in rapt attention as Knox unspooled the narrative slowly, embellishing the truth to make it more compelling. He was a natural storyteller, knowing when to pause for dramatic effect and when to build up the suspense. He concluded by describing the way he and Charlie had gotten locked in the storage room four weeks ago.

Charlie's dad kept nodding, like he was taking it all in. It was the same way he reacted when watching one of his favorite shows on the History Channel. He waited until Knox finished before speaking up. "A tale this fascinating needs to be included in the Historic Hauntings tour. Have you ever been on it?"

"Twice," Knox said. "The last time I went, Charlie joined me."

"It was so interesting," Charlie added. "Did you know they used to hang people in Bastion Square and then bury the bodies underneath?" Though she'd braced herself for a scary experience, she hadn't been that frightened. Maybe she was toughening up.

Her father refilled his glass with the last of the bottle. "Judge Begbie used to hold trials in that square. They called him 'the hanging judge' and named UVic's law school after him." He addressed Knox again. "You seem to have a keen interest in history. Did you study it when you were at university?"

"It was my minor. My degree was in creative writing."

Through a mouthful of apple pie, Randolph leapt into the

conversation, pointing his finger at Knox. "I knew it! Didn't I guess you were an aspiring author? Too bad it never panned out."

Charlie glared at him. She wished she could tell him the truth—that Knox had created an award-winning TV show—but it wasn't her story to share.

Knox shrugged. "My life didn't follow the path I intended, but I'm fine with where I ended up."

"Really?" Randolph said. "In my opinion, dealing with drunks hardly seems like a worthwhile ambition."

"I don't mind bartending at the Duchess. If I wasn't working there, I wouldn't have met Charlie." Knox favored her with a doting expression. She suspected he'd only done it to annoy Randolph, but she returned his smile with one of her own, hoping to make it obvious she cared about him.

She scraped the last bit of pumpkin pie off her plate. Another few minutes of small talk, and they could leave. But even if Knox had held his own at dinner, she could tell he wasn't happy about the way her mom had played Randolph against him. For now, there was nothing she could do about it. She'd just have to wait until they were alone to apologize properly.

Twenty

By the time Knox left the yacht club with Charlie, he was well and truly done. While he'd enjoyed talking with her father, and he'd found the Bouchards bland but inoffensive, Randolph had been more obnoxious than ever. It didn't help that Charlie's mother had egged him on, encouraging him to boast at length about his job.

They'd only been driving for a few minutes when Charlie spoke up. "I'm sorry."

"For what?" He knew damn well, but he wasn't going to make it easy on her. He was still annoyed she'd let her mom steamroll over her.

"I had no idea my mom would invite the Bouchards to join us. When she asked if you were free for Thanksgiving, she said she wanted to get to know you better."

"Funny how she never asked me anything about my life. Not one question." The only person remotely interested in him had been Charlie's father.

"I know. For what it's worth, my dad wasn't in on it. My mom's the one who handles their social calendar. When she pulled me into the ladies' room to tell me Randolph would be there, I threatened to walk out with you. I probably should have. Right?"

But instead, you did nothing. "That wasn't my call to make, but I would have gone along with whatever you decided."

"I didn't want to make a scene. My parents hate public displays of emotion. But that's no excuse for acting like a coward." Her voice wobbled. "Maybe...you should drop me off at my place."

"Is that what you want?"

"No, but I know you're angry, and you have every right to be. So, I'm guessing you'd prefer it if I went home."

His hands tightened around the steering wheel. He'd wanted to make her understand how much her mom's actions had hurt him. But if he ended their evening now, he'd spend the rest of the night brooding over it.

Then again, maybe this relationship wasn't meant to be. Their worlds couldn't have been any more different. But when he turned to look at her, the tears streaming down her cheeks weakened his defenses. Why was he punishing her like this? It wasn't her fault that her mom was a status-conscious snob who thought he wasn't worthy of her daughter.

He softened his tone. "I'd rather not be alone tonight."

"Are you sure?"

This conversation was too difficult to maintain while driving down a busy road. He put on his blinker, pulled onto a quiet side street, and parked his truck. "Answer me one thing first. Are you ashamed of me?"

"No. Never!" She wiped her eyes. "You work hard at what you do, and you're good at it. You also did a spectacular job telling everyone about the hotel's history. My dad was enthralled. Though you *did* embellish a few of the details."

His anger faded, replaced by an overwhelming sense of affection. "That's storytelling, sweetheart."

A tiny smile crossed her lips. "Well, it worked. And my mom's devious plan backfired. Tonight reminded me that leaving Randolph was one of the best decisions I ever made. Do you know how many dinners I sat through, listening to him boast about his accomplishments? He'd drone on forever and then joke about my 'little' job at the hotel, like I was a kid playing house. It was so demoralizing."

"Yeah, those cracks about the Duchess were uncalled for."

She fished a tissue out of her purse and dabbed at her eyes. "I'm sorry you had to put up with him. I promise nothing like that will ever happen again."

Could she honestly make that promise? He'd seen how desperate she was for her parents' approval. Then again, she'd told them about *Canada's Most Haunted* coming to the hotel, even if it meant facing her mother's scorn.

"If it helps, I'll remind my mom I wasn't okay with her inviting Randolph tonight." Charlie's voice hardened. "And if she ever pulls a stunt like that again, I'll walk out without a second thought, even if it means causing a scene."

The determined set of her jaw gave Knox hope. Maybe tonight would be a turning point for her. Rather than let her mom push her around, she'd take a stand. "Okay. Let's put the buffet behind us. If you're still up for spending the night, I'd like to have you over."

"Thanks. That would be nice." She crumpled up the tissue and tucked it into her purse.

He started up his truck again. Though he didn't want to give up on Charlie, the uncomfortable scene at dinner made him remember all the times he'd felt insecure around Lila. She'd gone from obscurity to fame in such a short time, whereas he'd remained a lowly screenwriter. Sure, he'd helped create the show, but most of the time, he worked behind the scenes. Even if Evan hadn't been in the picture, she still might have gravitated to someone better suited to her outgoing personality, like another actor whose star was on the rise.

Would that happen with Charlie? She might be done with Randolph, but there were plenty of other guys just like her ex-fiancé. Rich dude-bros with money to spare, fancy cars, and seven-figure salaries.

Enough self-doubt. Here he was, expecting the worst when nothing bad had happened. Tonight might have been rough, but in the end, Charlie was going home with *him*, not Randolph.

~

EVEN IF KNOX APPEARED TO HAVE FORGIVEN HER, Charlie couldn't shake her guilt at behaving so submissively during dinner. She hadn't stormed out in protest. Nor had she made any attempt to build up Knox. Instead, he'd done the heavy lifting, winning over her dad with his detailed recounting of the hotel's haunted history.

Since she hadn't wanted the night to end in tears and regret, she was grateful Knox was giving her another chance.

In the past, he'd mentioned living alone, in an area north of downtown Victoria. Other than that, she didn't know what to expect. She was pleasantly surprised when he drove up to an attractive four-story complex and parked his truck in the underground lot. And even more so, when she got her first glimpse of his place, which was spacious and welcoming.

The living room was outfitted with hardwood floors, a large navy couch, an inset brick fireplace, and a wall of bookshelves. Off to one side, a sliding glass door led to a balcony containing a bistro table and a couple of chairs. A sleek marble breakfast bar overlooked the kitchen, which was outfitted with a matched set of shiny, stainless-steel appliances. What struck her the most was how new everything looked.

She paused to gaze at a series of framed photos, taken at various spots around Vancouver Island: the Fisgard lighthouse, the shoreline at Mystic Beach, the lush rain forest along the Juan de Fuca trail. "Did you take all these pictures?"

"Yeah. You've seen me with my camera before."

"I have, but only when you came to take photos of the kids with Santa last Christmas. These are so artistic." She wouldn't have been surprised to see them hanging in a gallery.

"Thanks." He gestured for her to follow him. "I'll show you the rest of the place."

The larger of the two bedrooms contained an enormous king bed and a matching dresser. The smaller one was outfitted with a work desk, a couch, and more bookshelves. A quick peek at one of the shelves revealed numerous Stephen King books, along with some popular fantasy titles, and a hardbound edition of *The Lord of the Rings*.

She was dying to know how he could afford a place this size. But after listening to Randolph brag about his salary, the last thing she wanted to do was discuss money.

Knox ended the tour in his kitchen, where one corner housed a small bar, complete with shelves of liqueurs and mixers, a wine cube filled with a dozen bottles, and a cabinet containing different types of glassware.

"I love this setup," she said. "You have so many different types of liqueurs."

"This is where I practice making my cocktails. I don't indulge while I'm on the job, but after my shift ends, I like kicking back with a drink. Sometimes, it's an old favorite, and other times, I test out a new recipe. Would you like me to whip up something? Or would you rather have more brandy?"

While she was tempted to request a fancy cocktail, she was craving the taste of that sinfully good brandy. "I'd love a glass of brandy."

He filled two snifters and handed her one. Once they were settled on the couch, he turned down the lights. "I know it's not that cold out, but how about a fire?"

"I don't want you to go to any trouble."

"No trouble at all." He picked up a remote and aimed it toward the fireplace. In an instant, flames began flickering against the dark brick. "It's just gas. Not as fun as a bonfire, but a lot less work."

"It's perfect." She sipped her drink, luxuriating in the soothing warmth of the brandy.

He set his glass on the coffee table and stood up. "I'll be right back. I have something for you." When he returned, he handed her a tiny gift bag decorated with a design featuring colorful balloons and a banner reading "Happy Birthday."

Her mouth quirked up in a smile. "Thanks, but it's not my birthday."

"I know, but I always reuse my gift bags. I hate buying new ones."

She opened the bag and pulled out a tiny bookshelf containing four miniature Jane Austen books with intricately designed covers, so small they fit in the palm of her hand. "Oh my God. These are adorable. Where did you find them?"

"On Etsy. I was looking for a gift for my sister-in-law and somehow went down the miniature book rabbit hole. I figured you'd like these since they're romances."

She set them down, then leaned over and hugged him. "I do. They're going to look so cute in my shadow box. Thank you." She regarded him with admiration. "Is there anything you can't do, Mr. McIntyre?"

"What do you mean? This isn't a big deal. I just wanted you to know I was thinking about you."

She placed her hand over his. "You're really thoughtful, you're a talented mixologist, you wrote an award-winning TV show, you take photos worthy of *National Geographic*, you're very nurturing, and you're great in bed." The last statement made her blush, but it needed to be said.

He laughed. "Thanks, but I'm also a guy who'd rather stay

inside and read than go to a party. Or any big social events, for that matter. And I can't dance for shit. If you invite me to a wedding, you're not getting me on the dance floor under any circumstances."

"No dancing? Really? What if I played a romantic song on my phone right now? Wouldn't you be tempted to spin me around the room?"

"Nope." He gave her a mock scowl. "Don't even try it. And don't suggest dance lessons. Been there, done that."

With Lila, she assumed. Not that she wanted to bring up his ex. "That's okay. I can live without a dance partner." Honestly, she'd rather go out dancing with the Damsels than anyone else. Give Rosie a few drinks and she was all over the dance floor.

She snuggled closer to Knox. "How did you find this apartment? It looks so new."

"It's a condo. The complex was built three years ago. My sister-in-law works in real estate, and she told me about it. I was one of the first people to buy in."

He *owned* it? She tried to squelch her look of surprise, but it was impossible. Even if this place was a little far from Victoria's downtown core, it couldn't have come cheaply. "Oh, wow, that's... um..."

"Not what you expected from a bartender?" He raised his eyebrows.

"I wasn't going to say that. But I know for a fact Rosie makes more than most of us, since she's the hotel's assistant manager, and her place isn't nearly this nice." Charlie gnawed on her lip, hoping she hadn't messed things up again. "Not...that it's any of my business how you can afford it."

He placed his hand on her thigh. "It's okay to ask. I don't want you to feel like the subject of money is off-limits."

"Thanks. I just felt awkward after the way Randolph was boasting at dinner about his seven-figure job."

"Yeah, that was a lot. When he made that crack about me being an aspiring author, I was tempted to lay down the whole story—just to prove him wrong. But I'm not ready for that yet."

"I'll never reveal a word to anyone. If you feel like telling people, I'll support you, but I wouldn't expose your secrets." Though she wanted to brag about him, she could understand why he'd kept his accomplishments hidden.

"I appreciate it. The truth is, Evan and I got paid a decent sum for the pilot of *The Hidden Forest*. Once the show was picked up, our agent went to bat for us and made sure we were well paid. Evan went on a spending spree—bought a Porsche, a whole new wardrobe, a ton of shit—but I squirreled my money away. I grew up with frugal parents, and those habits were hard to break. My sister-in-law helped me invest some of it in a bit of property up island, and when its value doubled, I sold the land. I might not brag about it, but I'm doing just fine."

He hid it so well. The beat-up truck, the casual clothes, the utter lack of pretension. He was just a down-to-earth guy. "I'm glad to hear it. But even if you lived in a shithole with three roommates, avocado-green appliances, and a junky futon, I'd still want to spend the night."

He took her hand, lacing his fingers with hers. "Sorry I got bent out of shape about dinner, but I don't like being judged on the basis of my job. There's nothing wrong with working in the service industry."

She squeezed his hand. "You're preaching to the choir. My whole job is centered around customer service, and I'm proud of it. I'm a lot less impressed with someone like Randolph, whose primary goal is to make a ton of money for his millionaire investors."

"So, you weren't tempted by his fancy boat?" His tone was light, teasing her. "What about his BMW?"

"I'd rather spend all day in your truck than ten minutes driving around town with him." Looking into Knox's eyes, she couldn't hold back her feelings any longer. "In case it isn't obvious, I *really* like you."

"Sweetheart, the feeling is mutual." He gave her a sly smile. "Now, finish up your brandy so I can sweep you off to bed and show you exactly how I feel."

KNOX HAD TO HAND IT TO THE DAMSELS. WHEN THEY'D told him they were giving the Gilded Lily a Halloween makeover, he'd been skeptical. Based on the pitiful decorations they'd dredged up last year—plastic bats, fake spiderwebs, a few mini pumpkins— he didn't expect much. But they'd come through.

The high-tops and side tables had been adorned with antique brass lanterns and freshly carved jack-o'-lanterns, lit up with flickering LED candles. Along one wall, they'd hung a purple velvet curtain, backlit to reveal shadowy silhouettes. Another wall displayed vintage mirrors fogged over with ghostly outlines. The cobwebs draped over all the light fixtures looked like they'd been hanging there for decades. A hidden fog machine billowed near the photo booth; beside it was a big cauldron filled with masks and props.

Celia sat behind a wooden hostess stand at the entrance. Wearing an all-black schoolgirl dress, her hair in two braids, she looked like Wednesday Addams. "Good evening," she said in a low, drawn-out voice.

"Good to see you," Knox said. "Did Laurel ask you to help us out?"

"She was fully prepared to beg, but I said yes right away. I love Halloween parties. I'm checking IDs, handing out ballots for the costume contest, and making sure we don't exceed the room's maximum capacity." She raked her gaze over him. "Spiffy pirate costume. I saw Tinker Bell earlier, so I'm guessing you're Captain Hook?"

"Yep, except without the hook." He pulled his shiny metal hook from the pocket of his long red coat. "Too hard to mix drinks that way."

"We've got about twenty minutes before the Lily opens to the public at seven. Everything all set?"

"It's all good." He and Miles had come in early to prep, but he'd waited until the last minute to change. Even if his costume looked sharp, he was roasting in it. Having to wear a giant pirate hat didn't help. "I'd better hustle over to the bar and prepare myself for the onslaught."

Celia grinned at him. "Have fun!"

If that's what you want to call it. No doubt about it, tonight was going to be exhausting. At least he'd have Miles working alongside him, and Jordan was also coming in to help. To ease their load, Selena had recruited two of her staff to serve as cocktail waitresses.

Knox was grateful his duties were limited to one thing: mixing drinks. He didn't have to emcee the costume contest because Rosie's boyfriend, Drew, had offered to do it. Given that Drew usually volunteered to play Santa during the Christmas season, he was obviously the kind of cheerful soul who adored getting people pumped up for the holidays.

No, thanks. This wasn't Knox's scene. Too many people. Too much excitement. Getting through the next five hours would be rough.

His mood improved when Charlie flitted over to the bar. The sight of her dressed as Tinker Bell made his groin tighten. Wasn't her costume supposedly from a *children's* play? Or had she swapped it out for a "sexy fairy" outfit? Her pale green dress not only revealed a lot of cleavage, but it was so short that if she bent over, she'd give everyone an eyeful.

Not that he was complaining. But he couldn't deal with a hard-on right now.

She gave him a salute. "Ahoy there, Captain. Doesn't the Lily look amazing?"

"It does. But what the hell are you wearing?" His voice came out gruffer than he'd intended, but he couldn't help himself. He didn't want every guy in the bar trying to hit on her.

"I'm Tinker Bell, of course." Hands on her hips, she struck a pose. "I'll admit the costume is a little tight and a tad too short. I just have to be careful not to bend over." Her eyes sparkled. "Not until after the bar closes, and my lusty pirate captain can have his way with me."

You'd better believe it. "This is just pushing all your buttons, isn't it, sweetheart?"

"Absolutely." She came behind the bar and appraised him closely. "You look so sexy as Captain Hook. It's like all my steamiest pirate fantasies come to life." She ran her hands down his long scarlet jacket. "Seeing you dressed like this makes me all hot and bothered."

He pulled her closer and squeezed her ass, which was barely covered by the costume. "If you don't behave, you're getting a spanking tonight."

"Don't make any promises you can't keep, Cap'n."

"Hey, let's keep it PG over here." Rosie breezed up to the bar with Drew beside her. They were clad in matching gray *Ghostbusters* jumpsuits.

With a giggle, Charlie broke away from Knox. "Fine, we'll behave. I like your costumes, but you're missing the proton packs. How are you going to fight any ghosts without your equipment?"

"Those darn packs are too heavy," Rosie said. "So, we ditched them for now. We figured our outfits would be on-brand, seeing as how the hotel is hosting a ghost-hunting show next weekend. The only problem is…" She paused as their boss strolled into the bar. "Preston loved the idea so much he decided to follow our lead."

He was wearing an outfit like theirs, but with the hefty proton pack on his back.

"He's a total copycat," Drew said. "Though, to be fair, there were four ghostbusters in the movies, so I guess we can use one more."

"You still okay with running the costume contest?" Knox asked him.

Drew beamed. "Yeah, I can't wait. After Christmas, Halloween is my favorite holiday."

Knox cast his gaze around the lounge, taking in the full effect. The Lily could have easily served as the set for an eerie 1920s movie. "You all did an incredible job decorating. This is way better than I expected."

"Preston gave us a generous budget," Rosie said. "This stuff didn't come cheap, but we can store it in the basement and use it next year. Assuming this party becomes a tradition."

Knox rolled his eyes, but it was more to get a laugh out of the others. To be honest, he was glad the Duchess was going all out to celebrate Halloween. Last October, they'd barely acknowledged the holiday. At the time, Preston was still new to the job, and the hotel was struggling to attract guests. A lot had changed in a year.

"My cousin Benito's coming to act as our bouncer," Rosie added. "He's built like a tank and doesn't put up with any crap. If anyone gets too rowdy, he can deal with them."

Knox nodded. "Glad to hear it."

Charlie slipped out of his arms and went back to the other side of the bar. "We'll all be hanging out, but if you need a break or anything, tell one of the servers to come find us." She flashed him an affectionate smile. "Thanks for going along with this. I know it's a lot."

Her words filled him with a warm glow. She wasn't asking him to change who he was. All she wanted was one night where he was fully on board. "I'll be fine. But if I get too hot, I'm ditching the hat and jacket."

"That's okay. You'll still be my sexy pirate." When Rosie groaned, Charlie shot her a mock glare. "You think you and Drew are the only ones who can act all lovey-dovey? Not even." She looped her arm through Rosie's. "Come on. Let's see if there's a line forming outside the entrance yet." They walked away, with Drew following close behind them.

Lovey-dovey. Not an expression Knox would use to describe himself, but it fit. After the excruciating buffet at the yacht club and the reconciliation that followed, he and Charlie had grown closer. Squeezing in overnight visits when they could, trying to snatch a half hour here and there during their breaks, and sending flirty texts. He hadn't felt this happy in years.

His nephew, Jordan, scooted in just as the grandfather clock in the corner struck seven. Knox was glad he'd shown up on time, given the size of the crowd pouring into the bar. Everyone was dressed up, in costumes ranging from the bare minimum—three guys clad in cowboy hats and fringed vests—to the elaborate, like the group of women dressed as characters from *Alice in Wonderland.* Within minutes, Knox was up to his elbows in drink orders, working frantically with Miles and Jordan to keep the cocktails flowing. When he started getting overheated, he stashed his hat and coat in the back and rolled up his sleeves.

Occasionally, Charlie came by to check on him, but she spent most of the time circulating among the guests and hanging out with the Damsels. Seeing her so bubbly and cheerful, so clearly in her element, filled him with a pang of uncertainty. Once the novelty of dating him wore off, would his introverted behavior frustrate her? Events like this weren't to his liking. After tonight, he'd be happy to go back to his regular gig, tending bar at a cocktail lounge that was rarely crowded, except during happy hour.

Don't dwell on this now. You don't have the time.

Instead, he kept his focus on the bar as his muscle memory kicked in. Take the orders, mix the drinks, rinse and repeat. Two hours in, the place was packed to capacity.

Drew grabbed a mic and announced the rules of the costume contest. Once everyone had voted and turned in their ballots, the public judging would begin.

Preston sidled up to the bar. "Great party, eh? I can't get over the size of this crowd."

"It's something, all right," Knox said. "Need a drink?"

"Just a Coke. I'm on duty." Preston puffed out his chest. "Did you notice my costume? I'm one of the original ghostbusters."

"I noticed. You ready to go tackle the ghost in the haunted storage room? Be careful, or you might get locked in." Knox filled a glass with soda and slid it toward him.

Preston laughed. "Yeah, right. You don't honestly believe that room is haunted, do you?"

"Are you serious? Why else would *Canada's Most Haunted* be filming an episode here?"

"Because we're an old hotel. And because you and Charlie played up the grisly details of that murder-suicide. But I don't believe in ghosts. I never have." Preston sipped his Coke. "I just thought it would be a great way to draw interest in the Duchess. And it paid off, didn't it? I've gotta admit, it was a genius idea."

A genius idea that had required a lot of work. "Yep. But do me a favor. Don't tell anyone from the show that you're a total skeptic. We don't want to piss them off."

"Don't worry. I know how to keep a secret. After all, I've kept yours, haven't I?" Preston held up his glass in a salute before heading back into the crowd.

While Knox didn't appreciate the reminder, it no longer sent a chill down his spine. Now that he'd told Charlie about his past, he'd started wondering if he still needed to keep it hidden. Maybe it was time he shared his story with the rest of his coworkers. Once he got through tomorrow night's gala at the Grand Duke, he'd consider it.

After Preston left, Knox caught sight of a young woman sitting by herself at the far end of the bar, clad in a costume that must have been marketed as "sexy pirate," with an off-the-shoulder blouse, tight black bodice, and red bandanna.

"Hey, there," he said. "Can I get you anything?"

She looked up from her phone. "I'm not sure yet. Is that okay?"

"Sure. Just let me know when you're ready." He was about to turn away, but her expression gave him pause. Her dark eyes were glistening with tears. "Are you all right?"

She shook her head quickly. "Not really."

In the past, he would have done little more than nod in acknowledgment. But he thought about the compassionate way Charlie listened to everyone. "I've got a few minutes if you need to talk about it. I'm Knox, by the way."

"I'm Yvette. My friend was supposed to meet me here. She's the one who suggested dressing like this. And now she's not answering my texts, and I...um...feel so *stupid* wearing this costume."

He offered her a warm smile. "Nothing wrong with dressing like a pirate. I'm supposed to be Captain Hook, but I had to ditch my jacket and hat because it's so damn hot in here."

"Yeah, it's kind of warm." She glanced at her phone again. "I'm not sure if I should bail or wait for her. She's been flaking out a lot lately, so it's hard to know what to expect."

"Maybe she's running late. I'd give her a few more minutes. If she doesn't show, then you don't have to stay. No shame in leaving the party early."

She nodded. "Right. Thanks."

A trio of women dressed as the witches from the film *Hocus Pocus* approached the bar. "I need to take care of this group," he said to Yvette. "But let me know if you want anything."

As he mixed three blood orange martinis, he glanced back at Yvette, who was staring at her phone in dismay. Maybe he should ask Charlie to come over and chat with her. But once he'd served the witches, a group of young guys dressed in colorful T-shirts displaying matching condiment labels—Ketchup, Mayo, and Mustard—clustered around Yvette. At first, he was relieved, thinking they were friends of hers, but her anxious expression set off alarm bells.

He eased down to her end of the bar, side-eyeing the group as he cleaned up glasses.

Ketchup slung his arm around Yvette. "Hey, baby. What are you doing all by yourself?"

She tried to shrug him off. "I'm good, thanks."

Mustard flanked her on the other side. "Looks to me like you need a little company."

"Nope. Not interested." She stood up, but Mayo put his hand on her shoulder to stop her.

"Don't be in such a big hurry. Have a drink with us."

That did it. Knox charged toward them and used his extra-growly voice. "Did you hear her? She said, 'Not interested.' That means you need to leave her alone."

Ketchup flipped him the finger. "Fuck off."

"Yeah, get screwed," said Mayo.

While Knox had never gotten physical with anyone who caused trouble, he loved putting pushy assholes in their place. If they got out of line, he usually threatened to call one of the hotel's security officers. But it rarely came to that. He leaned over the bar. "I'll give you one minute to get out of here before I alert our bouncer. Trust me, you don't want to mess with him."

"You can't do that," Ketchup said. "We're paying customers."

"I can do anything I want," Knox replied. "It's my bar. Now, get lost."

"But the costume contest isn't over yet," Mustard whined.

"News flash, Mustard Boy. You're not gonna win. Now, get out and find another bar."

Ketchup glared at him. "Just for that, I'm leaving a one-star review of this dump on Yelp." But he and his friends slunk away.

After they left, Yvette graced Knox with a bright smile. "You didn't have to do that, but I appreciate it."

"No problem." He caught a glimpse of another young woman dressed in a pirate costume, who was hustling toward them. "Looks like your friend is here."

The woman came up to Yvette and gave her a side-hug. "I'm so glad you didn't leave yet. Parking was a shit show. It's like everyone in the world is downtown right now."

Knox nodded toward them. "I'll give you a few minutes to figure out what you want, then come back." He felt a sense of satisfaction, knowing that amid tonight's chaos, he'd made someone's night a little better.

As the costume contest played out, he barely paid attention. Even with the guests crowded around Drew, waiting on the results, the drink orders still came pouring in. A few times, he stopped to knock back a glass of water, but he kept going until last call. When the lounge's grandfather clock struck midnight, the servers ushered everyone out.

Knox surveyed the Gilded Lily with a critical eye. The place was a mess, awash in a sea of dirty glasses, crumpled-up napkins, and overturned bowls of candy corn and pretzels. No matter how hard the servers had tried to keep up, there had been too many guests to manage.

Rosie clapped her hands together. "Okay, everyone! Thanks for all your hard work. This is the best party we've ever hosted. Tomorrow morning, I've arranged for a few of our room attendants to take care of the mess, so you're off the hook for cleanup."

Perfect. All Knox had to do was tidy up the area around the bar, and he'd be good to go.

The others trickled out until only Charlie was left. She came around to his side, pressed him against the bar, and removed his cravat. Tossing it aside, she placed little kisses along the curve of his neck. "Thank you, Knox. That was a fabulous party."

"Easy there, Tink. I'm really sweaty."

"I don't care. I've been watching you all night, and I can't hold back any longer. I'm so grateful you agreed to do this. I know it was way out of your comfort zone." She stretched on her toes, flung her arms around his neck, and gave him a long, slow kiss. He kissed her back, threading his hands through her hair and groaning as she ground her body against his.

If this was how she intended to thank him, then he was glad he'd made the effort. He kneaded her ass, his fingers digging into the soft flesh as he kissed her even harder. At this point, he didn't care that they were both sweaty and exhausted. He wanted to bend her over the bar and make her cry out his name in ecstasy.

She pulled away and adjusted her costume. With a grin, she looked down at his tight black pirate pants, which barely hid his erection. "I wish we could keep going, but the Lily has too many security cameras. I'd rather not end the night getting fired."

"Same. You coming back to my place? I need to shower, but after that, I'm all yours."

"That's what I was hoping for." She grinned. "I want you to ravage me, Captain. Plunder my body like it's a lost treasure. You up for that?"

Hell, yes. He didn't care how tired he was; tonight, they were going to live out *all* her pirate fantasies.

Twenty-Two

WHEN CHARLIE'S PHONE ALARM WENT OFF, SHE silenced it with a groan. Beside her, Knox hadn't stirred. She peeked under the covers and ogled him freely. His broad back, the tattoos covering his shoulders, his thick tree trunk legs. Last night, she'd gotten to enjoy every inch of him.

Despite their exhaustion, they'd had sex in the shower. Then they'd enjoyed another round in bed. She'd let him take the lead, encouraging him to be a little rough, goading him until he spanked her, then demanding he ravage her thoroughly. And, damn, the sex had been even hotter than she'd expected.

Did that mean she was a weirdo? What kind of woman wanted to pretend she was being held captive by a pirate? Maybe it was best not to psychoanalyze her impulses. All that mattered was that Knox had been fully into it.

She placed a soft kiss on his bare shoulder. "Knox? Honey?"

"Mmmph."

"I have to go in to work at noon, and it's ten thirty now. You promised to drive me."

"Five more minutes."

"I'm gonna need coffee. Lots of it. Can we stop somewhere?"

Alma's was bound to be crowded, but there was a Tim Hortons drive-thru not far from Knox's condo. "Like, maybe somewhere with donuts?"

He rolled over to face her. "I'll buy you all the donuts you want. Thanks for spending the night."

"My pleasure. I wish I had the whole day off, but I promised Rosie I'd help her run Spooky Saturday at the hotel."

He brushed a wisp of hair from her forehead. "It's okay. I don't mind driving you. I'll pick you up at five, and we can head over to the Grand Duke for the gala."

"Thanks. I already stashed my costume in my office, so I wouldn't forget it."

"I can't believe I'm voluntarily dressing up twice in one weekend," he grumbled. "What have you done to me?"

By now, she could tell when he was using his grouchy voice to tease her versus actually being crabby. Even if he was still kind of a curmudgeon, he'd changed a lot over the past two months. Like last night, when he'd given his all at the Lily's costume party. Or during the times he'd confided in her, telling her stories about his life in Vancouver. Or listened to her when she was stressed about her mom.

"After this, I promise we won't have to dress up again until next Halloween. Unless you want to indulge in a little role play." She thought that might get a laugh out of him, but his brow furrowed. "Did I say something wrong?"

"I saw how much fun you had last night. Me, not so much. I could handle it for one night, but I'm not a fan of crowds or parties. I don't want to stop you from having a good time."

This had to be a Lila thing. Why else would he be so concerned? Was he afraid she'd tire of him? Or tell him their relationship lacked passion? Far from it.

"I like social events, but if that's not your thing, I'm okay with it," she said. "I have other friends who are into that stuff. But I love it when we spend time together, even if we're just walking in the park or lazing in bed. Being with you makes me feel special, and..."

I'm in love with you.

She hadn't told him yet. He might worry she was rushing into things. But she was sure of it. Though they hadn't been dating for long, she'd spent months yearning for him, hoping he'd eventually realize she was *right there*. Ever since they'd teamed up to work on the ghost-hunting show, her feelings had grown even stronger.

Maybe tonight, after the gala was over, she'd summon up the courage to tell him.

Or maybe in November, when their lives were a little calmer.

But definitely before Christmas.

He kissed her forehead. "You make me feel special, too. Now, go jump in the shower. Once you're dressed, I'll drive you to work, and we'll stop for coffee and donuts along the way."

AT FIVE, WHEN CHARLIE WALKED INTO THE LOBBY OF the Grand Duke Hotel, she could barely conceal her apprehension. Up until tonight, she hadn't worried that much about the gala. Even if it was a huge deal, she'd been too busy to think about it, what with everything going on at the hotel: Spooky Saturdays, preparations for the ghost-hunting show, and last night's costume party. But over the course of the day, as the event loomed nearer, she'd turned into a jittery mess.

While Knox's Phantom mask effectively hid his face, she was afraid of what might happen if Evan discovered him. Would he treat Knox decently or strike out in anger?

It didn't help that she'd barely eaten. In addition to her morning coffee fix, she'd only had two donuts, a bag of white chocolate pretzels, and a pumpkin bar from Spooky Saturday. While the sugar rush had given her a temporary high, the resulting crash was making her edgy.

Not that she'd told Knox any of this. Considering what a big risk he was taking, she needed to be the calm one.

Thankfully, her dress was light and comfortable. Not like poor Knox, who was stuck wearing a black tuxedo jacket, a long black cape, and a mask that covered most of his face. Following the signs in the hotel lobby, she led him to the ballroom, which she'd visited once for a friend's wedding. She remembered it being glamorous, but nothing like this.

The enormous ballroom had been transformed, containing dozens of realistic-looking oak trees, dripping with moss. Flickering candles appeared among the tree branches, and thousands of fairy lights twinkled above. Interspersed among the trees were round banquet tables, adorned with elaborate centerpieces, complete with vintage lanterns and rustic greenery. The total effect was like being in an enchanted forest, other than the wall at the front of the ballroom, which housed a raised stage and a huge projector screen.

"What do you think?" she asked Knox. "Does it feel like you're back in the forest?" The ethereal music, taken from the show's soundtrack, was a nice touch.

"A little, but we filmed most of the exteriors in an *actual* forest. This isn't bad, though."

She and Knox checked in with the event manager, a tall Black woman named Denise, who was dressed as Maleficent from *Sleeping Beauty*.

Denise led them over to a station in a corner of the ballroom and handed Knox a set of laminated cards. "Here are all the wines, beers, and ciders available, as well as the bottled liqueurs. We're also offering three specialty cocktails themed to match the show."

Knox reviewed the cards. "Alejandro sent me the list of cocktails earlier, so I got a chance to practice making them."

"Good to hear. Since it's an open bar, you won't have to worry about taking payment, but hopefully, our guests will still feel the need to tip. You can use this jar." Denise pointed to a mason jar painted with an elaborate forest scene and illuminated with more fairy lights.

Knox chuckled. "That's the fanciest tip jar I've ever seen."

Denise gave a delicate snort. "Isn't it, though? They were custom made. Anyway, the cash tips are yours to keep. There's also a card with a QR code if people prefer to use credit cards. Those tips will be split among all the bartenders, and you'll get your share once everything's settled up. If you need anything replenished, runners will be stopping by to check on your inventory. And—in case Alejandro didn't mention it—you need to act like professionals. No asking for selfies or autographs."

"Got it." Charlie looked over the laminated cards. The small selection of wines and liqueurs was minimal compared to the wide variety offered at the Gilded Lily. Once Denise had left, she addressed Knox in a low voice. "Does this seem doable?"

"Definitely, though I'm glad I practiced making those cocktails ahead of time. Otherwise, the setup is incredibly basic. Plus, I saw three other stations scattered around the ballroom, and a larger bar beside the stage. I guess they don't want anyone to stand in line for too long."

"Makes sense. At my friend's wedding, they didn't have enough bartenders. Once the dancing started, the drink line took forever." She glanced around the room, taking in the elaborate decor. "This event must have cost a fortune."

He shrugged. "Probably, but it's nothing compared to some of the outrageous stuff I've seen. Back when I worked on the show, we had a huge blowout after we won awards for the second season."

She wanted to ask him more about it, but her time would be better spent reviewing the list of instructions. Her role was to assist guests who had simple requests, like a bottle of water or a glass of wine. Earlier that week, she'd practiced her pouring skills with him, while he played the role of a snooty customer. They'd polished off an entire bottle of wine before tumbling into bed, all tipsy and amorous.

At six, she placed her hand on his arm. "You ready for this?"

"Yeah. It would be great to see some familiar faces, but I'm not sure who's still working on the show. I kept up with the gossip for a while after I moved here, but once I got hired at the Duchess, I shut it all out."

Though he made it sound like a simple decision, she knew how difficult the break had been. And how much it had weighed on him. "Whatever happens, I'm here to support you. We'll get through it together."

With any luck, he'd be able to make a few connections and feel like tonight had been worth the effort. While she was glad he was taking this step, she wouldn't be able to relax until they'd survived the entire event.

Twenty-Three

KNOX GREW ANTSY AS THE FIRST HOUR OF THE GALA passed at a glacial pace. Little by little, the guests entered the ballroom. The first to arrive were the crew members since the show's stars never liked showing up early.

"Do you see anyone you know?" Charlie asked.

"A few people from the crew, but that's it. No one from the writers' room. Logan told me Evan brought in some new writers after the fourth season, but I was hoping he kept a few of the old guard." Then again, it would be just like that bastard to clean house completely.

He spotted some of the show's secondary characters and pointed them out to Charlie. There was no sign of Princess Elodie's first love, poor Finn the Woodsman.

To Knox's surprise, he didn't feel much of anything yet. No heart-wrenching grief. No simmering resentment. No longing to be a part of it. It was like going back to a place he'd visited before, but without the desire to stay there.

As the guests stopped by his station, he greeted them and mixed their drinks but kept his Phantom mask in place. Fortunately, he didn't have to say much since Charlie was a pro at making small talk. She complimented everyone on their costumes and asked them about their favorite memories of *The Hidden Forest*.

An hour in, the show's stars made their appearance. Among them was Lila, all dolled up in a gorgeous, sapphire-blue ball gown and a tiara, looking radiant on Evan's arm. In Knox's opinion, her regal garb barely differed from the formal attire she'd worn for the show's High Court scenes. But seeing Evan dressed as her prince was a new look. A look that made Knox recoil in disgust. That smug fucker didn't deserve to swan around like royalty.

Knox's spine stiffened, his hands tightening into fists. How was he supposed to act like everything was normal when the asshole who'd ruined his life hadn't suffered one bit? The soft cadence of Charlie's voice took him out of his head. She placed her hands on his shoulders and kneaded them gently, soothing the rage and the bitterness. Once again, he was grateful to have her by his side. Getting through this on his own would have been a lot harder.

After tonight, he'd find a way to thank her. Not just in bed, but with another gesture that showed how much he cared. Like admitting he was in love with her.

Was it too soon? Maybe so, but he wanted her to know how he felt.

At seven thirty, he and Charlie were able to relax as the guests sat down to enjoy the plated dinner. The smell of roast chicken and vegetables made his stomach growl, but he ignored it. Once the gala ended, he was hoping to find an all-night diner where they could indulge in burgers and fries.

Halfway through dinner, the lights dimmed, and a video played on the screen. Knox could barely see it from his vantage point, but the audio came through clearly. The video contained a compilation of clips drawn from the show's best-loved scenes. He listened intently, smiling as he recognized dialogue he'd written. Included in the clips were the jaw-dropping final scene from the end of the second season, when the Fae King's devious plan was revealed, as well as the tender moment when Princess Elodie and Finn confessed their love for each other.

"I can't believe you wrote so much of this," Charlie whispered. "I'm so impressed."

His heart swelled with pride. How many people could make a claim like that? To have created a show that was part of the pop culture lexicon, that would be remembered long after it ended. Even if he didn't run into any of his old friends, coming here tonight had been the right move. It was a chance to bask in his accomplishments, to celebrate everything he'd achieved before Evan had stripped it away from him.

Once dinner ended, people flocked back to the beverage stations. A rush of drink orders kept him hopping until his line dwindled to just two people—the very writers he'd hoped to see. Zack Wilder—a tall, lanky guy with messy black hair—was dressed as the Grim Reaper, complete with a metal scythe. Beside him was Norah Chen, a petite woman with short dark hair and glasses, wearing a red polka-dot dress and Minnie Mouse ears.

"I can't believe they haven't kicked us out yet," Zack said to Norah. "When I ran into Evan, he gave me the biggest side-eye ever but didn't say a damn thing."

"Enjoy it while you can," Norah said. She smiled at Knox. "I'll have a gimlet."

Zack nudged her. "You're not going to try a Princess Elodie cocktail?"

She shuddered. "I hate anything with Midori liqueur. Too sweet."

"All these themed drinks are seriously over-the-top." Zack leaned his scythe against the bar and offered Knox an apologetic smile. "No offense."

"None taken. I'm just the bartender." Setting down his shaker, Knox took a deep breath. He'd never get a better chance than this one. He removed his mask and set it on the bar top beside him. "Though you might have known me in a different incarnation."

Zack gaped at him. "Fuck me. Is that you, Mac?"

"In the flesh. Though I go by my real name now. Knox McIntyre, at your service. And this is Charlie Fraser, my partner in crime. Charlie, meet Zack and Norah, my two favorite writers from *The Hidden Forest*."

Charlie waved at them. "Hi. Nice to meet you."

"Same here." Norah shot Knox an evil grin. "Are you planning to take down the gala? If so, then I want in. The show did you *so* dirty."

"Didn't it, though?" Charlie added. "But we aren't here to make trouble."

Knox nodded. "I actually signed up to serve drinks on the off chance of running into a few old friends. Like the two of you."

"I'm still trying to wrap my head around the fact that you're standing in front of us," Zack said. "You fucking vanished. Do you know how hard I tried to find you?"

Knox felt a twinge of regret. "Sorry. I shouldn't have cut everyone off. But..."

"We get it," Norah said. "I mean, your world went to shit. Especially after Evan did those vile interviews. If it's any consolation, the writers' room went downhill from there. Evan brought in a bunch of new guys, and those cocky assholes changed the whole tone of the show."

"I'll never forgive them for killing off Finn," Charlie said.

"Right?" Zack replied. "We got so much backlash."

"I was devastated when I found out what they did to that character," Knox added. "Poor Finn didn't deserve such an agonizing death."

"Everyone knew Evan did it because Finn reminded him too

much of you," Norah said. "When I pushed back, he had me fired at the end of the season."

"Same with me." Zack set down the laminated card listing the wine selections. "I'll take a glass of the Pinot Noir."

"Coming right up." Knox handed Norah her gimlet. "You both left the show? How did you score an invite to the gala?"

Zack laughed. "I'm here as Tyson's plus-one. We got married last year."

"That's great. Congrats." Knox had always liked working with Tyson, who'd headed up the design department. "What about you, Norah?"

"I'm good friends with Waverly Zhou, who works in costuming, so she invited me to join her. But I'm sure Evan isn't happy to see either of us. After you left the show and he spread those rumors about you going into rehab, we called him on his bullshit. Which left us with big targets on our backs."

"Sorry." Knox passed Zack his glass of wine. "I never wanted anyone else to suffer on my behalf."

"Don't apologize," Zack said. "My last year on the show was so unbearable I was glad to leave. I got a gig writing for *Siren Squad*, and it's been great."

Charlie clasped her hands together. "I love that series. It's so cool that it features female crime-fighters."

"I'm doing a script rewrite for a locked room thriller. It's got an Agatha Christie vibe." Norah took a business card out of her cherry-red clutch and handed it to Knox. "If you ever want to get back into the business, hit me up. Ever since I started working as a script doctor, I've got more projects than I can handle."

Knox could barely contain his relief in learning that Zack and Norah had never given up on him. "Thanks. I haven't written anything in years, but I'm starting to get that itch again."

"It never goes away, does it?" Norah said. "Now that you've got my contact info, don't be a stranger. I'm heading back to

Vancouver tomorrow, but the next time you come to the mainland, I'd love to see you."

Zack passed him a card. "Same here. Don't disappear again."

Knox tucked the business cards in his back pocket. "I won't. I'm not on social media, but you can find me at the Duchess Hotel."

Charlie grinned at them. "He's the head bartender at a 1920s-style cocktail lounge called the Gilded Lily. If you come back to Victoria, you should stop in for a drink."

"Will do," Zack said. "We're going to bounce in a bit, but we need to get together soon. This time, I'm not waiting five years to see you again."

"You got it. Thanks." Knox watched them leave, grateful no one was in line. This way, he could take a few minutes to process the feelings coursing through him. While he regretted the five years he'd spent in the wilderness, shutting out the people who could have offered him support, at least now he could finally make up for it.

"Knox?" Charlie gave him a gentle poke. "If you go to Vancouver to meet up with Zack and Norah, can you bring me with you?"

He regarded her with affection. "Sure, but we'll probably spend most of our time telling war stories. I wouldn't want to bore you."

"Are you kidding? I'd love a behind-the-scenes glimpse into the show. I promise not to act like too much of a fangirl."

"You can fangirl around me anytime, sweetheart."

At the sight of a group headed for his station, he grabbed his mask and put it back on. Even if he'd made the right call in revealing his face to Zack and Norah, he didn't want to press his luck.

At ten, the show's producers came onto the stage and addressed the crowd. They extolled all the ways in which the show had succeeded: major awards, merchandising opportunities, and devoted fandoms. Cast appearances at places like San Diego Comic-Con and Fan Expo Canada. The spin-off novels and plans for a feature-length film. They thanked the cast and crew for making *The Hidden Forest* come to life.

Even if Knox was attending the evening as a bartender rather than as a writer, he soaked up the praise. After all, he'd earned it just as much as the rest of them.

"Before we let you get back to the party, we'd like to shout out someone special," one of the producers said. "Usually, when a fantasy show becomes a hit, it's because the material was adapted from a best-selling series, like *Game of Thrones* or *The Lord of the Rings*. But *The Hidden Forest* sprang from the singular imagination of a brilliant writer who came up with the premise, helped turn it into a multi-year saga, and now serves as one of the show's executive producers. Evan Girard, come on up here and say a few words."

"What the fuck," Charlie said.

My thoughts exactly. By now, he and Charlie were alone at his station since all the guests had crowded around the stage. Knox's stomach churned as Evan told the crowd he'd come up with the show's premise on a whim and pitched it so masterfully it was picked up right away.

Sure, he'd thought up the concept. Knox would grant him that. He'd also done a fantastic job selling it. But when it came to writing the pilot, creating the story arc for the entire first season, and hammering out most of the episodes? That was all Knox.

He willed himself to stay calm. His costume was hot enough without him reaching the boiling point. Taking off his mask, he wiped the sweat from his brow, hoping to cool down.

But Charlie didn't attempt to hide her fury. "This is bullshit. Someone needs to call Evan out on his lies."

"It's fine. If he wants the credit, he can have it."

It wasn't fine. Without Knox, Evan's idea would have been just that—an *idea*. Knox was the one who'd turned it from a pipe dream into a full-fledged saga, especially during their first season when they hadn't relied on an entire writers' room to produce each episode.

All his good feelings vanished as Evan's words dug into him, reminding him of what he'd lost. He concentrated on breathing steadily and tuned out everything else—Evan's boastful speech, the applause that followed, the chatter of people as the presentation ended.

You can't lose your temper. Not again.

He tried to push past the hurt and the resentment, but it didn't help that Charlie had grown livid with anger. "Aren't you pissed? He didn't even mention you!"

"It's not worth getting upset about. Just let it go." Any minute now, guests would be making their way over to his station, requesting more drinks, and he'd have to focus.

"But Knox...it's not fair." Her voice shook with anguish. "You helped create *The Hidden Forest*. You deserve to be recognized for everything you did!"

"Charlie, stop. Please." He knew she meant well, but her outrage wasn't helping.

A soft voice made his blood run cold. "Knox? Is that you?"

Lila.

IN THE FIVE YEARS SINCE LILA HAD BROKEN HIS HEART, Knox hadn't seen her up close. He'd watched her on TV, but the effect wasn't the same. In person, she was dazzling, her beauty eclipsing everyone around her. Big, blue eyes the color of a tropical ocean, wavy blond locks, pale, delicate features. It was no wonder she'd captured the hearts of so many viewers.

She addressed him again. "Knox? What are you doing here?"

He reached for his mask, but it was too late. Even with the beard, he was instantly recognizable. And though he wanted to say something, he couldn't bring himself to speak. Coming face-to-face with Lila had knocked him off his axis.

Charlie nailed her with a ferocious scowl. "Why shouldn't he be here? *The Hidden Forest* would never have gotten off the ground if he hadn't put in so much work. But you let Evan act like he was responsible for all of it."

Lila reeled, her face crumpling in distress. "Who are *you*?"

Charlie jabbed her finger at Lila. "That's not important. What matters is that I'm here to support Knox. I can't believe he wasn't acknowledged."

Lila blinked. "I...I know. But I don't think you understand what happened."

"I understand plenty." Bright red splotches colored Charlie's pale cheeks. "Trust me, I know *all* about it. Consider yourself lucky Knox never exposed Evan's treachery."

Knox cleared his throat. Even if Charlie was right, he had to stop her from losing control. They were out in public, where anyone could start filming them. It was only due to sheer luck that no one else was in line at his station. "Charlie, please." When she refused to look away from Lila, he placed a hand on her shoulder. "This isn't helping."

Her voice trembled. "But...Knox, it's not right what happened."

Looking into her wide green eyes, he knew she was only speaking out because she cared about him. But she was in danger of screwing up everything. "I know, but this isn't the time."

"What the hell's going on here?"

Fuck. In attempting to talk Charlie down from her outburst, he hadn't noticed Evan barreling toward them. Knox braced himself for impact, but all of Evan's anger was directed toward Charlie. He leaned over the bar, his face mottled with rage. "You little bitch. Did I just see you yelling at my wife?"

Charlie backed up. "I...I wasn't yelling."

"I don't know who the fuck you are, but you have no right to talk to Lila Winstead that way. Get out of here before I throw you out myself."

Even if Knox had hoped to avoid a confrontation, he wasn't about to let his former writing partner bully the woman he loved. "Don't speak to her that way."

At the sight of Knox, Evan's lips thinned into a sneer. "Knox McIntyre? What the fuck are you doing here? Were you planning on sabotaging the party? You've got a lot of nerve."

"Who are you to talk about nerve?" Charlie demanded. "You

went up there and acted like you created *The Hidden Forest* single-handedly."

Knox's face flamed with a fiery heat. He couldn't imagine a worse scenario. He held up his hands, hoping to placate Evan. "I'm not here to sabotage anything. I wanted to see everyone one last time, and I thought—"

"What? That people would welcome you back with open arms?" Evan scoffed. "Hardly. You're even more pathetic than I remembered."

"*You're* the pathetic one," Charlie spat out. "Lying to everyone about your accomplishments. How do you even live with yourself?"

Ignoring her, Evan kept his focus on Knox. "I'm giving you five minutes to pack up your shit and get out, or I'm calling security."

Knox shook his head. "Just let me finish my job. I'm on duty until midnight. Then I'll leave, and you'll never see me again."

"Nope. Five minutes. Or I'll tell everyone how you snuck in here to ruin our evening." Evan crossed his arms and stared down Charlie. "That goes for you, too. I want you both out of here, or I'll have you arrested."

Arrested? Who the fuck did that asshole think he was?

While a part of Knox wanted to have it out with Evan, he knew when he was beaten. If this incident went viral, the humiliation would be catastrophic. Better to clear out now than be smeared with accusations that he was a vengeful prick intent on tanking the gala.

He grabbed his belongings, already knowing he'd get an earful from Alejandro for bailing early. He gestured to Charlie. "Come on. We're leaving."

She glared at Evan. "You're a horrible human being. I hope this comes back to bite you in the ass." Then she turned on Lila. "You're not much better."

Lila blinked again, as if fighting back tears. "I'm sorry, but you have to go."

Knox kept his head down and headed for the exit, with Charlie following behind him. Given how crowded the ballroom was, few people noticed their departure. After leaving the ballroom, he stood waiting at the hotel's entrance, shaking with agitation as the valet fetched his truck. A light rain was falling, and the air was cool and misty. Turning his face toward the sky, he savored the feel of raindrops on his cheeks.

When his truck pulled up to the entrance, he hustled Charlie toward it and helped her get in. He went around to the driver's seat and set his cape and mask in the back. Without waiting to see if she was buckled in, he sped away from the hotel, intending to put as much distance as he could between himself and the Grand Duke.

For a few minutes, Charlie said nothing. Was she still mad at Evan? Was she ashamed they'd been tossed out of the gala? As the rain beat down harder, he flicked on his wipers. The gloomy weather matched his mood. At least the drive would give them a chance to cool down. He didn't want to go to bed feeling this miserable.

When Charlie spoke up, it was clear her fury hadn't abated. "Evan was such an asshole. First, he takes all the credit for the show, and then he kicks you out. For no good reason! You didn't do anything wrong."

"Yeah, it sucks," he muttered, hoping she'd accept his response and move on. Blowing up about it wouldn't change anything.

"You seem so calm. Aren't you furious?"

"Of course I am, but what else can I do? You heard the acclaim he got. All because he twisted the narrative in his favor and people bought into it. It was better to leave now than let him make the situation even worse." A surge of resentment welled up inside him, so toxic it spilled over, tinging his words with acid. "And by the way, tonight wouldn't have ended so badly if you hadn't lost your temper."

"I was angry on your behalf! Because I care about you! I know you feel safer staying out of the spotlight, but it's time you fought back. You need to write *your* side of the story. You're a writer, for God's sake."

Like he needed her to tell him that? "Thanks for the reminder, but I'm not about to set myself up for more backlash. Do you honestly think anyone would believe me after all the lies Evan told about me?"

"Some people would. Like Zack and Norah. They were totally on your side. I'll bet they're not the only ones who feel that way. Don't you think it's time you stopped hiding in the shadows?"

He gripped the steering wheel so tightly his knuckles went white. The pressure built up inside him, like a volcano on the verge of erupting. He released a strangled breath. "That's enough, Charlie. Just stop."

Her voice softened. "I'm sorry, but I hate seeing anyone treat you like this. You need to stand up to Evan. That way, you can take back the narrative."

That did it. She'd pushed him over the edge. He turned on her, his voice thick with anger. "What would you know about standing up for yourself?"

"Wh...what are you talking about?"

As the light turned red, he skidded to a stop, his heart pounding. The driving rain had made the road slippery and treacherous. If he didn't calm down, he'd be putting them both in danger. But he couldn't stop himself from lashing out. "Come on, Charlie. Where do you get off, telling me to take a stand?"

"I was speaking up for you. Why is that so hard to understand?"

"Because you're asking me to do something that you don't have the guts to do for yourself. I know rent in Victoria is expensive, but in exchange for a place to live, you let your mom walk all over you. You're so afraid of making a scene that you won't challenge her. Isn't that what happened at Thanksgiving?"

She twisted her hands together. "I...I already apologized for Thanksgiving."

"But did you talk to your mom about it afterward like you promised? Did you tell her you wouldn't put up with it again?" From the way she recoiled, he knew she hadn't done it.

"I meant to, but...I..." Tears sprang up in her eyes. "This isn't about me."

"Isn't it? Here you are, demanding I fight back, when you won't even stand up to your mom." He hated that he'd made her cry. But his hurt and frustration had escalated to a point where he couldn't back down.

She was crying in earnest, tears streaming down her cheeks. "Take me home. *Now.*"

"Whatever you want." He made a quick U-turn, wincing as his tires skidded on the slick road. She braced herself against the passenger door but didn't utter a word.

The rest of the drive passed in agonizing silence. He wanted to rewind everything, to take back the horrible accusations he'd made, to apologize to Charlie for hurting her feelings, but he was too angry. Angry at her, at Evan, and at Lila.

But most of all, he was angry at himself.

CHARLIE GOT OUT OF THE TRUCK AND SLAMMED THE door shut. Knox, being the gentleman he was, insisted on walking her up the stairs to her apartment. The pouring rain made it hard to see, and she struggled to enter her door's key code. When she opened it, she hesitated, wanting to fling herself into his arms and ask for a do-over. But she resisted the urge and dashed inside, closing the door firmly behind her. The sound of his footsteps, descending the stairs, confirmed he wouldn't be trying to win her back tonight. He was done.

She plopped down on the couch and wrapped herself in a

fleece blanket. Though she needed to change out of her costume and hang it up, she couldn't make herself move. The tears kept coming until her entire body was heaving with sobs.

How could Knox have treated her this way? He'd dug in deep, attacking her where it would hurt the most. She should have been furious, but all she could feel was a crushing sense of regret.

Even if his words stung, they were justified. After Thanksgiving, she'd intended to talk to her mother, to tell her that inviting Randolph to the buffet had been an underhanded trick. But she'd lost her nerve. And then, after her mother had made yet another snide comment about Knox parking his truck in the driveway, Charlie hadn't defended her decision to have him sleep over. Instead, she'd started spending the night at his place to escape judgment.

Charlie Fraser, you're nothing but a coward.

That wasn't the worst of it. After promising to support Knox tonight, her ugly confrontation with Lila had attracted Evan's attention and gotten them kicked out of the gala.

If she hadn't lost her shit, they could have survived the night without incident. Once they were back at Knox's place, they could have ranted about Evan together. Called him horrible names, invoked curses upon him, and then tumbled into bed, grateful to have each other.

Instead, she'd ruined everything.

Knox woke on Sunday with a killer headache. As he sat up in bed, exhaustion crested over him like a wave. He grabbed his phone, hoping no one had texted him during the wee hours of the night. Right now, he couldn't deal with anyone—not even Charlie. Fortunately, his phone didn't display any notifications.

He couldn't remember the last time he'd sunk to this level of misery.

Oh, wait. He could. Five years ago, he'd gone through this exact scenario when he'd woken at Logan's place, the morning after Lila dumped him. At least this time, he'd resisted the urge to drown his sorrows in booze. Nothing worse than battling a hangover *and* a mountain of regret.

And right now, he was deeply regretting last night's fiasco. Given that he'd abandoned his station two hours early, he probably wouldn't get paid. Despite his joy at seeing Zack and Norah again, the night had ended on such a sour note that he hadn't gotten the closure he'd hoped for. If anything, his argument with Charlie had made him feel even more pathetic about the way he'd fled from Vancouver with his tail between his legs.

Worse yet, he'd taken out his anger on her. Though she should have eased up last night, he could have told her—gently—that he was done talking about *The Hidden Forest* until he was emotionally ready to discuss it. Instead, he'd struck her where she was most vulnerable.

He wanted to call her and apologize for his behavior. To tell her how much she meant to him. But before he talked to her, he needed to figure out his own shit. Even if she'd pushed him to the breaking point, she'd been right. He'd never be able to put his past behind him if he didn't tell his side of the story. To do so, he'd have to step out of the shadows and expose himself. The backlash could be terrible, but it was better than letting the resentment fester inside him.

Clearly, he wasn't going to be able to fall back asleep. He took a quick shower and made a pot of coffee. As he was downing his second cup, his phone buzzed with a text.

He read the message twice, unsure if he was being punked.

> Lila: Knox, it's Lila. Any chance you're free this morning? I'd like to get together.

How the fuck had she known how to reach him? After leaving Vancouver, he'd erased all traces of Mac Iverson, including his phone number. He'd only shared the new one with the few people he could still trust, like Logan.

> Knox: How'd you get this number?

> Lila: I tracked down the woman running the gala and asked for it. BTW, she was pissed at you.

Knox couldn't help but chuckle at her honesty. *I'm pretty sure her boss would like my head on a platter. He should be thankful I wasn't publicly arrested.*

> Lila: True. It wouldn't have been a good look. Anyway, can you meet with me?

> Knox: Sure. But only you. No Evan.

> Lila: He's still asleep. Let's meet in the gazebo outside the Grand Duke. 30 minutes?

> Knox: I'll see you there.

The timing was tight, but if he hurried, he could make it. He drove downtown, parked his truck in a public lot, and dashed over to the Grand Duke, wincing as the wind off the ocean buffeted him in the face. Last night's rain had given way to a sunny, chilly morning, the blue sky overhead dotted with fluffy white clouds.

The wooden gazebo sat amid a neatly manicured garden off to one side of the hotel. Lila was already seated on one of the benches, bundled in a black woolen coat and wearing sunglasses, black gloves, and a fur hat. Knox was about to suggest they take their conversation somewhere warmer, like Alma's Beanery, but she was probably trying to avoid being recognized.

As he sat beside her, he caught a whiff of her signature scent. A light, floral fragrance with a hint of jasmine, the same one she'd worn when they were together. Despite his unease at meeting with her, the familiarity made him smile. "Good morning, Lila."

"Hi, Knox. Thanks for coming." Her voice was as soft and melodious as ever, all the rough edges smoothed out.

He still wasn't sure why she'd asked to meet him, but he wanted to get his apology out of the way. "I'm sorry about last night. I wasn't trying to sabotage anything. I just wanted to..."

To what? Torment himself? Make things worse? He'd succeeded on both counts.

She placed her hand on his thigh. "You don't have to apologize. I'm the one who should be sorry. Not just for last night, but for all of it."

He froze, so taken aback he couldn't form a response. Back when he'd blown up at her and Evan, she'd apologized profusely, explaining how she'd never intended to hurt him. But Evan hadn't reacted the same way. Not once had that fucker ever said he was sorry.

"Knox?" she asked. "Please say something."

"You don't have to apologize. It all happened a long time ago. But..." Knox paused, trying to figure out how to justify his actions. "My coming to the gala wasn't about revenge. I wanted to be a part of *The Hidden Forest* one last time. When I left, I never got to say goodbye. Not to anyone, including the writers I'd worked with. Evan wanted me gone, so I left it all behind."

"I wish he hadn't been so insistent on that, but he didn't trust you. After you were promoted to executive story editor, he started getting paranoid that you'd get him kicked off the show and take all the credit for creating it. That's why he struck first. After you left, everyone kept asking when you were coming back. The only way for Evan to get the upper hand was to discredit you by making up that shit about you being an alcoholic."

He let her words sink in, reliving the agony as if it were only yesterday. "For what it's worth, I never would have kicked him out. Did I get annoyed when he didn't pull his weight? Sure, but I wouldn't have ousted him from his own show and then done my best to slander him."

The guilt on Lila's face spoke volumes. Like she'd realized—even then—how underhanded Evan had been. "After you left, I tried to find you, but you'd disappeared. I wanted to warn you I'd said some hurtful things in the interviews I'd given. I didn't mean them."

For so long, he'd hoped to hear those words. To know that his impulsive fit of temper hadn't distorted all her memories of him. He just wished she'd told him sooner. "Some of those articles were brutal, but I get it. You didn't want to look like the villain."

An elderly couple walked toward the gazebo, and Lila put her head down, as if shielding her appearance. When she spoke again, her voice was so soft he could barely hear her. "It's so much harder for women in this industry. Evan said if I didn't paint you as the bad guy, my reputation would suffer. I'd be called a slut or a cheating bitch. He told me the best way to spin the story, and I stuck with it."

A few of those interviews had dug deep into Knox's soul, making him question himself. After a while, he'd stopped reading anything about *The Hidden Forest*.

"Knox?"

"Sorry. I'd rather not remember that phase of my life. I appreciate the apology, though." He waited until the couple had passed the gazebo before speaking again. "Can I ask you one thing? Did you truly not feel any passion for me?" For years, that confession had hurt him more than almost anything. "Or was that what Evan coached you to say?"

She looked up at him, her ocean-blue eyes misted over with tears. "It was the truth. But that didn't diminish my affection for you. When we were first together, I needed someone to protect me and make me feel cherished, and you took such good care of me. But it wasn't true passion."

Her words hit him like a gut punch, swift and brutal. Would anyone ever feel that way about him? Or was he doomed to take care of women who'd move on once they found someone who offered them more?

She gave him a slight smile. "But Knox? That woman you were with last night? The one who stood up for you? She sounded very passionate."

That made him feel even worse. "Yeah, well, I fucked that up, too. After we left the Grand Duke, we got into an argument, and I drove her away."

He'd been such an idiot. Why had he turned on Charlie like that?

"You might be able to get her back. She knows about your past, doesn't she?"

"She's one of the only people I've told since I moved here. Other than my family." He braced his hands against the bench, knowing he needed to take the next step. "But I'm sick of keeping it hidden."

Charlie had been right in that aspect. He would never put old ghosts to rest until he came to terms with his past.

"Honestly, I can't believe you never spoke up," Lila said.

"Believe me, I thought about it. But after reading those interviews you and Evan gave—and then making the mistake of scrolling through the comments—I backed off. I also figured the truth might harm your reputation." Not that he'd owed her anything. But he'd never wanted to hurt her.

"It might have, but it won't matter as much now. Five years ago, I was still finding my footing. I've come a long way since then. If there's a little backlash, so be it. I'm tired of being Princess Elodie. I've agreed to do a couple of episodes next season, and then I'm bowing out."

Of all the things he'd learned this morning, this was the most startling. Lila Winstead *was* Princess Elodie. Though her star had risen steadily over the past eight years, she wasn't known for much else. "I thought you loved the show."

"I loved it when I first started and for five years after that. But over the last few years, I've done a few indie projects when we were on hiatus and realized I want more from my career. My agent sent me a few screenplays that look promising, and I'm ready for the next step. All of a sudden, I feel like the world is wide open."

She spoke with such passion that he remembered how much he'd admired her, back when she'd shared her dreams with him. "That's great. What does Evan think?"

She grimaced. "He's not happy. We spent months fighting about it. *The Hidden Forest* is his golden goose. It's all he's ever worked on, and he's not ready to let it go." She wiped her eyes with the back of her hand. "We're getting a divorce. We decided to keep it quiet until after the gala."

No matter what she'd done to him, Knox hated seeing her in pain. "I'm sorry."

"No, it's for the best." She gave a short laugh. "I can't believe I ever accused you of being controlling, when all along, Evan's the one who's insisted on controlling my career. I'm tired of it. So... this is just to say, if you want to write a piece exposing him for the backstabbing rat that he is, you have my blessing. I'll back you up, even if it tarnishes my image. I don't owe him anything now."

Knox swallowed, stunned at her admission. He'd never imagined she'd be willing to go to bat for him. But he also didn't want his confession to help fuel her personal vendetta. "Just so we're clear—this isn't me getting back at Evan. It's me reclaiming the narrative for myself. But I could use the support."

"I owe you so much more than that. Is there anything else I can do for you?"

He tried to think of what he could ask her, but nothing came to mind. After all these years, he couldn't conceive of returning to *The Hidden Forest*, even if he was invited back. Nor could he imagine pursuing Lila again. He was in love with someone else.

"I'm good. Just...take care of yourself, okay? I can't wait to see what happens with your career." He meant it, too. He'd never wanted anything but the best for her.

"Thanks, Knox." She leaned over and kissed his cheek, her lips chilly on his skin. She stood up. "Good luck with the story. And with your girlfriend."

He watched her leave but didn't get up to follow. By now, the chill was seeping into his bones, and he was desperate for a warm beverage, but he needed a few minutes to ponder over everything Lila had told him. At most, he'd come prepared to ask for her forgiveness. But instead, she was the one who'd apologized. While her confession didn't erase the torment he'd suffered, it had eased his conscience. Even though he'd been wrong to confront her and Evan in anger, that one incident didn't define him.

And now, if she was willing to back up his claims, there was nothing standing in his way. It was time for him to bring his story into the light.

He pulled out his phone, intending to call Charlie and share his news, but after staring at it for a few minutes, he held off. After their heated exchange, a little cooling-off period might be best. Besides, if he was going to dig deep into his past and bare his soul to the world, he needed to focus. Right now, the words were piling up in his head, ideas of what he wanted to say and how he wanted to frame it. He needed to make his story resonate without coming across as bitter and vindictive.

And he needed to ensure it got the maximum amount of exposure.

He pulled out his phone and called Logan. When he got his friend's voicemail, he left a message. "Hey, man, it's Knox. I know you're coming to Victoria in a couple of days, but I need to talk to you as soon as possible. It's about an article I'm planning to write."

Twenty-Six

CHARLIE WASN'T THE TYPE TO WALLOW IN MISERY. EVEN at her weepiest, she liked to take action. So, when she woke up on Sunday, her eyes raw from crying, her heart aching from her argument with Knox, she didn't go back to bed. She took a long, hot shower and forced herself to put on real clothes. Pajamas weren't an option.

She needed two things: strong coffee and someone to talk to. Otherwise, last night's disaster would keep playing on a loop in her head.

Though it was only nine, she figured Rosie would be awake. She sent her a text.

Charlie: Any chance you want to meet up for coffee? Last night's gala went sideways and I'm a hot mess.

Rosie replied immediately: Oh no! I'm sorry it didn't go well. I can't leave my apartment because I'm in the middle of a huge baking project. Do you want to come over?

Charlie: Sure. Should I bring coffee?

Rosie: I already made a pot. Just come prepared to frost dozens of cookies!

Charlie wasn't sure what this baking project entailed, but she grabbed a gingham apron from her kitchen and stuffed it in a tote bag before heading out.

Rosie lived in a small, one-bedroom apartment in a hip part of town known as Cook Street Village. Parking in her neighborhood could be tricky, but it was early enough that Charlie found a spot around the corner. When Rosie opened the door to her apartment, she was wearing an apron streaked with orange and black frosting.

"Come in," she said. "I'd hug you, but I don't want to get frosting on your sweatshirt."

"Thanks." Charlie surveyed Rosie's kitchen. Her breakfast bar was covered with trays of freshly baked cookies shaped like bats and pumpkins. "What's all this for?"

"Drew volunteers at a women's shelter downtown. Usually, he just plays Santa, but they need help with today's Halloween party. He signed me up to provide dozens of cookies, and we're bringing them over at two. I've got most of them baked, but they still need to be iced."

"I'd be glad to help." Charlie took out her apron and put it on. "Any chance I could get a cup of coffee first?"

"No problem. It's just Colombian roast from my coffee maker, but I've got pumpkin spice–flavored creamer." She poured Charlie a cup and handed her the bottle.

Charlie added a splash of cream to her coffee and settled on a stool at the breakfast bar. As the first hit of caffeine rushed through her system, she released a satisfied sigh. "I needed that. Once I'm done, I can pitch in."

"I'm glad you're here. Drew offered to help, but he was hoping to squeeze in a long run this morning. He's training for a half-marathon in December."

"Won't it be too cold by then?" Charlie asked.

"You'd think so, wouldn't you? Apparently, it's a very popular race. It's also Santa-themed, so it's right up his alley." Rosie grinned. "Now, drink up so I can put you to work. These pumpkins aren't going to frost themselves."

"Yes, ma'am." While Rosie's coffee couldn't compare to Alma's, the pumpkin spice creamer was a nice touch. Knox would have hated it. Thinking of him made Charlie's eyes well up with tears, but she wiped them away. Today wasn't for crying; it was for figuring out her next steps.

Drew came into the kitchen, wearing shorts over black running tights, a Northlife Fitness hoodie, and a fleece toque. Even bundled up, there was no denying his innate hotness. He was lean and muscular, with the cutest dimple when he smiled. Though he wasn't Charlie's type, he was a great match for Rosie.

"Hey, Charlie. Thanks for helping," he said. "Now I can go running without any guilt."

"Are you sure you're dressed warmly enough? Even with the sun out, it's chillier than I thought. The wind is vicious."

"I'll be fine. I consider it a challenge."

Rosie rolled her eyes. "I still don't see the appeal, but have a good run."

He leaned over and gave her a quick kiss. "Thanks. Save a cookie for me."

After he left, Charlie turned to her friend. "Things are good between you two?"

"They're great, though I'll never be into running. Hiking, sure. But running? Not unless someone's chasing me." She set a bowl of orange icing next to one of the trays. "You can start with the pumpkin cookies. Once you frost them, you need to decorate them with Halloween sprinkles. While you're doing that, I want to hear all about last night."

"I'll give you the full recap." Charlie finished her coffee and set down the mug.

She was glad Rosie had asked her to help frost the cookies, since focusing on the task at hand might stave off another round of tears. She spread the orange icing over each pumpkin cookie, describing the gala as she did so. When she got to the painful confrontation with Lila and Evan, her throat clogged with emotion, but she kept going. Right up to the heated argument in Knox's truck that had put an end to their evening. This time, she let a few tears fall before wiping them away with her sleeve.

When she was done, Rosie spoke up. "That sucks. I'm so sorry it turned out that way."

"Me, too. The worst part is it didn't have to end like that. If I hadn't gone off on Lila, Evan wouldn't have come to her rescue and kicked us out of the gala. I messed up everything."

The timer went off, and Rosie took another batch of cookies out of the oven. Since the breakfast bar and kitchen counters were full, she set the baking sheet on the coffee table across from her couch. "Maybe you said too much, but you were standing up for Knox. You really care about him, right?"

"I do. We haven't been together for very long, but I've never felt like this about anyone. Not even Randolph, and I was engaged to him."

"Then your reaction was justified. If someone hurt Drew that way, I wouldn't be able to keep quiet."

"But I still wouldn't let it go, even after we left the Grand Duke. And..." Charlie's breath hitched. "Knox got so mad at me." She dabbed at her eyes with a tissue, trying to get a handle on her shaky emotions.

Rosie frowned. "He shouldn't have treated you like that."

While Charlie appreciated her friend's support, she couldn't let Knox take all the blame. "It was harsh, but nothing he said was a lie."

Giving her a nod, Rosie wiped her hands on her apron and

picked up a bowl of black frosting. "So...do you want sympathy or advice? I'm happy to dole out either."

Sympathy might improve Charlie's mood, but it wouldn't solve anything. "Advice. Don't be afraid to give me some tough love."

Rosie dipped a knife into the frosting and began icing the bat-shaped cookies. "How long have you been living at your parents' place?"

Charlie cringed. "Three years. But before you say anything, you have to remember I was desperate when I moved into that apartment."

"That was after you broke up with Randolph, right? You didn't have anywhere else to go."

Charlie looked down, too ashamed to face her. She swirled her knife in the orange frosting to soften it up a little. "That wasn't the only reason. I've never told anyone this, but I was also dealing with a lot of credit card debt."

"Really? You always seem so careful with money. Other than your coffee addiction, which I can relate to."

That made Charlie laugh. She and Rosie had often joked that too much of their salary went toward supporting Alma's Beanery. But the credit card debt had been no laughing matter.

"When I was dating Randolph, he had high expectations. He pressured me into joining an expensive gym *and* a yoga studio so I'd stay in shape. He even hung a calendar in our kitchen and asked me to write down my workouts. If I missed a day, he'd give me a hard time about it."

"What the hell?" Rosie stared at her, gripping her knife tightly. "That's horribly controlling. Drew literally works as a personal trainer, and he'd never pull shit like that."

The memories made Charlie sick with anxiety. "It gets worse. For every social event we attended, he wanted me dressed in designer clothes. He didn't like me to repeat outfits, so I went shopping constantly. When I told my mom about it, she said,

'Don't worry. Once you're married, he can take care of you.' So I didn't. Until I was single and realized how much debt I was in."

"Oh shit, Charlie. I'm sorry." Rosie passed her a shaker jar filled with orange and black sprinkles. "Don't worry about making a mess because I can clean it up later."

"Thanks." Charlie opened the jar and shook it over the pumpkin-shaped cookies. "My dad offered to let me stay in the garage apartment, rent-free. Originally, he'd built it for his mom—my Granny Helen—who came to live with us when my grandpa died. Once she went into assisted living, the apartment wasn't being used. Dad told me to fix it up however I liked. I only intended to stay for a year, but somehow..."

Somehow, one year had become two and then three. Even when Charlie had chafed at her mom's intrusiveness, she hadn't made any steps to move out.

Rosie began adorning the bat-shaped cookies with sprinkles. "I don't blame you for taking advantage. Considering how much I pay for rent, I can see the appeal. That being said, even if my parents won the lottery and built me an apartment over their garage, I'd never live with them."

"I thought you liked your family. Didn't you say your mom stopped bugging you about being single after you and Drew got together?"

"That helped, but she can still be a lot. Lately, she's been asking when Drew and I plan to get married. And whether we want kids. It's better if I limit my time with her to holidays and family dinners. That way, I can retain my independence *and* my sanity."

Charlie remembered attending one of those dinners and envying Rosie's bond with her family. But she also recalled all the times Rosie had complained about her mom's matchmaking attempts. "Do you think I should move out?"

"It's up to you. If you're fine with the way things are, you don't have to change. But it sounds like your mom is up in your business a lot. And it's not cool she's been trying to get you back together with your ex."

"Yeah, even though I made it clear I'm not into Randolph, that doesn't mean she won't try again. Or attempt to set me up with someone more 'suitable' than Knox. In terms of money, I'm doing okay. I don't have any more debt, and I pay off my balance every month. But I still don't think I could afford my own place."

Rosie rummaged around in her cupboard until she found a couple of cookie tins. She set them on one of the counters. "What about moving in with Laurel? She told me she'll need a roommate in December."

Charlie recalled Laurel mentioning it during their coffee run to Alma's. At the time, she hadn't considered herself a possible candidate. "That would work. I'm surprised she hasn't found someone already."

"The timing's tricky because it's so close to the holidays. But if you're going to take this step, do it for yourself, not for Knox. You spent all that time trying to please your mom and Randolph. Make sure this is what you really want."

Charlie nodded. It might not be an easy transition, but it was the right move. No matter what happened with Knox, she needed some distance from her parents. This way, her mother wouldn't know whether she'd had a "friend" over to spend the night. And she wouldn't randomly pop in to invite Charlie to an event where she'd lined up a potential beau.

"I'm sure this is what I want." Just saying the words strengthened her resolve. "I'm going to call Laurel and see if she still needs a roommate."

"I'll bet she'll be glad to hear from you." Rosie set her bowl in the sink. "What about Knox? Are you going to try talking to him?"

"I want to, but...he might need a little more time to cool off." Things between them were so fragile she didn't want to push him too hard. "We don't work together until Tuesday, so I'll wait until then." Seeing him in person would give her a better sense of his mood.

"That's a good idea. And if things work out with Laurel, he'll probably be happy you took the initiative."

"I hope so." First, Charlie needed to apologize for getting him thrown out of the gala. Then she could tell him how their argument had inspired her to take control of her life. Surely, that would help him realize how much she cared about him. Even if their relationship was pretty new, she didn't want to lose him.

But before she tackled Knox, she needed to talk to Laurel.

And then she had to break the news to her parents.

That was the part that scared her the most. Not the act of moving out. But the conversation she'd need to have, to tell her mother what she'd decided.

Twenty-Seven

After spending the past three years living above her parents' garage, wavering over whether to strike out on her own again, Charlie didn't expect to resolve her dilemma so effortlessly. But by Sunday evening, it was done. All it had taken was a phone call with Laurel, a meet-up at her apartment, and a handshake agreement. Come December first, Charlie would be moving in with her. Though Laurel's building was on the older side, it was within walking distance of two coffeehouses and a fifteen-minute drive from the Duchess.

Only one step remained. Charlie needed to talk to her parents.

Maybe her news could wait. After all, she'd accomplished a lot in one day.

Don't be a coward.

If she didn't face them now, she'd probably put it off until the last possible minute. Better to give them plenty of notice. She went inside their house and found them seated in the living room. Her father was reading a thick tome about the Hudson's Bay Company while her mother leafed through a fashion magazine. Neither of them appeared to be dressed for an evening out. Charlie caught a whiff of something savory and heard activity from the kitchen.

Her father looked up from his book. "Would you like to join us for dinner? Magda's making hunter's stew and steamed dumplings."

Magda was a Polish chef who cooked for the Frasers three nights a week. On those occasions when Charlie had joined her parents, the food had been excellent. The hunter's stew was among her favorites, with its mixture of kielbasa sausage, potatoes, bacon, and sauerkraut.

"Thanks, but I'll pass." She sat down on the stiff, floral-print armchair across from the couch and took a deep breath. "I wanted to let you know I'll be leaving the apartment at the end of November. I'm moving in with my friend Laurel, who works with me at the Duchess."

"Are you sure, muffin?" her father asked. "Even if you're sharing a place, rent in Victoria can be quite steep."

"I'll be okay. I created a preliminary budget to keep my spending on track." She'd borrowed the template from Rosie, who was a whiz at spreadsheets. "I'll still come visit, but I'm ready to try living on my own again."

Her father's warm smile crinkled the corners of his eyes. "Obviously, we'll miss having you around, but it might be time for you to spread your wings."

"Thanks, Dad."

Her mother slapped the magazine on the coffee table with a loud whack. "Really, Art? Last time Charlie was left to her own devices, she racked up a significant amount of debt."

Charlie clenched her jaw. Of course her mother would bring that up. "Only because I was trying to meet Randolph's expectations. But I paid off all my credit cards."

"Is this about that...boy? The one with the truck? Are you moving in with him?"

Had her mother heard nothing? "No. I just told you—I'm moving in with my friend Laurel. This isn't about Knox."

"Then why move out now? Was this *his* idea?"

Even if Charlie's argument with Knox had led her down this path, she'd still made the decision on her own. Now that she'd set her course, she couldn't believe she'd waited this long. "No. I felt like it was time. But since we're on the subject of Knox, I'm not happy with that stunt you pulled on Thanksgiving."

Her mother waved a hand in dismissal. "That was two weeks ago. Water under the bridge."

"Not to me. When you invited Randolph to join us and encouraged him to brag about his promotion, you made Knox feel uncomfortable. Like he paled in comparison." Charlie rubbed her forehead as the first inklings of a headache nagged at her. "Knox is a really nice guy. I don't understand why you're set against him."

"Because he's a man with a dead-end job. How do you expect him to take care of you?"

"To take *care* of me?" What kind of old-school bullshit was that? "This isn't the 1950s. I can take care of myself."

"That remains to be seen. Even if you manage to stay out of debt, your future is hardly secure. What if the Duchess goes out of business? Marrying a man like Randolph would ensure you never have to worry about money again."

Why was her mother so fixated on this? It wasn't as if she'd grown up in poverty.

Charlie addressed her father, hoping he'd take her side. "Dad? What do you think?"

With a drawn-out sigh, he set down his book, as though he wasn't keen on mediating between the two of them. "About you moving out? Or about the fellow you're dating?"

"About Knox."

"I rather liked him." He took off his reading glasses and polished them with a handkerchief. "He was well-spoken with an excellent knowledge of local history. But regardless of what I think, you're old enough to decide for yourself. The same goes for your choice to strike out on your own. I have faith in you."

Charlie's eyes welled up in gratitude. Receiving his validation was a huge win. She gnawed on her lip, wanting her mother to agree with him. "Mom? Please don't be upset. It's not like I'm moving to Toronto. I can come back and visit anytime you want."

"I just worry about you," she said. "You haven't always made the best decisions."

Like dating Randolph? Or spending an exorbitant amount to keep him happy? In both instances, Charlie had been heavily influenced by her mother, but she also bore some of the responsibility since she hadn't possessed the courage to stand up for herself. "That's true. When I was with Randolph, I let him bully me into spending too much. He used to get annoyed if I wore the same outfits too many times. Or if he thought my clothes looked cheap. He insisted I get my hair and my nails done all the time. Just so I'd look good when we were together."

Her mother frowned. "Do you really think it's fair to place all the blame on Randolph?"

"No, because I should have stood up to him a lot sooner. I was so afraid of upsetting him that I put up with all his criticism, no matter how bad it made me feel." She gave a short laugh. "I don't even like skiing, and I spent a fortune on all that equipment, just to make him happy."

She wished she could take back the money she'd spent. After she and Randolph had broken up, she hadn't kept most of the clothes because they didn't suit her. Instead, she'd donated them to a women's shelter.

"But Knox doesn't make you feel this way?" Her mother's voice was more curious than adversarial. Like she was actually trying to understand Charlie.

"He likes me just as I am. But like I said, this isn't about him. It's about me wanting my own place. I'll be okay, and I promise I'll reach out if I need help."

"Very well. But if you don't have any plans tonight, you should join us for dinner. You love Magda's cooking."

While her mother wasn't exactly gushing with praise, this

invitation was an olive branch. Charlie wasn't about to turn it down. "You've convinced me. I'll join you."

Given that she'd skipped today's grocery store run, the alternative was a can of tomato soup or a bowl of cereal. Magda's hearty stew sounded infinitely better.

ON MONDAY MORNING, KNOX WOKE WITH A SENSE OF purpose. After spending much of Sunday outlining the article he planned to write, he forced himself to deal with the most painful aspect of it. Buried deep in his closet were two cardboard boxes, containing three years' worth of memories from his time at *The Hidden Forest*. Old scripts, notebooks crammed with ideas, memorabilia from various events, free merch, and his own personal journals. Before leaving Vancouver, he'd packed everything up and almost tossed the whole lot in the dumpster. In the end, he'd taken the boxes with him but never opened them.

He couldn't avoid them any longer. If he wanted his story to be accurate, he needed to revisit his old memories, no matter how excruciating.

Today would require more coffee than usual, so he made a whole pot. Taking a cup with him, he went into the guest room, where he'd set the boxes. He opened them and tipped them out, spreading the contents across the floor. As he started leafing through his old journals, his phone buzzed with a text.

> Logan: Got your message. Work's crazy right now, but if you're ready to spill everything, I'm all for it. I'll call you tonight.

> Knox: No rush. I haven't started writing yet.

He was tempted to text Charlie. She might be glad to hear what he'd decided. Unless she was still simmering with anger over

Saturday night. For now, he'd hold off contacting her until he'd written the article, just so he wouldn't get derailed. Before getting started, he found Zack and Norah's business cards and emailed both of them, telling them what he was up to. He wasn't sure whether they'd want to be involved, but he figured they might appreciate the opportunity.

After three hours, he'd written a very rough draft. A few times, he'd been tempted to say, "fuck it" and forget the whole thing. Reading through his journals forced him to relive the humiliation all over again. To recall the hurt he'd experienced when he realized how badly Evan had betrayed him. But he pushed past the pain and kept going.

When he needed a break from rehashing his past, he threw on a fleece jacket and headed outside. Though the wind was brisk, the chill revitalized him. He walked to Chuck's Deli and picked up an Italian meatball sub for lunch.

He was just heading back when his phone rang. Pulling it out of his pocket, he peeked at the caller ID: Alejandro Rivera, the AGM of the Grand Duke.

Fuck me. Knox had forgotten he was due for an ass-kicking. Better to deal with it now.

"Hello, is this Knox?" Alejandro asked.

"Hey, Alejandro. I'm sorry about Saturday night, but I..." Knox hesitated as he scrambled to come up with a plausible excuse for leaving early. He couldn't risk revealing the truth until he published his article.

Alejandro's terse voice broke the silence. "How is it that you know Lila Winstead personally?"

This was *not* how Knox had expected the conversation to go. "It's a long story, but we're old friends. Years ago, we worked together in Vancouver. Why do you ask?"

"She sought me out yesterday and told me you weren't to blame for leaving your post early." He clicked his tongue. "For a bartender, you certainly have friends in high places."

Damn. Knox couldn't help but smile. Oh, to have been a fly on the wall when Lila reached out to Alejandro. He could only imagine the smug hotelier's stunned reaction. "Did she tell you what happened?"

"She said her useless husband was drunk and unruly and that you tried to calm him down. When he threatened to call security, Lila suggested you and Charlie leave before things got ugly. For that, you have my profound thanks. Dealing with celebrities is difficult enough without getting caught in a tawdry scandal."

A rush of gratitude engulfed Knox. Lila hadn't been kidding when she'd promised to have his back. "You're welcome. Does that mean Charlie and I will still get paid?"

"Only for the hours you worked. No exceptions. But since your 'friend' Lila promised to leave a glowing review of our hotel, I'd like to offer you a gift certificate for our restaurant. It's one of the most highly reviewed dining establishments in Victoria."

Of course it is. "Sounds good to me. Should I come by and pick it up?"

"No need. I'll have one of our peons drop it off at your bar. Good day."

After Alejandro hung up, Knox stared at the phone. The fact that Lila had already come through for him increased his resolve. If he kept working on his article, he could send it to Logan for review before he arrived at the Duchess on Friday with the crew from *Canada's Most Haunted*.

Once again, Knox was tempted to text Charlie, but he held off. Better to wait until after the article was done. Then he'd make it up to her by using that gift certificate to treat her to a five-star meal.

<h1 style="text-align:center">Twenty-Eight</h1>

Now that Charlie had decided to move out, she wanted to tell Knox as soon as possible. Preferably in person. All day Monday, she was itching to text him, but she forced herself to wait. Once he came in to work on Tuesday, she'd seek him out. She'd also apologize for causing a scene on Saturday night. At least the incident hadn't gone viral. She'd been following coverage of the gala—including stalking Evan and Lila on social media—but she hadn't seen one mention of Mac Iverson's unexpected return.

But come Tuesday, she barely had a moment to breathe, let alone send a text. Wednesday and Thursday were even worse. The hotel was at one hundred percent occupancy, filled with guests who'd booked rooms after learning the Duchess would be featured on an episode of *Canada's Most Haunted*. Thanks to the episode's teaser, which mentioned the hotel's haunted storage room, the front desk had received dozens of requests for a "private tour" of the room. So far, Preston had denied them all.

Meanwhile, the Gilded Lily had been so busy Charlie had only crossed paths with Knox twice. Though he hadn't seemed angry, he hadn't lingered to talk to her, either. Both times, he'd greeted her with a slight smile and a quick "Hey, Charlie," as if they were acquaintances rather than lovers who'd spent last Friday night in each other's arms.

Then on Wednesday, he'd sent her a cryptic text:

> Sorry for the silence. I'm not mad, I promise. I just need time to work some stuff out. Talk soon.

While his texts were often short and to the point, they usually made sense. Not this one. What kind of "stuff" was he talking about? Did it pertain to the two of them? Was he trying to "work out" whether they should stay together? Maybe after Saturday's debacle, he'd decided romantic relationships weren't worth the trouble.

She wanted to ask him more but decided against it. Given that she'd already pushed him over the edge on Saturday night, demanding answers wouldn't help her case. She needed to trust him and give him space. By next week, they'd have more breathing room to talk things over.

Being patient sucked. But it was better than forcing a confrontation that neither of them had the bandwidth to deal with right now.

On Friday afternoon, she waited at the front desk for the film crew from *Canada's Most Haunted*. When Logan had called her earlier to confirm the logistics, he'd mentioned they'd be arriving between three and four. The team planned to do a preliminary walk-through of the storage room and get baseline readings, followed by three in-person interviews: Charlie, Celia, and Gertrude. Charlie had already asked the two women to show up at seven.

When Preston stopped by, Charlie forced a courteous smile on her face. If dealing with needy guests wasn't bad enough, her boss had also been more demanding than usual. Three times today, he'd reminded her to contact him the minute the film crew showed up.

"Good afternoon, Mr. Hargreaves," she said. "They're not here yet."

"I'm aware of that. While you're waiting, I think you should visit the storage room one more time. I want to make certain it hasn't been disturbed."

"I don't see how that would be possible. No one can get into that room without a key."

Preston rocked back on his feet. "Well...I might have lent out a key to one of our guests. A VIP with important ties to the hotel's owners."

Charlie repressed a groan. "He went up there by himself? Did he get locked in?"

"No. He told me he took a stroll around the room but didn't get stuck there. He was rather disappointed, even though I warned him it didn't happen every time. Anyway, I made sure he returned the key." He took it out of his suit jacket pocket and handed it to her. "Why don't you go take a peek?"

"Sir, I don't think that's necessary."

Preston crossed his arms and stared her down. "It's not a request, Charlotte. I need you to go up there and make sure everything is in order."

Given that she'd been on edge all week, she had no desire to worsen her distress by getting locked in a haunted room. "Do you want to come with me? To make sure I don't get trapped inside?"

"Are you seriously that worried about it?" His voice dripped with condescension. "Just prop the door open. At most, it'll take you ten minutes."

Easy for him to say. He'd never gotten stuck there before. But she knew better than to disobey a direct order. After asking the front desk clerk to watch out for the film crew, she took the elevator up to the third floor. She approached the storage room with trepidation, still remembering how tense she'd felt when she and Knox had gotten locked in. How her initial fear had morphed into despair and then into an abrupt burst of anger.

At least she wouldn't erupt in another sneezing fit. In anticipation of escorting the ghost hunters up here, she'd taken a preemptive dose of allergy meds.

She unlocked the door and propped it open with an old wooden chair. While she would have preferred to leave it that way, a passing guest might decide to poke their head in. Instead, she found an old, musty hardcover and wedged it in the doorjamb before closing the door. This way, it couldn't slam shut and lock her in.

Shaking off her nerves, she flicked on the light and made a slow circuit of the room. As far as she could tell, nothing had been disturbed. A layer of dust still covered the furniture and the cardboard boxes. Atop an antique dresser was the wind-up phonograph Knox had noticed before; beside it was a stack of vinyl records in faded brown paper sleeves. Like last time, the faint scent of rose-scented soap tickled her nose. But even if there was a stash of hotel soap somewhere in the room, by now, it would have faded. The scent had to be coming from Maeve.

A sudden bang made her pulse race. The door had slammed shut, sending the book flying across the room.

She froze in place, her heart hammering in a frantic rhythm. Was someone playing a prank on her? Or had the ghost trapped her in here again?

"Maeve, is that you?"

No response.

Approaching the door cautiously, she turned the knob. Like last time, it refused to budge. Nor did her key succeed in opening the door.

Damn you, Preston. What was he thinking, sending her up here alone?

Despite the warmth of the room, an icy sensation danced along her spine. She plopped down on the antique settee facing the door. Reaching into her blazer pocket for her phone, she braced herself for the worst.

Just as she suspected. No bars. No Wi-Fi.

"Joke's on you, Maeve. This time, I'm prepared." She unclipped the two-way radio from the waistband of her skirt. "I've been carrying this sucker around all day."

She turned it on, but it didn't light up. *Shit.* Was Maeve interfering with it? Or had she forgotten to replace the batteries? What with everything going on at the hotel, the second explanation was totally plausible.

Wrapping her arms around herself, she closed her eyes and tried to find a sense of balance. *It's okay. It's going to be okay.*

If she didn't return to her post, Preston would come looking for her. Or the team from *Canada's Most Haunted* would arrive and ask to visit the storage room. At that point, someone would bring them here and open the door. All she had to do was wait it out.

Right?

A sense of dread crept over her as she recalled her interview with Gertrude, who'd vacillated between misery and rage during her three hours in captivity. Rather than spiral into a full-blown panic attack, Charlie kept her breaths steady and even.

But her attempt at relaxation was no match for the crushing sadness that engulfed her, like a dark cloud blotting out the sun. With it came a fresh resurgence of guilt.

Admit it, you drove Knox away. You pushed him too hard, and he's done with you.

No. Maeve's spirit was preying upon her worst fears.

You saw how beautiful Lila was. How did you think you could compete with her?

It wasn't a competition. Knox was completely over Lila. Wasn't he?

You ruined everything, and now it's too late.

"Stop it!" She felt foolish yelling at an empty room, but she couldn't think of how else to fight back. "Just because you messed up your chance at love doesn't mean you have to make everyone else miserable! Why can't you be a force for good?"

Was it fair to blame these feelings on a ghost? Weren't they the fears she'd been secretly harboring since Saturday night?

As Maeve's spirit battered her with negativity, the tears came of their own accord, and she was powerless to stop them. She placed her head in her hands. "I was going to tell him I was in love with him, and now it's too late. He probably doesn't even want me anymore."

As the door creaked open, her spine stiffened. Had Maeve relented?

Knox stood in the doorway, brandishing the other key. "Of course I want you. Nothing about that has changed."

Her joy at seeing him was chased out by a sudden, vicious anger. Like someone had flipped a switch, setting her emotions ablaze. "You've barely spoken to me since Saturday! All you did was send one lousy text! What's wrong with you!" She clenched her hands, trying to fight off the fury Maeve was generating inside her. "Stop it! Go away!"

Knox flinched, visibly stricken by her words. He took a step back. "If that's what you want, I'll leave. But it's not safe for you to stay here on your own."

"No, I didn't mean you! I meant *her*. Maeve. I...I just." Black spots dotted her vision. Knox became a fuzzy blur.

She closed her eyes as a wave of dizziness took hold.

Twenty-Nine

What the hell just happened? One minute, Charlie was yelling at him, and the next, she looked like she was about to pass out.

Knox rushed toward her, letting the door slam shut behind him. He sat beside her on the settee. "Charlie? Are you okay?"

With infinite slowness, she opened her eyes and rubbed her forehead. "Knox? I just...got so dizzy. What are you doing here?"

He took her hand, gripping it tightly, as if his touch could keep her from fading away. "I came here because I was worried about you. When I got in at three, I stopped by the front desk to see if the film crew had arrived. Preston said he'd sent you up here, so I wanted to make sure you were okay."

Charlie wiped the tears from her eyes. "Thanks for coming to check on me. I tried to wedge the door open, but it slammed shut. Then the ghost got to me. I was hit with a barrage of emotions—none of them good. I couldn't control any of it."

He placed a gentle kiss on her forehead and inhaled the familiar scent of her lavender shampoo. "I've got you, sweetheart. Why'd you come here all by yourself?"

"It wasn't by choice. Preston insisted on it because he let a VIP visit the room earlier. When I told him I was scared to go on my own, he dismissed me as if my fears didn't matter."

"That's because he doesn't believe the storage room is haunted." At Charlie's shocked look, he nodded. "He thinks it's all bunk, but he's going along with it to draw guests to the hotel. He's such a tool."

"No kidding. But the thing is...even if we forced him to face this room alone, he might not feel anything. When I called Celia yesterday to set up the time for her interview, we started talking about Maeve and the way her negativity only seems to affect women. When you and I were stuck here the first time, I'm the one who got frightened and angry. Neither you nor Glen were affected when you went in here with Celia. And all the staff who were written up for refusing to go into this room were women." She frowned in concentration. "Is the room affecting you at all? Any powerful feelings of misery or rage?"

"Nope. But I didn't feel those things the other times, either."

"But you believe me, right?"

"Absolutely." For all his skepticism, he couldn't discount the way this room had affected Charlie. Or the evidence she'd uncovered of women who'd reacted similarly. He stood up. "I should check the door. I meant to keep it open, but I was too worried about you."

"Thanks, Knox." Her affectionate smile made him glad he'd rushed in after her, even if it meant being locked in again.

When he turned the door handle, it didn't budge. Since Charlie's key was already sticking out of the keyhole, he tucked his key in the pocket of his pants. "Looks like we're stuck, but we'll be all right. The crew will be here soon, and once they get the other key, they can unlock the door." He paused. "*Is* there another key?"

She wrung her hands together. "I think so? Maybe Rosie has one. Or Joe from Facilities? I'm pretty sure there's at least one more." She scanned the room furtively. "Being trapped doesn't scare me as much as losing control of my emotions. I don't want to say something I'll regret."

He sat back down and took her hand again, stroking it softly. "Speaking of regret, I'm sorry I've been shutting you out."

"It's okay. When I yelled at you earlier—that wasn't me. Maeve got into my head. I know we've both been busy. I could have texted you myself, but I wanted to give us some time to cool off after Saturday night. And...I was kind of worried you might want to break up with me." She looked away, as if afraid to meet his eyes. "I wouldn't blame you, either, not after the way I botched everything at the gala."

Guilt swamped him. He'd been so fixated on finishing his tell-all he hadn't taken the time to explain why he'd been so distant. "I'm not mad about that. I was just trying to get my shit in order before I talked to you. After I dropped you off on Saturday, I wasn't sure what to do. But on Sunday morning, Lila reached out to me, and we met up for a bit. It was eye-opening, to say the least. She and Evan are getting a divorce."

"Oh." Charlie blinked quickly, then wiped her eyes again. "Um...that's great. If you want her back, I understand."

Jesus, he was making a mess of this. "*No.* I don't want her back. I'm in love with *you*, Charlie."

Not the way he'd intended to proclaim his love, but her sweet smile made his heart soar.

"Oh, Knox. Really?"

He gave her hand a quick squeeze. "One hundred percent. But let me finish. Lila wanted to apologize. Not just for the gala, but for all the shit that happened after she dumped me, like those interviews where she painted me as the bad guy. She only said those things because Evan insisted on it. When I told her I was thinking of writing a piece explaining the real reason I left *The Hidden Forest,* she agreed to back me up."

"You're going to do it? For real?"

"Yep. Feel free to say, 'I told you so,' if you want."

She gave him a sassy grin. "Nah, it's enough to hear you admit it. Then what happened?"

"After I talked to her, I contacted Logan. He got back to me on Monday night and said he'd reach out to a few places to see if any of them would be willing to run my story. I also emailed Zack and Norah, who agreed to comment on Evan's behavior. Since then, I've spent every spare minute working on the article. That's why I've been so distant—it wasn't easy delving into my past, and I knew if I let myself get derailed, I might not finish the piece. With Logan's help, it should come out next week. Lila's also going to release the news about her divorce around the same time. The internet will have a field day."

"Yes!" Charlie pumped her fist. "A big one-two punch to Evan! I'm so proud of you."

Though he was glad to be shaking off the chains of his past, he still had unfinished business to take care of. Like apologizing to Charlie for hurting her. "I'm sorry I was such a jerk on Saturday night. I should have been grateful you were standing up for me, but I took out all my anger and frustration on you. I was way out of line."

"I'm sorry, too. I didn't mean to be so pushy. As it turns out, you're not the only one who needed a little pressure to get their act together. I decided it was time to leave the nest, so I arranged to move in with Laurel, starting December first. I also told my mom I wasn't okay with her springing Randolph on us at Thanksgiving."

While Knox was pleased she'd stood up for herself, he didn't want her to suffer financially. "This won't be a hardship, will it? I know rent's expensive."

"I can handle it. I'm looking forward to sharing an apartment with Laurel. And I won't miss having my mom scrutinize my every move. Especially if a certain someone sleeps over."

"You can count on it." Pulling her closer, he brushed his lips against hers. Soft at first, and then with a little more pressure, his hand curling around the back of her neck. She tasted sweet and delicious, with just a hint of peppermint. Though only six days had passed since he'd last kissed her, it felt like months. With a groan of pleasure, she nipped at his lower lip and then deepened the kiss, twining her tongue with his.

When they broke apart, she peeked at the door. "Darn. I was hoping our positive energy would be strong enough to break Maeve's hold. I think that's what happened last time."

"What do you mean?" he asked.

"We were arguing, and you almost kissed me. Remember?"

"I remember." At the time, he'd cursed himself for not sealing the deal and giving her a proper kiss. "Is that why you kissed me back just now?"

"No, silly. I did it because I've missed you. But I also figured good vibes couldn't hurt."

To think he might have lost this extraordinary woman to his own pigheadedness. A woman—as Lila had said—who felt passionately about him. "Good vibes, hmmm? I'm happy to keep kissing you. Or you could unzip that skirt and give me a little more access?"

"Tempting, but kind of risky." She bit her lower lip, a gesture that made her look even sexier. "How about some music? That always livens up the mood. Like in *Elf,* when they start singing Christmas carols so Santa's sleigh can get off the ground."

Not going to happen. "I can't sing worth a damn. That's why I never do karaoke."

She leapt up from the settee. "I've got it. There's an old-timey phonograph in here. I wonder if it still works."

"I'll bet it does. You have to crank the handle first."

The player sat atop the dresser, still collecting dust. He wound it up, and Charlie pulled a 78 record from a faded paper sleeve. "Try this one. It's from the 1930s."

When he put it on the turntable and set the needle down, it

gave a satisfying crackle. A woman's sultry voice filled the room, and he instantly recognized the tune from an old Steven Spielberg movie. "This is 'Smoke Gets in Your Eyes.' I love this song."

She gave him a bemused smile. "You *love* this song? You realize it's very sappy, right?"

He didn't care. Nor did he pause to consider his actions when he beckoned Charlie toward him. "Dance with me."

She stepped closer and put her arms around his neck. He grasped her waist, pulling her tight against him, and swayed with her. The fragrant aroma of her lavender shampoo was like a balm to his senses. He didn't care how long they were stuck in this room. He was just so fucking grateful to have her back.

"I was going to wait until next month to tell you," she said. "But I can't hold out that long. I'm head over heels in love with you."

"Me, too, sweetheart. This time, I'm not letting you go."

With a pop, the key burst out of the lock and clattered to the floor. The door swung open. Knox released Charlie and scrambled to grab the door before it misbehaved again. He leaned against it, letting a wave of fresh air into the room.

Charlie clasped her hands together. "We did it! And you danced with me!"

"If you tell anyone, I'll deny it." In actuality, he'd enjoyed every second, but he had his grumpy reputation to uphold.

"Your secret's safe with me." She took the record off the turntable, placed it back inside the paper sleeve, and set it on the dresser. "Let's get out of here before Maeve changes her mind."

He scooped up her key from the floor and waited until she was safely in the hallway before closing the door behind him. He still couldn't figure out Maeve's endgame. Was she vengeful or just plain lonely?

Charlie pulled out her phone. "It's working again! Good thing since the front desk just left me a message. The crew is here."

Taking her hand, he ran with her toward the elevator. A

lightness flowed through him, like a weight had been lifted from his shoulders. At the front desk, Logan and the four members of the film crew stood chatting with Preston. After a quick round of introductions, the clerk on duty handed the guests their key cards.

"Let me know when you're ready to check out the storage room," Charlie said to them. "I'll take you up there so you can see the space and set up your equipment."

Knox handed her one of the brass keys. "You need me to come with?"

"I'm good. I'm going to contact Joe from Facilities and have him meet us there. I need him to set up a barrier around the room so no one tries to get in. He can also make sure the door stays open while the guys are setting up. But thanks. I'll stop by the Lily when I get a break."

While the other members of the ghost-hunting team left to go up to their rooms, Logan lingered behind. "Got a minute?" he asked Knox. "I have a few updates for you."

"Sure." Knox gestured for Logan to follow him toward the Gilded Lily. "The bar's not open yet, but I can fix you a drink."

Logan grinned. "I wouldn't say no to a cocktail."

The entrance was closed off with two metal stanchions and a thick velvet rope, along with a sign declaring the lounge opened at four. Knox pushed past it. "I'll be going on duty soon, but if your team needs anything tonight, let me know. Another bartender's coming as backup."

"If Charlie's good with taking them to check out the haunted area, then we'll be fine. After we break for dinner, we've got three interviews scheduled. You're not doing one, right?"

Knox flicked on the lights and headed for the bar. "Nope. I didn't experience any psychological turmoil when I was stuck in there. It seems like the room doesn't affect men the same way it does women. Charlie, Celia, and Gertrude all said the storage room messed with their emotions. That never happened to me."

"Interesting. The female member of our crew couldn't make it for this visit, so I hope we still get some kind of ghostly activity. At least the others have plenty of experience with the paranormal." He settled himself on a barstool and picked up a laminated card with the happy hour specials. "I'll take a bourbon cranberry cocktail."

"Good choice." Knox went behind the bar and grabbed the bourbon. "One other tip about the storage room—if the negative energy gets too overwhelming, music seems to help. Charlie and I were locked in there just now, but when we started dancing to an old record album, the door opened."

"You were dancing? Voluntarily?" Logan laughed. "What has this woman done to you?"

"Hell if I know." Knox couldn't help smiling. He slid the drink over to Logan. "You said you had some updates?"

Logan sipped his cocktail. "Ah, that's good. Brace yourself. I reached out to a bunch of places, and *Entertainment Weekly* responded right away. They were all for it."

"Are you shitting me?" Knox had been reading *Entertainment Weekly* since he was a kid, way back when it had been a print magazine.

"No lie. It helps that Lila promised them an exclusive interview, spilling the news about her divorce. I'm glad you were able to persuade Zack and Norah to contribute."

"They also put me in touch with two other writers. I can't believe the level of support I've gotten." The more people Knox heard from, the more memories came flooding back, making him remember all the things he'd loved about working on the show.

"You totally deserve it," Logan said. "Hell, everyone deserves a second act."

"Thanks, man. I owe you."

"You don't owe me a damn thing. Except you need to start writing again. The world needs more Mac Iverson."

Knox couldn't help but smile. "Funny that you mention it. Last month, I started tooling around with a horror screenplay I wrote ages ago. But I'll be writing it as Knox McIntyre. After this article comes out, that's it for Mac."

For so long, he'd worried someone would discover his alter ego, but not anymore.

He was done keeping secrets.

Thirty

When Charlie escorted the show's film crew up to the storage room, she left nothing to chance. Joe from Facilities kept the door cracked open and stood guard, shooing away the few hotel guests who tried to peek inside. The crew set up their stationary cameras and digital recorders, then took baseline readings of the room's temperature and electromagnetic energy. This time, Charlie didn't catch the scent of roses or experience any emotional turmoil, which made her suspect Maeve was absent. Hopefully, she'd return for tomorrow night's lockdown.

At seven, Charlie unlocked the Duchess's breakfast room and ushered Celia and Gertrude inside. Since the room was usually off-limits to guests when not in use for the hotel's daily breakfast buffet or occasional afternoon tea, it offered the crew the best chance at a little privacy. Along one wall, a row of tall windows provided a view of the back garden, including an old wooden gazebo that had once been used for outdoor events. Another wall displayed framed photos of Victoria, from the 1920s up through the present day. Charlie made a mental note to ask Knox if he'd be willing to add a few of his photographs to the room since they captured the natural beauty of the nearby beaches and forests.

Gertrude peered around the room. "Ooh, it's nicer than I remembered in here. I'll bet the food's better, too."

"We take pride in our breakfast buffet," Charlie said. "The banana pecan muffins and lemon poppyseed loaf are baked fresh every day. Since the coffee is locally sourced from Alma's Beanery, it's better than the swill you get at most hotels."

"Maybe Glen and I will have to spend the night here, just to take advantage," Celia said.

"No need. Remind me before you leave, and I'll give each of you some free coupons for the buffet." It was the least Charlie could do, seeing as how Celia had refused payment for all the research she'd done.

"Thanks." Celia sat at a table facing the window. "And thank you *so* much for offering to move in with Laurel. I'm glad she won't be stuck with a stranger. She's a great roommate. It's just that..." She trailed off, a dreamy smile crossing her face.

"You're in love with Glen and can't wait to move in with him?" Charlie asked. "That's wonderful. How long have you two been dating?"

"A little over a year. But after our first month together, I knew he was the one. Which isn't like me because I'm not a romantic at heart."

"When you know, you know, right?" Gertrude said. "That's how I felt with Rupert. A few weeks after he started courting me, I was already imagining our wedding."

Charlie could relate. Even if she'd spent over a year pining for Knox, she hadn't expected to fall in love with him so quickly. She was glad she'd followed her heart and told him how she felt. And equally glad he felt the same way. Now that they'd both admitted their feelings, she was looking forward to everything that lay ahead of them—more nights in his cozy king bed, more hiking excursions and picnics in the park, more sexy teasing and quiet moments of relaxation.

As Logan and the other members of the team came in, she

beckoned them over. The one carrying a handheld camera positioned himself at a table across from theirs. All the others sat beside him except the leader of the crew, a tall, bearded guy with a shaved head and a firm build that suggested an intense weight-lifting regimen. He was the first one Charlie had recognized when she met the team earlier since he'd featured prominently in the episodes she'd watched with Knox.

He greeted the women. "Good evening, ladies. I'm Burke, the lead investigator, and I'll be conducting the interviews. Fair warning—they're always edited for brevity, so you might not see much of yourself on the screen by the time the show airs."

"That's fine," Charlie said. Based on the episodes she'd seen, she'd expected as much.

Celia went first since she was the one who'd discovered the tragic secret behind room 309. Gertrude followed, describing the harrowing incident when she'd been locked in for three hours. When it was Charlie's turn, she summarized the research she'd done, including the accounts of numerous female staff members who'd had unsettling experiences in the room. She concluded by recounting the two occasions when she and Knox had been trapped in there.

After she finished her testimony, Burke addressed them while the camera was still rolling. "Thanks for sharing your stories. Given what you've experienced, what would be your best guess as to the source of the emotional manipulation? Is it coming from one of the people who died during that devastating event?"

Celia nodded. "I believe Maeve's ghost has been the entity haunting the room."

"I agree," Charlie added.

"What makes you say that?" Burke asked. "Why couldn't it be the spirit of Frances Delacroix since she committed the murders? I would have assumed she'd be the one who'd stick around as a vengeful spirit."

"That would have been my first guess, but unlike Maeve,

Frances wasn't forgotten," Celia said. "Her obituary appeared in the paper, and she's buried at Ross Bay Cemetery next to her husband, Howard, where you can find their headstones. Since they came from prominent local families, they would have been mourned. Maeve—not so much." She went on to describe everything she'd learned about the young clerk. "I don't know why she hasn't crossed over. I think she's not just devastated at what happened to her, but also angry at being forgotten."

Burke nodded enthusiastically. He turned to Charlie. "If that's the case, why did Maeve allow the door to open when you and Knox were in the room?"

"I don't know. I think our...love might have diminished her power." Charlie's face crackled with heat at sharing something so intimate on camera. "Both times, the door opened right after Knox and I grew closer."

"All right, I think we've got all the testimony we need," Burke said. "Do you have any advice for us when we're locked in the room tomorrow night?"

Charlie frowned. "I'm not sure. Maeve doesn't seem to affect men the way she does women, so I'm worried you might not experience the same sensations." She turned to Celia. "Any chance you could join them?" Since Celia was so attuned to the supernatural, she would be a huge asset to the team.

Celia shook her head. "Originally, I was hoping to participate, but that was before the filming was set for the thirty-first. Every year, my family throws a huge party on Halloween night, and all our relatives attend. Missing it isn't an option."

Burke responded with a condescending smile. "We'll be just fine without a female team member. Trust me, we've been doing this for years, and we rely heavily on our equipment. If there's a spectral presence, we'll detect it."

His smugness made Charlie uneasy. She didn't want him to grow frustrated if the room didn't deliver a ghostly encounter. But she kept quiet. By now, she'd done everything she could.

"We're planning to take some B-roll footage around the outside of the hotel tomorrow morning," he said. "We'd also like to get some shots of the lobby and the front desk. Charlie, any chance we could grab your boss for a few minutes to get his take?"

Knowing Preston, he'd be all over it. "It shouldn't be an issue, but I'll check his schedule and let you know when he's free."

"Excellent. Tomorrow night, three of us will be locked in the storage room for four hours. We've already set up two digital recorders and two wireless cameras; one of our guys will also be circulating around the room with a handheld. Meanwhile, our 'base camp' team will monitor everything from one of the hotel rooms. That way, if things go sideways, they can break us out. It usually doesn't happen, but you never know."

"Can Knox and I stop by your 'base camp' and take a peek while you're filming?" Charlie asked. "We promise not to interfere with anything."

"No problem. Thanks for comping us the rooms. It sure beats doing surveillance out of our van."

Once the film crew left, Charlie escorted Celia and Gertrude to her office, where she gave each of them a handful of coupons for the breakfast buffet. Though she didn't know when the episode would air, she promised them she'd be in touch.

After they left, she congratulated herself on a job well done. Tomorrow night, an actual ghost-hunting show would be filming an episode at the Duchess, thanks to the efforts she and Knox had made. For someone who'd never considered herself brave, she'd ventured far beyond her comfort zone. Heck, she'd been locked in that scary room not once, but twice. Along the way, she'd also had the courage to pursue a relationship with Knox.

Not bad, Charlie Fraser. Not bad at all.

Before returning to the front desk, she popped into the Gilded Lily. Inching her way past the crowds—who filled every chair and high-top in the place—she sidled up to one end of the bar. Both

Miles and Knox were slinging drinks, so she waited for a break in the action before gesturing to Knox.

He reached over the bar top and took her hand. "How'd the interviews go?"

"They were great. Tomorrow night, Logan and one of the crew members will be monitoring the lockdown from their hotel room. Do you want to stop by and watch? Burke said it would be okay."

"Hell, yes. I already talked to Logan about it. They're going to start at ten. Miles and Jordan will be here at the bar, so I should be fine. I wish I could be in the storage room with them when they're investigating. What a rush that would be."

A full-body shudder coursed through Charlie. "Are you kidding? What if something bad happens?"

"Good point. I guess we'll have to settle for watching it from a distance. What time do you get done tonight?" At the sight of a patron approaching him, Knox held up one finger in the 'just a sec' gesture.

"God only knows. I want to make sure the crew doesn't need anything else before I head home. What about you?"

"Eleven or thereabouts." He cast his gaze around the bar and scowled. "I'll be glad when all this is done. The Lily's been too damn busy for my liking."

Typical Knox. But she wouldn't change a thing about him. "Why don't you stop by my place after work?"

"You sure? I might not get there until midnight, and I know you've had a long day."

"I don't mind. If I'm not awake, you can use the code to let yourself in and join me in bed." Even though they'd reconciled in the storage room, all they'd done was kiss.

That got a smile out of him. "I'd like that. We need to make up for lost time."

Thirty-One

CHARLIE WOKE AT SEVEN, SURROUNDED BY A STURDY pair of arms. With a hum of satisfaction, she nestled her body into Knox's. Last night, upon getting ready for bed, she'd stripped down to nothing and waited for him to arrive, eager to offer him a delightful round of make-up sex. Despite her best efforts to stay awake, she'd drifted off before he showed up.

Knox's arms tightened around her waist. He nuzzled her neck. "Good morning, my little ghostbuster."

She giggled. Like her, he was naked, his rigid length pressing into her back. A rush of heat flooded through her, settling squarely between her legs. "Morning, Knox. Can you believe today's the day? The Duchess is going to be on TV. And it's all because we did such a great job proving it's haunted."

He kissed the tender spot behind her ear. "We make a good team, don't we?"

"We sure do. Maybe we should start planning the hotel's Christmas activities. Remember those events we did last year? The family Saturdays with Santa and the hot cocoa bar? All those festive holiday-themed drinks? I'll bet you can't wait to get started."

With a growl, he flipped her over so she was flat on her back. He hovered above her, giving her his stormiest, don't-fuck-with-me glare. "I just got through one holiday season, and now you want me to dive into another? How am I supposed to catch a break?"

Even if he sounded like an angry bear, she knew he didn't mean it. "Admit it. You secretly loved that sparkly vest I made you wear."

He brushed his thumb over her nipple. "I admit nothing."

When he gave it a tweak, little tingles settled low in her belly. "Maybe this year, I could convince you to wear a Santa hat. You'd look so cute in one."

"Not. Another. Word." Lowering his head, he ran his tongue over each bud, sucking on them until she moaned in submission.

She wove her fingers through his thick hair, arching her back as he gave her breasts his full attention, his beard tickling her bare skin. She wanted to keep teasing him about Christmas, but she could barely form the words. Not when each swipe of his tongue, each nip and caress, was driving her wild.

"You...you know you love all those holiday events," she gasped.

He nudged open her legs and dipped a finger inside her. "Nope. I did it for you. So you wouldn't think I was a Grinch."

"Oh, Knox." She closed her eyes, surrendering to his touch as he found the right spot. Stroking it with the perfect amount of pressure. She clenched her thighs as he took her close to the edge and left her hanging. With a whimper, she wrapped her hand around his wrist, desperate for him to keep going. But he pulled his fingers away with a throaty chuckle that let her know exactly who was in charge.

"You're so impatient. The longer you wait, the better it'll be." His breath was warm on her skin as he trailed kisses along her rib cage and down her stomach. Parting her legs wider, he teased her with little pecks along the inside of her thighs until finally seeking out the warmth and wetness between them. When he placed his hands under her ass and gripped it tightly, she writhed beneath him.

"My greedy little pixie," he murmured. "You want this so badly, don't you?"

"Yes. Oh my God, yes. *Please*, Knox." If he wanted her to beg, she'd beg for it.

But already, he was working his magic with his tongue, bringing her so close to ecstasy that her breath came in little gasps. How was it possible that it felt this good, every damn time? She babbled his name incoherently, completely lost in sensation, so close she could hardly bear it. As the orgasm rushed through her, she tumbled over the edge and released the air from her lungs in a cry of pleasure.

When he looked up and met her eyes, she couldn't help but laugh. He looked so damn smug. Like he'd thoroughly enjoyed pushing her to the point where she was at his mercy.

You win, Knox. No more Santa hats.

As he got off the bed and opened the nightstand drawer to retrieve a condom, she grabbed his arm. "Let me return the favor. Please."

Knox eased back onto the pillows and placed his hands behind his head. "You won't get any argument from me." He enjoyed taking the lead in bed, and he loved those few occasions when he'd gotten the chance to put Charlie over his knee and spank her. But there was something unbelievably hot about letting her take control.

She ran her tongue along his shaft, then stroked it with her fingers. Just the softest of touches, driving him up the wall. At this rate, he was going to come before she even wrapped her lips around him. But when she took him into her mouth, the wait was worth it.

"Fuck, Charlie, that feels incredible."

He twisted his hand in her hair, tugging on it until she moaned and took him deeper. This, right here, was as good as it got. If she wanted him to wear a Santa hat this Christmas, he would. And he'd wear a shiny vest embellished with holly berries. Hell, he'd even dress up like Santa.

Wait. Where had that come from? Now was *not* the time to be thinking about this shit.

He was so wound up that he wasn't going to last. Not when that hot little mouth of hers was pushing him over the precipice. He loved that his sweet, sunny Charlie secretly possessed a wicked streak. And that she enjoyed giving pleasure just as much as receiving it.

"I'm coming," he groaned. But she kept going, keeping hold of him as he allowed himself the sweet bliss of release. He shuddered as the pleasure soared through him.

When she sat up and grinned at him, he shook his head in resignation. "You win, sweetheart. I'm helpless around you."

"I think the feeling's mutual. But I'll take the win."

He pulled her toward him, and she rested her head on his chest. A sense of peace washed over him. Like the past no longer mattered. Right now, this was precisely where he needed to be.

She traced her fingers along his bicep. "Do you want to come by the front desk tonight? Maybe around ten thirty? That way, we can go check out their base camp. I'm curious to see what kind of footage they get with their equipment, like the thermal-imaging monitor and the electronic voice phenomenon detector."

"I wonder if they'll get any messages from Maeve on the EVP."

"They might not since it's an all-male team, but maybe they'll get lucky." She shivered. "I'm just glad they're the ones handling it."

～

Despite his best intentions, Knox wasn't able to stop by the front desk until just before eleven, when the Lily was about to close. He'd had Miles and Jordan helping him, but it didn't matter. The fact that it was a Saturday night—and Halloween, to boot—meant there had been a big crowd and an even bigger demand for his ghost-themed cocktails. Though the lounge had already hosted a costume party last week, lots of guests had come dressed up. With all the booze being consumed, he'd had to keep an eye on things to ensure no one got out of line.

When he came to get Charlie, she was so hyped up she was practically vibrating. She set down a stainless-steel tumbler. "You're here. Finally! I'm dying to go upstairs."

"Sorry. Things got a little nuts." He motioned to the tumbler. "That isn't coffee, is it?"

"It sure is! I'm so wired. I already worked a full shift, took a break for dinner, and came back here to wait for you. If not for this coffee, I'd be crashed out in my office."

"You okay to leave the front desk? It looks like you've got enough coverage." He pointed to the two clerks working the night shift, who were dressed for Halloween. One wore a witches' hat, while the other sported black cat ears and drawn-on whiskers.

"I'm not on duty or anything. I was just waiting for you to show up." She came around to his side. "Let's do this! I'm so excited."

He took her hand. "Easy there, sweetheart. The film crew would probably prefer it if you were a little more chill."

"Right. Sorry. But I hope they get some good footage. What if they pick up words with the EVP? What if Maeve says something sinister, like 'leave this place' or 'get out'? Or what if the temperature gauge thingy shows a huge spike in temperature? Wouldn't that be awesome?"

She was still amped up, but he didn't have the heart to ask her to calm down again. Despite his relaxed demeanor, he was equally excited. They took the elevator up to the third floor and walked down the hall. When they knocked on the door to room 308, Logan opened it right away.

"Come on in," he said.

A large monitor took up most of the space on the work desk, displaying footage from the three different cameras. One guy sat behind the desk, observing everything. Logan gestured for Knox and Charlie to come closer. "So...it's not looking too good."

"What do you mean?" Knox said. "Did something bad happen?" From all the accounts Charlie had shared with him, the staff members who'd been trapped in the room had never suffered physically.

"Nothing's happened. That's the problem." Logan swiped a hand through his wavy blond hair. "Burke and the others have called out to Maeve, but she hasn't responded. No readings, no cold spots, no unknown voices. Nada. This investigation might be a bust."

"Shit." Knox fought back a wave of guilt. He'd warned Logan the room might not pay off but still felt like he'd wasted their time. "Sorry about that."

"No, dude, it's cool. We knew the risk going in. We'll just have to play up the interviews and the backstory. Sometimes this happens."

Through the cameras displayed on the monitor, Knox could hear the two team members conversing in the dark room while the other one scanned it with an infrared camera. Though the storage room looked creepier in the dark, it was a far cry from some of the eerie locales the show had visited in the past.

Charlie spoke up. "You know what the problem is? You're relying on male investigators. That's why Maeve isn't reacting."

Logan tilted his head to the side. "What?"

"This is what I warned you about when Burke interviewed us yesterday. Maeve only responds to a female presence. But you and the others wouldn't listen." Her expression darkened. "I wish Celia was with them. I'll bet you'd get some activity then."

Logan scratched his chin. "Well...we're only an hour in. This isn't how we usually run our lockdowns, but do you want to join them?"

Charlie's eyes widened. "Me? Join a paranormal investigation?"

"Sure, why not?" He shrugged. "You've already had two freaky experiences in that room. What's one more?"

"Do you have any idea how unnerving it was?" Her voice rose. "I hated getting stuck in there."

Knox put a hand on her shoulder. In the grand scheme of things, the show wasn't that important. He'd rather keep her safe. "You don't have to do anything you're not comfortable with. This isn't on you."

The man viewing the monitor turned to face them. "If you think it'll help to send her in there, I'll let them know. They might be up for it. Otherwise, we could end up with three more hours of nothing." He gave an exaggerated yawn.

Charlie scrubbed her hands over her face. "I...I don't know. I'm not sure I could stick it out for three hours."

"How about for a half hour?" Logan asked. "All we need is some kind of response from Maeve. Didn't you say she bombarded you with negative vibes when you were in there?"

Knox frowned. Even if Charlie did experience a strong emotional response to the ghost, her feelings wouldn't manifest as evidence. "I don't think that'll be enough. And it's not worth it to put Charlie through all that turmoil." He kissed the top of her head. "Not unless you want to."

"If I start panicking, can you let me out of the room?" she asked. "I don't want to have a heart attack or anything."

A heart attack? *Jesus*. He'd just gotten her back. He didn't want to lose her. "You don't have to do this."

"It's okay." She tucked a stray lock of hair behind her ears. "I'm just going to freshen up first. To make sure I look good for the cameras."

When she dashed into the washroom, Knox glared at Logan. While he appreciated everything his friend had done for him, he didn't want to put Charlie at risk. "This is a bad idea."

"Let her try it. She's braver than you think."

Knox mulled over that thought. She *was* brave. And not just when it came to diving into the hotel's haunted history. At the gala, she'd stood up for him, challenging both Lila and Evan. She'd followed that act of defiance by standing up to her mom and deciding to move out, after years of not wanting to rock the boat with her folks. For all the people-pleasing she did, she was pure steel underneath.

"Okay," he grumbled. "But understand this. I refuse to stand by and let anything bad happen to her. If she's in danger, we need to pull her out of there. Got it?"

His voice must have come across as sterner than he intended because Logan flinched. "Understood. I won't let her get hurt."

Knox wanted to trust him, but he wasn't sure what their ghost had up her sleeve.

Thirty-Two

CHARLIE STOOD OUTSIDE THE DOOR TO THE STORAGE room. It was one thing to go in there with Knox or to show the crew around. But to deliberately provoke a ghost? What if she got possessed? What if Maeve's spirit attached itself to her after she left? Based on what she'd read about spectral encounters, the possibility existed.

"You okay?" Logan asked. "Knox would murder me if anything happened to you."

"It's all right. I'll give it my best shot, but I can't promise I'll get results."

"Hey, it's better than three more hours of nothing." Logan rapped on the door four times, and it swung open. Burke ushered her in and closed the door swiftly behind her. As it clicked shut, Charlie's spine stiffened. That click sounded more ominous than ever before.

"This isn't our usual protocol," Burke said to her. "Once we go into lockdown, we don't like to compromise our findings by introducing new elements or people. You left your phone behind, right? And your two-way radio?"

"Affirmative. I even took off my watch." She was still wearing her work clothes—a button-down shirt, a navy skirt, and matching heels—though she'd ditched her blazer in the hotel room. Good call since the storage area was as stifling as ever. "What do you want me to do?"

"Introduce yourself." He directed her to one of the cameras. "Tell our viewers why you're here."

"Okay." She took a second to conjure up the sunny persona she used at work, then waved at the camera. "Hi, everyone. I'm Charlie Fraser, the front office manager of the Duchess Hotel. Over the past two months, I've visited this room twice. Both times, I've gotten locked in. I tried using the key, but it didn't work." She let out a nervous giggle. "When I got trapped in here, my partner, Knox McIntyre, was with me. He couldn't open the door either."

"What else happened the last time you were here?" Burke asked.

"I smelled the faint scent of roses, which seems to be a pattern since the other women who were locked in here experienced the same thing. But the most notable effects were the extreme mood swings I went through. Sad one minute and angry the next. It was hard to control. I think the ghost—Maeve —was manipulating my emotions. She's one of the people who was murdered in this room, and I believe her spirit still haunts it."

Burke gestured to the familiar settee. "Is this where you were sitting the last time? Why don't you take a seat?" He gave her a handheld device. "This is a temperature sensor with a built-in thermometer. If there are any spikes, they'll show up here."

She eased into the settee and tried to relax. Maybe tonight, Maeve would stay dormant, since there was so much testosterone in the room. She might also choose to hide from the investigators out of pure spite. But within a minute, the scent of roses returned, stronger than ever. A gloomy fog settled over Charlie. Like her own personal raincloud. Bleak thoughts crowded into her head, pushing everything else out.

Knox threw you under the bus, didn't he? For the good of the show. He's just using you.

She knew it wasn't true. Or was it?

He'd only acted protective for a few minutes before letting her leave with Logan.

As a wave of sorrow seeped into her consciousness, an anguished moan escaped her lips. Accompanying it was an arctic chill that felt like walking into a freezer. She trembled all over, and the monitor beeped in her hands.

Burke leaned over her. "The temp's going down. Good job. Try talking to the ghost."

"Maeve," she called out. "I know you're sad. You wanted to be with Howard, didn't you? Did he promise to marry you? To take care of you?"

Goose bumps prickled her arms as she recalled her mother's words. How she always wanted to ensure Charlie had someone to take care of her. Was that what Maeve had wanted? It couldn't have been easy, coming on her own from Ireland to Canada. Had she been lonely? Seeking out love from whomever offered it, even if he was already taken? Had Maeve truly loved Howard, or had he just offered her security?

"Maeve, why are you still with us? What's stopping you from crossing over? And what's making you so angry?" Charlie tried to imagine what might be troubling her. "Are you mad because Howard and Frances ended up together in death, and you were forgotten?"

A book sailed through the air, barely missing her head. Trembling, she stared at it in disbelief. Her stomach clenched tightly, bringing with it a pang of agony. She gripped the arm of the settee, willing herself not to bolt from the room in a panic. Another book flew past her, smacking into the side of an old dresser. Either Maeve had bad aim, or she wasn't actually intending to hit Charlie.

Behind her, the team members were whispering epithets, like "Holy shit" and "Bro, did you see that?"

Be brave. You can handle this.

She got to her feet. "Maeve? I don't blame you for being upset. It's not fair that you were left behind. Is that what's making you angry?"

A third book came at her, and she ducked just in time. Was one of the crew doing it to play up the scare factor? In the darkened room, she couldn't make them out very well. Not that it mattered. Right now, she needed to stay focused on Maeve.

"Even if everyone else has forgotten you, I'm going to keep you in my memory," she said. "You're part of a sisterhood, like all the women who've worked here over the years. I'll make sure you're not erased from history." She needed a way to ease Maeve's grief. "We could put a stone marker outside, next to the back garden. To honor the service you gave to the hotel. I know that won't help with the heartache, but every time someone sees it, they'll think of you."

Charlie's head spun with a sudden rush of dizziness. She sat back down as the emotions barraging her—sadness, anger, helplessness—made her senses reel. Images flooded her mind, and she envisioned herself in Maeve's shoes. Toiling away as a hotel clerk in the 1920s, with no family around to support her, hoping one day her situation would improve.

Around her, the men were talking—about EVP readings and EMF fluctuations and other jargon. She didn't care about any of that. She just wanted to be free of the frenzied emotional turmoil battering her brain.

"I'm sorry, Maeve," she whispered. "I only want you to be at peace."

Once again, a bone-chilling cold flooded her body, like diving into an icy river.

Then nothing.

No sadness. No pain. No anger.

The fog lifted like a blue sky breaking through the clouds. She released the air from her lungs and opened her eyes. The team members were staring at her in awe.

"Are you all right?" Burke asked. "That was intense."

"It was. I'm not sure if Maeve is still with us." Had she left for good? Or had Charlie appeased her enough that she'd relented? For now, Charlie was grateful the darkness had lifted, setting her free. "I think I'm done here."

As she stood up, her legs wobbled, and she braced herself on the arm of the settee. Burke contacted Logan, and within minutes, four raps came at the door. Logan opened it; behind him was Knox, with a thunderous expression on his face. "Damn it, Charlie, are you okay? You had me scared shitless."

She launched herself into his arms, taking solace in the warmth of his body. "I'm fine. You saw what happened, right?"

"I wanted to burst in there and tell Maeve to back the hell off. She almost beaned you with those books."

Charlie didn't know whether Maeve or one of the crew had thrown the books at her. At this point, she didn't care. "It's all good. I'm not sure if she'll be back, but I've done enough."

"You did plenty," Logan said. "Unless something else happens, your interaction with Maeve will be the highlight of the episode."

"Good." She rested her head against Knox's broad chest. "Will you take me home? I've had enough ghost hunting for one night."

"You got it, sweetheart."

Usually, when Knox slept over, Charlie couldn't wait to have sex. Tonight, she just wanted him to hold her. Though she'd regained control of her emotions, she was still shaken by what she'd experienced. She rested in his arms, letting the tension ease from her body as he stroked her hair.

"You sure you're all right?" he asked. "That ghost didn't mess with your mind, did she?"

"No. I feel like myself again, just exhausted. Maeve was tossing a lot of powerful feelings at me. I hope I was able to help her." Charlie wanted to believe her words might have eased some of the ghost's misery but didn't know for sure. The only way to find out would be to subject herself to the room again, and she was in no hurry to do that.

"How'd you know what to say?"

"I tried to think of why she'd be so worked up. It's not just that she was murdered so young, but also that she was forgotten. I couldn't find anyone connected to her—no family whatsoever. That's why I felt so sorry for her."

Knox nuzzled her hair with his lips. "That's because you're so compassionate. You care about everyone, even ghosts. But I like the idea of commemorating her by ordering a plaque or a memorial stone with her name on it."

"Thanks. I figured we could plant it in the hotel's back garden." There was no guarantee the gesture would satisfy Maeve, but at least she would have something to mark her death.

"You were so gutsy," he said. "Don't ever call yourself a scaredy-cat again."

She laughed. "I still can't stomach horror movies, and I've only read two Stephen King books."

"That's not what true bravery is. It's standing up for yourself and for the people you care about. Like you did at the gala. You weren't afraid to call out Lila and Evan for their actions. I've never had anyone go to bat for me like that."

"I'd do it again in a heartbeat. I love you, Knox." The words spilled out before she could stop them, but she knew in her heart that it wasn't too soon.

He cupped her chin, tilting her head until she was looking up at him. His eyes shone with affection. "I love you, too. You made me realize that for all my horror-writing chops, I was the real coward. For too long, it was easier to hide in the shadows than reveal myself. You gave me the courage to speak out. Thank you."

"You're welcome. Putting yourself out there is a big risk, but the rewards are worth it."

Back when Preston had assigned her to work on *Canada's Most Haunted*, she hadn't known what it would entail. She'd only agreed to help so she could get closer to Knox. She'd never imagined getting locked in a haunted room or confronting a ghost. Or taking the initiative with Knox by asking him over to her place and then inviting him into her bed. Or standing up to her mother and striking out on her own. Two months ago, she couldn't have conceived of doing any of those things. She was incredibly proud of how far she'd come.

With a yawn, she nestled against Knox. "I'm getting sleepy. Tomorrow, I'll make it up to you, I promise."

"No rush," he murmured. "I'm not going anywhere."

Thirty-Three

THREE MONTHS LATER

After Knox learned that *Canada's Most Haunted* would be airing the Duchess Hotel's episode in late January, he met with the Damsels to organize a viewing party. Initially, he'd suggested they hold it at the Gilded Lily, but the lounge wasn't outfitted with a TV. He'd always preferred it that way, especially during hockey season, when fans could get rabid. As a compromise, Selena suggested the breakfast room, which housed two TVs. She arranged the room's seating to accommodate most of the hotel's staff, along with a few special guests like Logan, Celia, Glen, and Gertrude, along with two of her great-grandchildren.

When the big night arrived, the attitude was festive, the crowd eager to see how the Duchess had fared during the filming. Charlie sat next to Knox at the front of the room. "I'm so excited. But also really nervous. What if I look like a total idiot? Everyone's going to see me talking to a ghost."

"You were the star of the show. Without you, the episode would have been a bust." According to Logan, once Charlie left, the team's equipment hadn't registered anything else unusual. The three ghost hunters had spent the last two hours waiting for the lockdown to end.

"I know, but I kind of lost control. I just wanted to help Maeve find some peace. I'm glad we found a way to remember her and to commemorate her service to the hotel."

At first, Preston had dismissed the idea as unnecessary, but Knox and Charlie had worn him down until he allowed them to order a granite memorial stone. At the top was an engraving displaying Maeve's name, along with her date of birth and passing. They'd placed it in the hotel's back garden a few weeks ago.

Was Maeve aware it existed? Had it made a difference? Knox wasn't sure. But when he'd accompanied Charlie up to the storage room last month—to fetch the antique phonograph—she'd been unaffected.

Since Logan was attending the watch party on behalf of the show, he offered to say a few words before the episode aired. He stood at the front of the room and addressed the group. "Hi, everyone. I'm Logan Cantrell, one of the producers of *Canada's Most Haunted*. I want to thank all of you for letting us film our show at the Duchess Hotel."

The room resounded in whoops and cheers. Charlie's was among the loudest.

Logan grinned. "I appreciate the enthusiasm. When our ghost hunters go into lockdown to film an episode, we never know precisely what will happen. Certainly, the Duchess was a prime candidate for investigation, given the shocking events of 1924 and the anecdotal evidence surrounding the unusual occurrences in the third-floor storage room. Even so, we didn't know if any spirits would manifest. I'd like to give a shout-out to Charlie Fraser, who was brave enough to reach out to the hotel's ghost."

"Her name is Maeve," Charlie called out.

Logan nodded her way. "Right. Sorry about that. Because Charlie had the courage to address Maeve directly, she put herself at risk, as you'll see in this episode. I do believe Charlie's offer to ease Maeve's pain helped diffuse what could have been a dangerous situation. In any case, I hope you enjoy the show. And I apologize for taking so long to get it on the air. We were hoping to release it before Christmas, but we got backlogged."

Rosie spoke up. "Don't worry about it. January's better anyway since we were slammed in December. Weren't we, folks?" Around her, other staff members voiced their agreement.

Her candor made Knox chuckle. Even if Preston didn't appreciate it, the guy needed to be reminded that he occasionally pushed them too hard.

Charlie whispered in Knox's ear. "I'm glad she said it. As much as I love Christmas, this year's events were a lot."

That was an understatement. Though Knox hadn't donned a Santa hat, he'd suited up in his shiny red vest to help pitch in for the holidays. He'd been pleasantly surprised when Preston had allowed both him and Charlie to take a few days off, starting on December twenty-fourth so they could spend Christmas Day with Knox's family. The McIntyre clan had adored Charlie (how could they not?), and she'd fit right in, entirely at ease amid the boisterous chaos.

In return, Knox had joined her and the Frasers at a New Year's Eve party at the yacht club. Despite secretly dreading the event, he'd enjoyed it thoroughly. Hard to complain about a party featuring lavish hors d'oeuvres, expensive champagne, and an open bar. It also didn't hurt that Randolph was nowhere to be seen since he was still recovering from a broken ankle he'd gotten while skiing at Whistler.

But after the bustle of the holidays, Knox was glad to return to his regular routine, albeit one that now included Charlie. His favorite moments with her were the low-key ones they shared together—reading books by the fire, talking in bed, visiting flea markets, exploring Victoria's hidden coves. She'd become an integral part of his life.

As the show's opening credits unspooled over the screen,

Charlie gripped his hand tightly. The episode started off with a recap of the murder-suicide, complete with a shadowy reenactment of the incident. After a brief overview of the modern-day Duchess, snippets from the three interviews followed. When Gertrude's face appeared, her great-grandchildren whooped loudly, to the delight of everyone in the room.

Back in September, Knox hadn't wanted anything to do with the show. But now? He was glad he'd been roped into it. If not for the opportunity to spend time with Charlie, he might have let her slip through his fingers. Thanks to her, he'd stopped lurking on the sidelines and taken a leading role in his own life. If asking her out had been risky, then coming clean about his past had been an even greater challenge. But both risks had paid off.

That wasn't the only change. For the first time since he'd started working at the Duchess, he felt like he was a part of something. It was similar to the experiences he'd had back when he was deeply invested in *The Hidden Forest*. While he still had a reputation to uphold as the city's surliest bartender, now his grouchiness was more of an act.

With the backstory and interviews complete, the show moved on to the main event—the much-anticipated lockdown in the storage room. When Charlie entered the room, Knox tensed up, as if experiencing it all over again. The producers had manipulated the footage to make it seem like she had stayed longer than ten minutes. When the books came flying at her head, people gasped. Thanks to the lighting and camera angles, everything looked more dramatic than when Knox had first viewed it.

Laurel sat on Charlie's other side, riveted by the ghostly showdown. "Holy shit, Charlie. And to think, I still can't get you to watch horror movies with me. This show is scarier because it happened in real life."

Charlie shuddered. "This was a one-time thing. No more ghosts for me."

"Knox, you have to convince her," Laurel said. "She's seriously missing out."

He chuckled, knowing it was a lost cause. Fortunately, both women loved fantasy films. Ever since Charlie had moved in with Laurel, retro movie nights at their apartment had become one of his favorite traditions. Charlie would make a huge batch of popcorn, Laurel would bake cookies, and he'd bring the candy. Then the three of them would settle in together for a rewatch of a classic flick like *The Fellowship of the Ring* or *Labyrinth*. He was glad the two women were getting along so well and that Charlie didn't have any regrets about leaving her parents' place.

Toward the end of the show, Burke played back the recording he'd taken with the EVP during the few minutes when Charlie was recovering from Maeve's emotional assault. Knox could barely make out what it was saying.

"What did that sound like to you?" he asked Charlie.

"Goo-buh? It sounded like nonsense."

Burke played it again and announced, "Maeve is saying 'goodbye.' Could it be that she's finally at peace and is bidding us farewell?" The other investigators responded with enthusiasm as he replayed it two more times.

Knox thought "goodbye" seemed like a stretch. But if that was the narrative they wanted to spin, who was he to argue?

As the show came to its conclusion, Burke faced the camera. "To the best of our knowledge, tonight's investigation brought us in contact with the spirit of Maeve, an Irish hotel clerk who was murdered in 1924. Based on what we experienced during our lockdown, it seems as though she might have left this earthly plane and crossed over to the other side. Does this mean the Duchess Hotel is no longer haunted? Or will Maeve return—with a vengeance—at some point in the future? Only time will tell."

Way to dramatize it. Knox stifled a laugh but joined the others in a thunderous round of applause. While the show might have been a bit hokey, it had certainly been entertaining.

Once the TV was shut off, Preston strode to the front of the room and raised his hand to silence the crowd. "Thank you, everyone. And Logan, thank you so much for featuring our hotel in *Canada's Most Haunted*. We're proud we were able to participate. As far as we can tell, Maeve's ghost seems to have departed. But if she chooses to return, having a resident ghost associated with our hotel shouldn't hurt business. Why should the Grand Duke be the only one capitalizing on their ghostly lore?"

Knox secretly wondered if the hoteliers at the Duke were jealous that they'd passed up the opportunity to star in *Canada's Most Haunted*.

Preston continued. "Before we break for a little celebration, I want to recognize the two employees who helped make this happen. Knox McIntyre and Charlotte Fraser, stand up please."

Charlie turned to Knox in astonishment. "No way."

Knox couldn't ever recall receiving this kind of acclaim from his boss. But he wasn't about to pass it up. Taking Charlie's hand, he stood beside her. Together, they waved at the group, which erupted in another round of applause.

"Thanks for watching," he said. "We're glad it worked out so well. Right after this, there's a private party in the Gilded Lily. Just give me about ten minutes to get things ready."

Charlie grinned at everyone. "Knox and I had a blast getting involved in *Canada's Most Haunted*, but I'm turning in my resignation as one of the hotel's ghostbusters. If anyone else wants to tackle that storage room, have at it."

Knox tugged at her hand. "Want to help me set up?"

"Sure." She waved at the audience again. "See you all in a bit."

As they left, people started chatting amongst themselves. Did they believe the ghost was real? Or did they consider it an elaborate hoax? Regardless, the episode had served its purpose as a half-hour of spine-chilling entertainment.

Knox walked with Charlie to the Gilded Lily, pushing past the sign that announced the lounge was reserved for a private party.

Once he was behind the bar with her at his side, he took her in his arms. Though they didn't have long before the others came streaming in, he wanted her to himself for a few minutes. "We did it."

"You really think I looked okay on TV?" Charlie asked. "I should have touched up my lipstick before I went in there. And one of the camera angles made my butt look kind of big."

He gripped her ass, relishing the feel of it under his palms. "Your butt looked amazing, as always. You were fierce and wonderful."

"Ooh, fierce. I like that."

"The camera loved you. Maybe Hollywood's calling?"

She laughed. "No thanks. I have no ambition to be on TV again. And after all the dirt you told me about *The Hidden Forest*, I can't imagine working in the entertainment industry. But if you ever want to return to it, I would understand. Now that everyone knows the real reason you left, you'd probably be welcomed back."

"I'm glad the truth's out there, but I'm happy where I am." Last November, he'd taken a big risk in exposing his past online. Fortunately, it had paid off. Zack, Norah, and two other writers from *The Hidden Forest* had contributed to the article. Not only had it generated a ton of buzz, but Knox had also been invited to share his story on a two-hour episode of a podcast devoted to the show.

Two days after his tell-all hit the internet, Lila dropped her own bombshell. In addition to announcing her impending divorce from Evan, she called him out for damaging Knox's reputation. Her news was followed by two other articles blasting Evan for his toxic behavior. He'd subsequently been fired from *The Hidden Forest*, and his name hadn't been attached to anything new. In the meantime, Lila had ended her commitment to the show and was filming a Victorian-era mystery set in London.

While Knox had no desire to return to his old gig, he'd gotten back into writing again. After revising his horror screenplay, he'd contacted his former agent, who'd been pleased to hear from him. With any luck, she might be able to sell his script, but there was no urgency. What mattered most was that he'd dragged his past into the light and had shaken free of it.

He smoothed his hand along Charlie's cheek. "Thanks for going on this ghost adventure with me. I still can't believe Preston gave us so much credit. Maybe he's changing his tune."

With a grin, Charlie broke away from him and pointed to the cash register. "That's debatable. Seeing as how he left you one of his notes."

Knox peered at it.

Hey, Knox,

Loving those wintry cocktails! They're snow much fun! But now that February's almost here, it's time to pivot. How about some romance-themed drinks? I'm sure if you put your "heart" into it, you'll come up with something swoony.

Charlie laughed as she read it over his shoulder. "The guy never knows when to quit, does he? You gonna be okay with this? Aren't you the one who called Valentine's Day a Hallmark holiday?"

Knox crumpled up the note. "That couldn't have been me. Clearly, it was some fool who doesn't have any faith in romance."

She looked up at him, her eyes sparkling. "And you do?"

"You'd better believe it, sweetheart."

THE END

Acknowledgments

Like Charlie at the start of the book, I don't consider myself a particularly brave person. I'm scared of a lot of things: bees, wasps, ghosts, drowning, and being buried alive in an underground tomb (okay, so maybe that's oddly specific, based on my experiences as an archaeologist). One of the scariest things I ever did (besides babysitting in a haunted house—really!) was deciding to share my books with the world. What if no one ever read them or liked them?

Now that it's been four years since the publication of my first book, Blue Hawaiian, I can say with certainty that I'm so glad I took the leap. It hasn't always been easy, but there are few things I enjoy more than crafting a story and sharing it with readers. A lot of it is thanks to readers like you. Without my readers, I'd just be sticking those manuscripts in binders on a shelf, and they'd never see the light of da. So, if you've read this far—thank you!

As with all my books, I owe a huge debt of gratitude to my creative team. When I told my cover artist, Bailey McGinn, what I wanted for my cover, she went above and beyond. The colors, the details, the characters—all of them bring this book to life. My copy editor Serena Clark, went over the manuscript so diligently and helped me smooth out so many rough edges. And finally, Sandra Dee, my proofreader, helped me fix those pesky typos and comma flaws.

Thanks so much to my beta readers: Liz Czukas, Michelle McCraw, Brandy Shaw, Jennifer Rupp, and Janiah, and John Luna. All your comments and feedback made for a much stronger book. Thanks to Jackie Lau for help with the opening chapters.

And thanks to my critique partner, Tricia Quinnies, for helping me to create this story and encouraging me every step of the way. A huge thanks to my writer friends for all their encouragement and support, including Liz L., Natalie, Liz C., Brandy, Michelle, Carrie and Megan.

In researching this book, I went down the ghost hunting rabbit hole, watching episodes of *Ghost Hunters* and *Ghost Adventures*, and reading lots of books on this subject. Thanks to fellow author Natalie Caña for sharing the information she gleaned from the Paranormal Investigators of Milwaukee, and to my brother, John Luna, for sharing his stories of leading ghost tours in Victoria. For those interested in Victoria's haunted history, I highly recommend *Victoria's Most Haunted* by Ian Gibbs.

Though the TV show *The Hidden Forest* is purely a project of my imagination, I did a lot of research into writers' rooms to learn more about the process of writing for TV, including watching both seasons of *The Writers' Room* on AMC. Thanks to Jeff Messerman for his insight into the world of screenwriting and the nitty gritty of writing partnerships. For those interested in the toxic behavior that goes on in real-life writers' room, I recommend *End Credits* by Patty Lin (a writer who worked on *Freaks & Geeks, Friends,* and *Desperate Housewives*).

Finally, thanks so much to my family—Mike, Tasmine and James—for all the love and encouragement.

<h1 style="text-align:center">About the Author</h1>

Be our Ghost is being published posthumously following the unexpected death of Carla Luna Cullen. This is the second book in an intended three book series set in the fictitious Duchess Hotel in Victoria, British Columbia. Carla grew up in Victoria and drew on many of her life experiences in creating this series.

Carla's passing has left a huge hole in the hearts of her family and friends. Carla was a passionate writer who imagined stories and characters throughout her entire life. Her voice lives on in *Be Our Ghost* and in all of her writing.

The following was written by Carla to describe herself and her writing:

Carla writes contemporary romance with a dollop of humor and a pinch of spice. A former archaeologist, she loves to travel to far-off places and uses her traveling experience as the settings for her stories. Her books have been called "escape reads," perfect for perusing during a beachside vacation, a long flight, or a relaxing weekend at the lake. In addition to being a voracious reader, she loves baking, Broadway musicals, whimsical office supplies, and pop culture podcasts.

THE ROMANCING THE RUINS SERIES

Field Rules

Digging up the past takes on a whole new meaning when graduate student Olivia Sanchez is forced to team up with her ex, Rick Langston, while working at an archaeological dig in Cyprus. Given that their last fling almost led to their academic ruin, they can't afford to repeat their past mistakes. But as they work together under the scorching Mediterranean sun, the heat between them proves impossible to ignore.

Troy Story

For years, Dusty Danforth has harbored a secret crush on her best friend Stuart Carlson. Hoping to take things further, she jumps at the chance to join him on an archaeological dig at the legendary site of Troy in Turkey. But keeping the excavation on track is harder them either of them expected. Just as their long-simmering passion ignites, their boss's treacherous behavior puts the entire project in jeopardy.

Tour Wars

Sparks fly when archaeologist Emilia Flores gets stuck working alongside her infuriating nemesis, TJ Mayer, at the ancient ruins of Pompeii. Despite their fierce rivalry, they agree to co-lead a ten-day bus tour across Southern Italy to pay down their student debts. As the trip unfolds, their animosity gives way to an unexpected passion. But what happens when the tour ends and the real world steps in?

w meaning when graduate
m up with her ex, Rick
gical dig in Cyprus. Given
cademic ruin, they can't
at as they work together
n, the heat between them
ignore.

a secret crush on her best
nings further, she jumps at
gical dig at the legendary
ne excavation on track is
st as their long-simmering
s behavior puts the entire
dy.

Flores gets stuck working
ayer, at the ancient ruins of
y agree to co-lead a ten-day
wn their student debts. As
s way to an unexpected
ur ends and the real world

About the Author

Be our Ghost is being published posthumously following the unexpected death of Carla Luna Cullen. This is the second book in an intended three book series set in the fictitious Duchess Hotel in Victoria, British Columbia. Carla grew up in Victoria and drew on many of her life experiences in creating this series.

Carla's passing has left a huge hole in the hearts of her family and friends. Carla was a passionate writer who imagined stories and characters throughout her entire life. Her voice lives on in *Be Our Ghost* and in all of her writing.

The following was written by Carla to describe herself and her writing:

Carla writes contemporary romance with a dollop of humor and a pinch of spice. A former archaeologist, she loves to travel to far-off places and uses her traveling experience as the settings for her stories. Her books have been called "escape reads," perfect for perusing during a beachside vacation, a long flight, or a relaxing weekend at the lake. In addition to being a voracious reader, she

loves baking, Broadway musicals, whimsical office supplies, an
pop culture podcasts.

THE ROMANCING THE

Field Rules

Digging up the past takes on a whole n
student Olivia Sanchez is forced to te
Langston, while working at an archaeol
that their last fling almost led to their
afford to repeat their past mistakes. E
under the scorching Mediterranean su
proves impossible tc

Troy Story

For years, Dusty Danforth has harbore
friend Stuart Carlson. Hoping to take
the chance to join him on an archaeo
site of Troy in Turkey. But keeping
harder them either of them expected. J
passion ignites, their boss's treacherou
project in jeopa

Tour Wars

Sparks fly when archaeologist Emilia
alongside her infuriating nemesis, TJ M
Pompeii. Despite their fierce rivalry, th
bus tour across Southern Italy to pay d
the trip unfolds, their animosity giv
passion. But what happens when the
steps in?